Precious

Other books by Douglas Glover

The Enamoured Knight
Elle
Bad News of the Heart
Notes Home from a Prodigal Son
16 Categories of Desire
The Life and Times of Captain N.
A Guide to Animal Behaviour
The South Will Rise at Noon
Dog Attempts to Drown Man in Saskatoon
The Mad River

PRECIOUS

DOUGLAS GLOVER

GOOSE LANE

"Faithless Love," by John David Souther © 1974 (renewed) WB Music Corp.
(ASCAP) and Golden Spread Music (ASCAP). All rights reserved. Used by
permission. Warner Bros. Publications U.S. Inc., Miami, FL 33014.

First published as a Seal Book by McClelland and Stewart-Bantam Limited,
Toronto, 1984. This edition published by Goose Lane Editions, 2005.

Cover design by Kathleen Peacock. Photo by Kyle Cunjak.
Book design by Lisa Rousseau.
Printed in Canada by Transcontinental.
10 9 8 7 6 5 4 3 2 1

Library and Archives Canada Cataloguing in Publication

Glover, Douglas, 1948-
Precious / Douglas Glover. — 2nd ed.

First published: Toronto: M&S, 1984.
ISBN 0-86492-414-3

I. Title.

PS8563.L64P74 2005   C813'.54   C2004-907314-1

Published with the financial support of the Canada Council for the Arts,
the Government of Canada through the Book Publishing Industry Development
Program, and the New Brunswick Culture and Sports Secretariat.

Goose Lane Editions
469 King Street
Fredericton, New Brunswick
CANADA E3B 1E5
www.gooselane.com

*For Mal Aird, Barry Johnson, Peter Leney, Mike Clugston,
Garth Wilton, Peter Walker, Walt Christopherson, and the
rest of the night desk at the Montreal* Star, *1975-1976.*

And for Laura.

Precious

1

Jerry Mennenga's bar hid like an overlooked misprint amid a block of jutting bank towers off King Street not far from where the *Toronto Star* building used to be. Jerry's was a quiet place compared to most downtown bars. It boasted neither neon nor television. Two old mirrors reflected the weather from the streets, and behind the bar, in a niche surrounded by autographed pictures of hockey and football stars, was a bronze statuette of Jerry himself, thirty years younger, coiled in the pose of a discus thrower.

I was pondering the statue, thinking some woman had done it, that it was the product of some romantic, artsy liaison from the barkeep's past, and trying to imagine Jerry as a marble torso in the Athenian room at the Royal Ontario Museum, when he started in on me again.

"Precious, you look awful. You look like you just got outta jail."

"Bull's eye," I said. "Now are you going to give this poor ex-con a break or kill him with neglect?"

Jerry stuffed the stump of a burnt-out cigar into the corner of his mouth and wheezed asthmatically to express the pleasure he took in his own perception and my repartee. In the mirror over his shoulder, a ghostly face hovered, staring back at me like a fish in a bowl. It was pale, feverish, and needed a shave. Anne had often said I resembled one of those handsomely ravaged French poets gone to hell on drugs and absinthe. But now I looked like a corpse.

"You in trouble, Precious?"

There he was again. Ask the guy for a loan and he thinks he's got a right to paw through your private life like an amateur detective.

"Just broke," I told him.

"I heard you talking to Bellfield about some job in Ockenden.

You desperate or sumpin? What do you want to go to a place like that for? Why not stay here? We got doctors and hospitals in Toronto, you know."

Jerry was always thinking of his clients' welfare. He had the idea that civilization stopped somewhere just east of Greenwood Raceway.

An expatriate Genoan with a Play-Doh face like Jack Dempsey's, Jerry had ministered to generation upon generation of regulars, from Bay Street lawyers to newspaper publishers, from advertising flacks to office girls moonlighting as hookers, since the Second World War. He was already something of a legend in the sixties, when I first came to Toronto from the provinces to work a swing shift on the old night editor's desk at the *Star*. A series of syndicates had owned the licence, using local jock celebrities as front men. But Jerry's statue had occupied pride of place no matter who was in or out. By way of an avocation, the barkeep was a loan shark.

It had been a week since my fortieth birthday and less than thirty-six hours since the aforementioned Anne Delos and her crooked notary had arranged my release from the jail in Salonika. It cost her four thousand dollars in bribes, besides medical and legal fees. And I was cheap at that, the notary told me proudly when he came with the good news. The Lebanese wars had flooded Greece with a surplus of easy money, and my pet case of ambulatory pneumonia had turned me into a liability, one that might die any time at the state's expense.

We had met at the courtesy bar of a Mediterranean shipping convention. She was a biggish American woman with a face like Ingrid Bergman's and a shy lisp. According to the line she fed me, she was a female version of the old remittance man, running away to Europe to escape a failed marriage and nervous breakdown while her long-suffering relatives paid the bills. Apparently they had decided to suffer no longer because the money had dried up and she was destitute.

I count it a major personality defect, pernicious naïveté, if you want to give it a name, that after two decades of adulthood, a career in the papers, three marriages, and countless skirmishes with the perfidy of human nature, all I could do was look into her eyes and believe every word she said. The trouble was that, like most of us, Anne's quota of self-knowledge was strictly limited, and much of what she did know about herself she kept secret from me. It was the stuff she didn't care to talk about that landed me in jail.

Her real husband turned out to be a bad-tempered Greek economics professor who owned three oil tankers and had friends in the justice department. One night I was dragged, kicking and shouting, press card in hand, to the local prefecture and charged with sedition and crimes against the state. This meant I could be held without trial indefinitely while the prosecutors and police dissected my recent past for every possible subversive act from fomenting revolution to littering. The cops beat me twice out of curiosity to see whether I would confess to anything indictable. I took sick instead and threatened to succumb if they touched me again.

Anne's notary was a comical little fellow of advanced years who had lost one and a half lungs and part of his rib cage to cancer. Desiccated and bent, he nevertheless managed to conduct himself with great charm and courtliness in a white linen dinner jacket that must have dated from the Austro-Hungarian Empire. On visiting days, after earnestly inquiring about my chest, he would chain-smoke black Turkish cigarettes that smelled of rotten plumbing. He told us he had relatives in the police and launched an energetic campaign of payoff and arm-twisting that only made the authorities more suspicious than ever.

I have to credit Anne for her loyalty in a situation like that. She may have been sinfully reticent about her family affairs, but she was also true blue. It was her grand gesture, pawning her grandmother's emerald pendant, that finally did the trick. The old confidence man was touched to his gentlemanly core. He suddenly found the right magistrate to bribe, and my prison doors sprang open.

I was sick and broke, and they put me on a Lufthansa jet bound for Frankfurt, Paris, and Toronto with orders not to let me off until we reached the end of the line. Anne was at the airport to say goodbye. She placed an elegantly gloved hand on my forearm, looked at me with those innocent New England-bred eyes, and begged forgiveness for the trouble she had caused. I said not to mention it, which was pretty chivalrous considering that she had nearly been the death of me. I said I would write.

All of which doesn't tell you why Rose Oxley was murdered a month later, or why people insist on calling me Precious. But it does explain why I happened to be in Toronto that January with nothing but thirty-nine dollars and an out-of-date UPI card in my pocket, a stained London Fog raincoat over my shoulders, and a pair of tinted Italian sunglasses. It also explains why I borrowed all that money from Jerry Mennenga and why I took a newspaper job in Ockenden on Bellfield's say-so. Which is how the story really began, if you'll forget the inquest and those tabloid epics the big-city journalists churned out on their word processors long enough to hear my side of it.

"Are you going to lend me the money or not?" I asked. "You've known me a long time, Jerry."

"I ain't seen you in three, four years."

"I've been away."

"Some kinda foreign despondent or sumpin, right?"

"Yeah, a roving foreign despondent."

"I heard the boys talking about it."

Jerry chomped on his cigar and gazed at the ceiling, turning this earth-shattering piece of intelligence over in his mind. The man was a well-known incurable evader. I saw my chances of extracting a loan disappearing like lead slugs in a melting pot.

"I need cash to live on until I get a job. I haven't even got enough for a hotel room in this godforsaken town, damn it."

"You just got a fifty from Bellfield."

"What if I don't get a job right away?"

"You want sumpin to eat, Precious? We got a nice Swiss steak."

I slumped against the bar in disgust.

An hour earlier, alerted by my frantic call from the airport, Bellfield had bounced into Jerry's, beaming like a caution light. A pudgy, pot-bellied man with a yellow bulldoggy face, he had been in the RCAF with me just out of high school. Now he ran a public relations firm called Richard Bellfield Himself, which boasted two stunning typists, both taller than Dickie. In the years since I had last seen him, he had switched from leisure suits to three-piece pinstripes and someone else's old school tie.

"Oh ho, Precious, my lad!" This was how he greeted my re-emergence from the slipstream of history. "You look like somebody dragged you through a car wash without the car. Lord, how the mighty have fallen. And now you've come to old Dickie Bellfield to get you out of a jam."

Hoping that Jerry wouldn't notice, I flashed my ingratiating smile and did an imitation of a limp doormat while Dickie gloated. Envy had been his long suit ever since he washed out of pilot training and I didn't, back in Base Caribou Heart, Saskatchewan, when we were both still ignorant of womankind and lying like mad about it. That was when the Precious thing got started.

Out of some quirky instinct for revenge, Bellfield set me up on a blind date with the acting colonel's niece, an elephantine, hysterical woman ten years my senior. I reacted badly. I drank too much. After a long and embarrassing evening, full of painful silences, I was steering her toward her uncle's porch light when she lurched and pinned me against the picket fence.

"I adore chess," she said, lapsing into baby talk and kneading my ribs. "I adore piwots. Hold me, my pwecious! Oh, my pwecious!"

Her voice rose with the urgency of impending crisis. "Take me, pwecious! Have your way with me, my dawling!" And then the old acting colonel himself came hotfooting it from the house with a bird gun to save her.

On isolated prairie air bases such incidents rarely escape notice. I never saw the lady again, but the nickname has pursued me through twenty years of evasive manoeuvres, a dozen or so jobs, those marriages, and five armed conflicts. My real name, if you can remember it, is Moss Elliot, after my father and a primitive form of plant life. There is also a "C." in the middle sometimes that stands for Claude; I once went out with a girl from Quebec City who called me Clo-Clo. Some people are not lucky with names.

Bellfield was only too happy to see I hadn't yet become a roaring success in life. I didn't have to ask; he jumped right in, offered me money, and then made a big to-do about getting Jerry to cash a cheque. Needy as I was, I was doing Dickie's ego a world of good. He even wanted to help me find a job.

"But you won't get one in the city, Precious," he said eagerly. "You'll have to go back to the boonies. The news game has passed you by. You're a regular Rip Van Winkle. You spent too much time in the yellow-fever belt, playing correspondent, chasing fire engines. It's all mass marketing, journalism school, and video display terminals now. You ever write a story on a TV before?"

"Doesn't sound like the good old days," I said, trying to pitch the proper mixture of misery and awe into my voice. A few feet down the bar, Jerry was polishing glasses, listening intently. "I can always slash my wrists and charge admission."

"Wait a minute. Like I said, there are still the boondocks. And lucky for you I've got contacts. Ever hear of a guy called Burton Spandrell?"

"Not in this life."

"Came to Toronto from Fleet Street three years ago. He's as Canadian as you and me but he affects one of those mid-Atlantic accents and pretends he grew up in the shadow of Big Ben. He pulled down a big money job at the *Daily News* running a string of investigative reporters, and for a while he was making a name for himself as an A-one cast-iron incorruptible muckraker."

The *Toronto Daily News* was an upbeat tabloid paper that specialized in crusades, government exposés, and cheesecake. It was sued a lot, most recently by a provincial MP over allegations involving a bid-rigging scandal. Sometimes the *Daily News* won these lawsuits, sometimes the plaintiff. But it had a reputation for taking chances while the other city papers were looking the other way. Next to the *Sun* and the *Star*, the *News* was the most popular paper on the subways during the morning rush hour.

I only half-listened as Bellfield rattled on. In his excitement he had spilled some of his drink, and I dabbed absentmindedly at the reddish puddle it made on the bar with a napkin while thinking about my second wife, the only one who lasted long enough to hurt. She and Dickie had come from the same world, though they'd disliked each other at first sight. They both had *contacts*, as well as *conferences*, *meetings*, *lunches*, and *projects*. I myself never had contacts. When I went out to get smashed with a friend, Rini *had drinks* with a *colleague*. In moments of drunken excess I am still liable to suggest the marriage died of incommensurate vocabularies.

". . . quit just like that," said Bellfield, snapping his fingers. "Surprised the hell out of everybody."

"No kidding," I said, not certain what he was talking about but willing to share in the general astonishment at a sudden twist of fate.

"Claimed he wanted to be his own boss. Story was that he'd inherited a bundle when his first old lady kicked off a year ago. She was some kind of English county bluestocking, too good for mere mortals — nobody I know ever met her. He hired a sharp corporation lawyer, set up a company called Bar-Tor, and took over an independent daily, the *Star-Leader*, in Ockenden.

"I handled his PR during the takeover. On paper he looked

really good, but between you and me, Precious, Spandrell's no publisher. People management, employee relations, whatever you want to call it, he hasn't got the knack. Can't keep his hired help. The extra cash he brought to the operation has been going into new plant, computers, offset, photo labs. His back shop keeps walking out. He makes do in editorial with a bunch of tired hacks, kids out of journalism school, and steno girls dragged upstairs from classified."

"What you're telling me, Dickie," I said, with heat, "is it's a lousy job with a rotten boss, but I can have it because no one else wants it. What's wrong with Spandrell? He a lush, a martinet . . . "

Bellfield smiled triumphantly. "Take it easy, Precious, my friend," he said. "He's just an old-time hard-ass editor who likes to fire you every afternoon and hire you back every morning. Just the thing to soothe your shattered nerves."

With those words as a parting shot, he wrote Spandrell's number on the back of a business card and left Jerry's bar, promising to call the guy later in the afternoon to give me an introduction. The way he looked as he skipped out the door, the Cheshire cat grin, struck me as a bad omen. But there I was: too old for the army, too young for a pension. I didn't have a lot of alternatives.

I went into a coughing jag and lit a last French cigarette to clear my lungs. Jerry was looking at me with a mixture of pity and skepticism, as though he knew what was coming and didn't like it.

"Listen," I said, "all I need is a little capital to keep me going until I set up a cash flow. Doesn't that sound sensible?"

He looked pained and disappointed.

"Geez, Precious, I want to help, you know, but not in business."

After veering out of control, our conversation was getting more or less back on track. As soon as he mentioned business, I knew Jerry was getting ready to negotiate. He always had a soft place in his heart for regulars.

"I'll pay it back right away. You want me to go to somebody else and run the risk of getting my legs bent?"

He shoved his cigar into the kink of his mouth with an air of authority.

"I wanna show you sumpin, Precious." He turned away and shouted toward the back of the building. "Hey, Marty, come out here a minute, will ya?"

A monstrous primate, something between a gorilla and a neanderthal but uglier, dressed for the Queen Street disco scene, entered from the nether regions. He was built like a fullback, all wrapped up in platform shoes, brushed denim dungarees, and a silk shirt open at the chest. Nestled there in a mat of thick black hair, suspended from a gold chain, was a little corno to ward off the evil eye. He stared blankly in my direction.

"I wanted you to see another aspect of the business," said Jerry. "On account of Marty I can do business with some very high-risk clientele. You might say he's my default insurance like they have for car accidents. I just wanted to show you, Precious, in case . . ."

"Okay. Okay. Put it back in the box. I get the picture. This isn't some damn B movie, you know. I'm just taking out a loan."

Jerry dealt me two hundred dollars from the community chest. That made two hundred and fifty dollars for the day. I ordered the Swiss steak and fries and stood myself another drink. But somehow the atmosphere had turned chilly and officious.

2

It seemed to me that I had spent a lifetime, more or less, in towns just like Ockenden, changing buses to get to other towns.

A small branch-plant city of about forty-five thousand on the shoreline of Lake Ontario between Toronto and Kingston, it boasted a decayed waterfront that hadn't seen significant shipping since the 1890s, a ponderous close-built Victorian midtown, and a helter-skelter collection of brick or stucco subdivisions. At the ragged urban fringes there rose grey low buildings that housed a cable factory, a tractor assembly plant, a foundry, a knitting mill, and the regional warehouse for a grocery store chain, all owned by American conglomerates.

Approaching by road, you threaded rows of cut-rate gas stations, fast-food outlets, cheap motels, craft stores, and shopping malls surrounded by acres of parking lot. In the centre of town there was a bandana-sized park where pigeons disported between the War of 1812 cannon and a blue and gilt bandstand. Looking hopelessly out of place against the aged sedateness of its backdrop, a chamber of commerce banner loudly proclaimed Ockenden's annual winter carnival, complete with snowmobile races on the lake and an ice-fishing derby. From either end of the green space, the Anglican and Baptist churches glared at each other through a lattice of bare maple trees, rubbing shoulders with a railway hotel, a restaurant called the Ritz, a tavern called the American House, an art gallery, and the *Star-Leader*.

The newspaper occupied a squat two-storey building cheerfully decorated with patterns of brickwork in two tones of grey. From the upper floor, suspended over the sidewalk, hung a combination clock-thermometer advertising a local insurance agent who shared the office space. Neither device was working the next day when I arrived in Ockenden, or any other day for that matter. The time read 7:18, the temperature was eighty-two degrees.

Bellfield had been right about Spandrell. He was nasty and he needed a journeyman editor badly.

"Your friend says they call you Precious. You a pansy or something? I can't stand pansies. I won't have homosexuals working on my newspaper."

That was the first thing he said to me.

"Anyway, I wouldn't hire you in a million years on that idiot's recommendation."

That was the second.

It sounded bad, but it was difficult to take the man seriously because of the wig he was wearing. It was a cheap, ill-fitting specimen that looked like a small flat fur-bearing mammal which had taken refuge at the summit of Spandrell's bald head.

I said, "At least we agree on Dickie's mental ability."

Under the hairpiece my future employer was about forty-five, over six feet tall, and constructed along the lines of an over-the-hill sumo wrestler: bulging torso, thighs like fire hydrants, a skull that sat squarely on his shirt collar without the intervention of a neck. His eyes were small, angry, and almost hidden behind the thick black rims of his glasses. The lower part of his face was covered with a beard that only missed matching the colour of his wig by about a third of the spectrum.

He was sitting behind an antique Underwood typewriter in a glass office behind the U-shaped "rim," or editorial desk. His door was open; he had been poring over the day's page proofs, which littered the floor.

"I hate people who make wisecracks," he shot back in a voice that was trying to make up for the toupee.

He resumed stabbing his proofs with the stub of a grease pencil. The sheets on the floor bore the scars of his attacks, irritable circles, illegible hieroglyphs. He hadn't told me to leave, so I sat back and waited.

"Can you edit copy?" he demanded finally. "That's what we need to find out. Lay out pages, write headlines, size photos? You've been out of this end of the business a long time."

Instead of reciting my resumé, I picked up one of the proofs and held it in front of his face.

"You've got two busted heads and somebody doesn't know how to spell the capital of Nicaragua. On yesterday's front page — I read it outside — the council story lead was buried in the fifth paragraph. The picture should have been blown up over three columns and the story played beside it. Who does that page, anyway?"

"I do," said Spandrell. "Think you're smart, don't you? I want to show you something."

He placed a heavy hand on my shoulder and led me to the doorway.

It was a newsroom like any other newsroom, a little older, a little scruffier: scuffed tiles, banks of vinyl-topped desks, the chatter of aging typewriters, telephones ringing, the low buzz of conversation, and the suck and whoosh of pneumatic tubes. Along the length of the window ledge there were stacks of yellowing *Star-Leaders*, empty Styrofoam cups, cobwebs, and curled photographs. In one corner an office had been partitioned off for the sports department. Two doors led through the side wall to the composing room and the morgue.

Spandrell gestured grandly with the hand that wasn't gripping my clavicle and muttered, "The troops." The place suddenly went quiet, everyone looked up expectantly.

"Gratz, city desk," he said, nodding at a Teutonic youth who had just entered from the reception area rubbing his hands with a paper towel. "Spends a lot of time in the bathroom.

"You see that guy at the end of the rim with his mitt in a sling? That's Kercheval, the wire editor. Tried to run himself through a blender. See that empty desk? That's Millicent Pietrowski, my women's editor. She just eloped with her little theatre director.

"See that fat kid in the blazer? That's Wishty, court reporter. He's been here four months and we spike ninety percent of his stories because he's unreliable. That guy beside him? The one in tweed with the apple cheeks? Ashcroft. Here two weeks. Don't know about him yet. He hasn't turned in a story.

"My best photographer is a wino with a wooden leg who won't go near fires because he's inflammable. My sports editor takes drugs and thinks he talks to God. The old guy trying to hide by the coat rack? That's Damon Barrett. Pen name, you know, as in Damon Runyon. Maybe you heard of him. He keeps talking about when he was nature writer for the *Toronto Star*. He plagiarizes his copy from *Field and Stream*.

"Now, Precious," he said, turning to me, "I don't like you, but I think you'll fit right in. You get me? You can start on the women's pages and sub on the desk when you get the time. You know what a puck is?" He didn't wait for an answer. "I'm grooming you for sports when that guy in there flips out."

He tightened his grip on my shoulder for emphasis.

"And I don't want to hear another peep out of you. That's how I know things are working properly. I don't get any complaints. Okay?"

I looked around the newsroom. Nobody made a move. They were all terrified of Spandrell.

"Okay," I said.

The publisher's eyes narrowed suddenly as though he detected an element of insubordination in my answer. They were poker player's eyes, they gave away nothing but his anger. Then he dismissed me with directions to Payroll and Personnel, where a jolly fat lady with hair like fire, a moustache, and at least eight rings seemed to think my hiring on at the *Star-Leader* was the funniest thing since the invention of plastic doggy-do.

"Sorry, honey," she said, her mirth subsiding in a series of tremors that shook various parts of her anatomy independently of the whole. "Welcome to the Foreign Legion. You must be running away from something really awful to end up in a dump like this. What was it, hon? A woman? Booze? Drugs? Murder? Nobody wanted to publish your memoirs?"

"All of the above," I said, "and more, much more, too sordid to relate." She bit her lip to suppress another explosion of laughter; judging from the colour of her cheeks, the effort was nearly fatal. "You get a lot of that class of talent passing through?" I asked.

"Oh, honey, you don't know the half of it," she said, pausing to wipe tears from her eyes and take a deep breath. "We turn over more bodies than a massage parlour." She stretched out an arm the size of my leg and opened a filing cabinet. "See there? I don't file them alphabetically; I bet on how long they're going to last with Burton Spandrell. See! I had Millicent's folder at the front of the drawer. Of course, she was a friend so I knew what was coming. You taking her job?"

The fat lady erupted into hiccups when I nodded, then handed me a sheaf of forms and questionnaires.

"You have to fill out every one of these, even if you only stay a day, honey. Otherwise the tax people have epileptic fits. Here's a *Star-Leader* pen. It's the only thing you'll get around here that's free, except me." She winked coquettishly. I started to read some fine print dealing with loss of limbs in pursuit of my occupation. "You don't have to do that now, beautiful. I'll put you on the payroll. Just drop them off sometime before you quit."

"Thanks," I said edging toward the door. "Anything else I should know before I sign the lease?"

"That skinny blond in classified?" she asked with a giggle. "Name's Alice Varney. Don't try anything on her. Varney's got the clap."

"I'll try to remember," I said. "How about a map to the press-room? I'd like to look the place over."

"Second door past the food machines and back of the loading bay. You're not a union man, are you?" she asked. "Old Burton Spandrell hiring a union organizer. That'd be a laugh and a half. Say! Aren't you the guy they call Precious? What a riot!"

I left her lolling helplessly like an upturned turtle in a sagging office chair that shrieked metal fatigue every time she moved. The sound followed me along the corridor until I was almost out of earshot, when she shouted, "And don't eat outta those machines, honey! Stuff's poison. Couple a years ago I coulda been Miss Universe."

The pressmen were replating for a second edition when I pushed through the last fire door into the double-storey cavern that housed the *Star-Leader* printing plant. The steel floor shook; the air was thick and sharp with the heavy throb of machinery, like the beating of a heart, and the acrid newspaper smells of oil, ink, and hot lead. For a moment or two I gazed in awe at the intricate pile of cogs and wheels and giant cylinders like a kid in a museum staring at his first dinosaur skeleton.

The first press I had ever seen was an ancient creaking Campbell flatbed that crowded the tiny shop at the back of my Uncle Dorsey Elliot's house. Dorsey was a stereotypical hack newsman; his blood was eighty proof, his family life zero. That his wife had left him was history; no one ever talked about it except Dorsey when he was drunk, and then he talked too much. I could never tell whether he missed her or wanted to kill her.

In 1945, for reasons of economy, my mother and I moved in with Uncle Dorsey, soon after my father and his Hurricane were shot down over the Netherlands. Neither of them seemed much enamoured of the arrangement. My mother's name was Nicolle, although everyone called her Nickel. She was a black-clad proto-beatnik who made her living painting portraits at a hundred dollars a shot. Uncle Dorsey published the local weekly, a chronic money-loser known affectionately by its subscribers as the Ameliasburg *Times and Distemper*. Nickel spent so much time at the Parmesan Bar and Grill, the town night spot, that she made a serious attempt to have the bar legally designated as the final repository for her ashes. Dorsey did all his drinking in his office with a mangy misanthropic golden retriever bitch called Adolph. Often Mother and Dorsey would go for days without saying a word, stumping around the house lost in their separate worlds, like the proverbial ships that pass in the night.

Yet that little newspaper and the cluttered printing shop enchanted me: the holy of holies where the silent press stood like an altar, its black rollers as high as my head, the stern cabinets with their neat gunmetal type trays, the Ludlow machine for casting heads, the small galley press with a brayer for inking, bales of newsprint, drums of ink, cubbyholes along the walls for column rules, space slugs, and stand-up lines, and the smooth-surfaced stone, always mysteriously cool. As a boy I rummaged there for hours, mixing the fonts, printing messages on bits of scrap, carving lead pigs, watching my uncle's hands flutter over his composing stick.

When I was old enough, I went to work for Dorsey part time after school to earn pocket money, and it stood to reason that I had my eye set on a career in the papers. But Mother had other ideas. She had decided I would follow my luckless father into the air force. When I asked her why, all she could do was sniffle into a paint-smeared rag and mutter something about men in uniforms being nothing but heartbreakers. Unaccountably, Uncle Dorsey backed her up. The day I left Ameliasburg for basic training he dragged me into the pressroom, spilled gin into two cracked coffee mugs, and said, in his inimitably pickled voice, "Moss, don't ever become a newsman, and never fall in love." It was there they found him a few years later, face down, dead, in the litter and ink.

I stayed where I was a few minutes longer to see the hands lock down the last plates, hear the warning bells, and watch the freshly folded newspapers flooding off the line. Twenty years had fled. I hadn't listened to Uncle Dorsey. When I got out of the air force, I had my wings and a ticket to a gold mine. In the early sixties airlines were offering a million bucks, fifty grand a year, to ex-servicemen who wanted to fly passenger jets. But the thought of turning into a glorified bus driver at the age of twenty-three chilled me. And somehow I thought the money would always be there.

On a whim I took a job covering the police beat for a small city daily not unlike the *Star-Leader*. Inside of a month I was hooked on the steady rhythmic surge of the deadline, dropping

Dexedrine tablets and working eighty-hour weeks, drifting through my free Sundays in the company of chain-smoking, liverish veterans, their hoarse endless talk echoing in my ears and dreams. I got married; I got divorced. The years accumulated like spent butts in an ashtray. When I finally pulled my nose out of the rat race long enough to grasp the situation, when I finally realized Dorsey had been right all along, it was too late to change and too late to kick.

Twenty years.

But, as the French say, even the most beautiful woman cannot give more than she has.

3

I took a room over the American House, where I could roll downstairs to the bar if I had to, and started working the early-morning shift at the *Star-Leader*. Each day I wrapped the raincoat around my body like a winding sheet and plodded wearily to the newsroom. Yellow street lights blazed at irregular intervals. My shadow waxed and waned like successive incarnations of a soul. My ulcer played up. I caught a cold which threatened to revive my pneumonia.

Yet, if the truth were told, I was relieved and content to be back in harness to the daily press. In the aftermath of my collision with Anne Delos, I needed a place to hide out and nurse my rumpled self-esteem. By the time a month had passed, I had lapsed comfortably into the anonymity of the editorial desk, the diurnal tussle with blank dummy pages, and the stubborn syntax of faceless wire service rewrite men.

I took Spandrell's advice and stayed out of his way. I was only being pragmatic. What I worried about was losing my temper at him. Although my recent stint in a Greek jail had taught me the wisdom of accommodation, I wasn't sure that would be enough to prevent me from offering constructive criticism if he started pushing me around. But I soon discovered a couple of regular paycheques had turned me into an addict, and I didn't relish the thought of a sudden decline in prosperity. After paying my debts to Jerry Mennenga and Dickie Bellfield, I had opened a savings account.

Afternoons I spent in the American in the company of various colleagues, usually Kercheval and Barrett. I liked these men, tough old birds flying upwind against time. The wire editor, his sliced hand held in front of his chest like a puppet, was one of those stolid types who stuck with one paper for forty years, hated unions, belonged to the Legion, invested in duplexes, and moved to a prefab in Arizona when he turned sixty-five.

Barrett, on the other hand, was a bona fide burnout, an aging hack who swore undying friendship as soon as I let on I did remember his fishing columns in the *Star*. A sad-faced, teary-eyed man with a nose like a strawberry, he had grown up in Ockenden, where he had apprenticed at the *Star-Leader*, arced briefly into the big city limelight, and finally subsided into familiar obscurity. No one remembered his real name, possibly not even Damon himself. What he had done for entertainment before I came along, I'll never know. I would sit for hours listening to his stories, drinking his booze, vaguely hoping someone would do the same for me twenty years down the line.

When I rented my room, the woman at the desk (who also doubled as barmaid and dinner hostess) told me that there wasn't much happening in Ockenden. The young people with any get up and go usually got up and went to Toronto. The rest played musical marriages, stagnated in the plants, bought motorboats and trail bikes on time, and raised fat cells in front of their TV sets. The only thing that ever got them excited was the town hockey team, the Oaks, which hadn't had a winning season in eight years.

As January quietly congealed into February, I began to enjoy myself. It was lonely at times but I got to enjoy that too. I took my meals at the Ritz and drank beer at the American. I made some friends and dated a checkout girl at Food City. I avoided writing Anne, and except for a couple of postcards, I didn't hear from her.

I read a lot. The Ockenden Heights Secondary School English department was leaning heavily on Dickens, Yeats, and Hemingway that winter. As the school year wore on, the book and supply store a block down from the tavern began letting its overstock go at half-price. When I was bored I took walks around town, especially along the waterfront, where I got all the excitement I wanted watching the lake freeze. In a short while, Barrett told me, the little bay would come alive with ice-fishing shacks and buzzing snowmobiles. But for the time being I had the place to myself.

It was then, in the middle of February, armpit of the year, with the weather closing in and spring nothing but a weatherman's stale joke, it was then Rose Oxley was murdered.

The shrub borders in front of the newspaper knocked their icy branches together in the wind. The sidewalks were choked with snow. The clock-thermometer read 7:18 and eighty-two degrees. The real time was one p.m., Friday. I had just returned to the newsroom from a trip to the doctor about my sick chest. He was one of these modern doctors, fit and tanned enough to make most normally healthy people feel terminally ill. His wife sold real estate, and he gave me her card in case I needed a house. He seemed bored with my cold, told me to buy a warmer coat.

The office was deserted. Not the ghost of a hand passed its immaterial fingers over the keys of a typewriter. Telephones jangled at half-a-dozen unoccupied desks. Spandrell had taken the day off, and the rest of the staff had followed his example after putting the paper to bed. The *Star-Leader* was that kind of organization. Harry Gratz, the city editor, would leave the phone number of some bar, but he was never there. The kids might be out digging up deathless features for the time bank. That was giving them the benefit of the doubt.

I shucked my coat and started answering phones from the reception door to the editorial rim. They were mostly callbacks until I reached the city line.

"Gratz?"

"No can do, Wishty. He's gone home."

"Oh God, I've been trying to reach him for an hour. Who is this?"

"Elliot."

"Who?"

"Women's page."

"Who?"

"Precious, damn it! What do you want?"

Wishty was excited. If possible, his thinking was even more confused than usual. He had been on the paper five months and still hadn't figured out how to put a subject and verb together to make a two-word sentence. He and Gratz were symbiotic, Gratz the patron, Wishty the toady, otherwise Wishty would have been fired long ago for his chronic inability to copy names and addresses correctly from the police charge sheet.

"There's been a murder, for God's sake," he said, almost shouting, before adding, as an afterthought, "I think."

"What do you mean, 'I think'?"

"The cops were talking about it in the can. I can't get anything official."

Wishty's voice was harassed and self-important. A trifle myopic on the topic of his own shortcomings, he believed his court notices ranked somewhere near *Crime and Punishment* as mirrors of the human soul.

"Hold it," I said. "Don't you guys have a police band radio in here?"

"Somebody stole it."

"Well, at least get an address for this alleged homicide and take a ride over there. What are you waiting for? Ever hear of initiative?"

"I can't leave, Precious. Municipal court's been held over; there are seven drunk-driving charges to come up this afternoon. What would Harry say?"

"He'd say you left your news sense in the toilet when you came to work this morning. You can get those verdicts from the court secretary Monday. Let's see you hit the track running, Wishty!"

"I can't. I want to talk to Harry."

"Wishty!"

"I'll call if I hear anything."

The phone went dead. I looked up to see young Blythe Ashcroft amble into the newsroom from the morgue with a sandwich thrust into his face.

"What's all the excitement?" he asked innocently.

Ashcroft had joined the paper because he wanted to be a novelist. Of course every young reporter worth his salt has an unfinished novel in his desk drawer awaiting bestsellerdom, but Ashcroft had tried to show me sections of at least five, all based on the theme of a young man finding himself in the rough and tumble demimonde of the newspaper world. Born to money, he had taken great pains to let me know he was one of the Oakville Ashcrofts, just in case I confused him with the Rosedale Ashcrofts, who were much richer but not as nice. He had graduated *cum laude* from the posh precincts of Upper Canada College, dropped out after two years of university English, and then spent a further year in Paris making the acquaintance of large numbers of Left Bank cockroaches. All this I learned because Ashcroft, like Damon Barrett, was willing to buy the booze as long as I listened to his stories.

I quickly explained about Wishty's call and tactfully suggested he ought to get onto the story pronto. Ashcroft started for the door, then turned back, dismayed.

"Where am I supposed to go?"

"Jesus, call the radio station. If there's been a murder, they'll have a man out there by now."

"But that's the competition."

"Not where the *Star-Leader*'s concerned, kid. In this thing we're non-starters. Let's hope they're in a good mood over there and think you're some kind of joke."

Swallowing his pride along with the rest of his sandwich, Ashcroft dialled the CQPR News Hotline. Their police band radio had not been stolen and they had gotten wind of something big an hour earlier, according to the news editor. A CQPR radio car was at the scene, but no word had come back.

Ashcroft scribbled down the address on the edge of town and bolted for the door.

"Holy shit!" he said, stopping to don his coat and galoshes. "I've never had a story like this. It's a scoop."

"Not exactly, kid. Close enough, though. You deserve it."

"Thanks, Precious."

"Kid, don't call me Precious."

"What do I do?" he asked, pausing in mid-galosh to peer at me anxiously.

"What do you mean?"

"Well, how do I investigate a murder? Where do I start?"

"Kid, just go over there and ask a cop what's going on. Don't get in the way. Get a statement, then call me." I looked at my watch. "I'll wait."

I hated to admit it, but if Kercheval and Barrett sometimes reminded me of the gloomy surcease toward which my slapdash career was headed, Ashcroft often looked like a ghost from my past. As he stampeded out the door, already half-blinded with visions of banner headlines, I recalled my younger self, vomiting on a riverbank while a meat-faced detective called Flaherty fished out the decomposed body of a once-pretty high school co-ed. That was my first murder. My first floater.

When I look back now, it's obvious that novelty was the chief charm of youth. Everything I did was a first; everything was exciting by virtue of being new. And while I was rushing around like that, piling up trophies and trying to keep track in my head, I didn't have to think much about myself or whether I was doing any good. It came as quite a shock to discover that housewives really did wrap today's haddock in yesterday's headlines and that a newsman's life could end up being nothing but a series of one-night stands.

Needless to say I tried to break the mould. I sold math texts and wall projection units for a Toronto publishing house. I wrote ad copy for a Japanese automaker, striving to interest the Canadian consumer in a new line of subcompacts named after venomous snakes. One winter I published a gossip sheet on a Caribbean cruise ship. I even taught journalism at a place called Martin Frobisher Community College north of Timmins, training Eskimo kids to churn out leading articles on the price of butter in the EEC.

My biggest break came when I married Rini, and she finagled me a job as a provincial government information flack at Queen's Park. That lasted precisely five and a half months, after which I was hastily terminated when my too-lucid gloss on the announcement of a budget deficit caused the party in power to drop three points in a Gallup poll. Struck by the vanity and fallibility of all human desire and aspiration, I ceased forever to kick against the pricks. I spent my severance pay in Jerry Mennenga's bar and then proceeded to run up a tab that took me a year to work off.

Pondering the many twists and turns a life could take between a riverbank, a Greek prison, and my present servitude, I coughed my way back to the reception desk and browbeat the blue-haired dragon who lived there into giving me a staff list with addresses and phone numbers.

I tried the American first; Barrett came on the line with a cheery, "Goddamn, Precious, I sure would like to help out. I could probably give Ashcroft a lot of pointers. But I'm tied up at the moment." He chuckled, making a sound like gas escaping a valve. "I'm interviewing a rum and coke."

I dialled Spandrell's number. Since his first wife's death, he had remarried. The new Mrs. Spandrell, voice like a street hawker, curtly informed me he was out and not expected home until late.

Telephones shrilled all around me. I answered the nearest: it was a female, bursting with spleen because her paper was late. I slammed the receiver down on her distant squawks.

The city line rang — it was Ashcroft.

"Give me a rewrite man! Fast!"

"This isn't the *New York Times*, kid. What have you got?"

"I'm at the scene."

"Yeah."

"Do you want me to read my story?"

"Yeah."

"This reporter arrived at the scene at approximately 2:45 p.m. From where I sat, just outside a police barricade, I could see the house, a brick farmhouse about a quarter mile from the edge of town. The house was threatening, make that 'sinister,' with its ivy-choked windows —"

"Cut it out, Ashcroft," I said. His voice had taken on the laboured tone of a TV news documentary. "This isn't Live-Action Cam. What happened?"

"At 2:47 p.m. I approached Constable Rick Myers of the Ockenden Police Department at the barricade. He confirmed that a murder had taken place. They haven't caught anybody yet. Precious, I think I can get a good sidebar on what it's like to man a police roadblock."

"Shut up," I said. There was definitely something wrong with the way Ashcroft thought. "Take a deep breath, look at your notes, assuming you took some, and tell me who was killed, where, when, how, and why. Very simple. The-quick-brown-fox-jumped-over-the-lazy-dog. Now you do it."

"I was coming to that." He sounded hurt. "She was a Rose Oxley, sixty-eight, widow. The address is a rural route number, but everybody calls this concession road the Blue Line. She was found before noon by a daughter."

"Anything else? Suspects?"

"No. Nothing like that. Uh-oh! Wait a second!" I could hear paper shuffling at Ashcroft's end of the line. "The cops sent for a tracker dog. That's something, eh? A trail. Maybe the killer left a glove or something."

"Get real, kid. How was she killed?"

"Renner, that's the assistant chief of police, Renner won't say. But . . ." There was more paper shuffling. "Here it is — a fire!"

"She was burned to death."

"Not exactly. There was a fire, but it had nothing to do with

. . . at least, I think . . . well." The kid sighed deeply. "Well, anyway, it wasn't really a fire. Some old newspapers and junk smouldering in another room. Hey! I'll bet the killer set a fire to cover up his crime. You know — no body, no murder!"

"Ashcroft," I said, "I just can't break your code. You read too many damn detective stories. You want to be a newsman or a paperback dick or what?"

"A newsman, of course." Now he sounded insulted.

"Then try to resist this fatal urge to spin fiction into the tangled plot of life. Leave the theories and cover-up angles to the police. You just get a story."

There was a long silence as Ashcroft, clearly impatient with me, reined himself in.

"What should I do then?" he asked finally. "Come in and write it up?"

"Are you tired of working? What's the radio reporter doing?"

"He's just hanging around, talking to cops," said the kid.

"Well, why don't you just do that for a while? Deadline isn't until eleven a.m. tomorrow. I'll find somebody to look after things here."

There was a long pause.

"Sure, Precious," he said, "I mean Mr. Elliot. I mean . . ." His voice quavered doubtfully. "Isn't there anything else?"

"That's the business, Ashcroft. There never is anything else. Nothing else at all. Just stand around and talk. If you want romance, take your girl to the movies. Well, maybe there is one other thing you should know."

"What's that?" he asked eagerly.

"Don't piss in the wind."

"What? Oh."

I hung up. I hoped Ashcroft would have the sense to do the same.

4

By the time I finished talking to Ashcroft, typing notes for Gratz, and filing a three-paragraph lead (story to follow) to the Canadian Press regional desk in Toronto, it was four o'clock, two hours over my shift. I dialled the American: Barrett had achieved considerable spiritual enlightenment since we last talked and cheerfully promised to trot across the park "*toot sweet*" with a bottle of Hennessy. Another half hour slid by before it dawned on me that he had capitulated much too easily. Chances were high that Damon had lingered to toast his good intentions and forgotten his holy mission. I tried Spandrell's number once more; no one answered.

An empty newsroom is a lonesome place. The sea-glow of fluorescent lights, the vacant desks, the idle typewriters, the silence, broken only by an occasional chatter of wire-service machines, contrast sharply with the chaotic hubbub of deadline. I was just recalling how Uncle Dorsey had dealt with professional solitude by sipping neat gin from an ancient Benylin cough syrup bottle, and considering the application of some such ruse in my own case, when the receptionist (hair like smoke, chest like a cowcatcher) burst through the door with a bundle of correspondence clutched to her breasts.

This aging force of nature was Lana Deptford, aka Miss Lana, spinster. During business hours she handled the publisher's calls, repelled visitors, censored letters, and otherwise interfered with the chores of news-gathering in a glass alcove in the hall lobby. Because of her strategic position, she had an effect on the paper out of all proportion to the importance of her job. If Miss Lana didn't think a tip or a press release was newsworthy, it generally didn't get over the threshold. If she didn't like you, you didn't get any mail.

"You forgot to check your box again, Mr. Elliot," she said, hissing through her teeth.

"Oh darn," I said, taking a defensive position behind the rim.

Miss Lana was also a frustrated gossip columnist and took an inordinate interest in the women's pages. It was a constant source of pain to her that I failed to share this enthusiasm for the Byzantine entanglements of Ockenden society.

"There was another card today, Mr. Elliot," she added, her voice dripping with reproach. She fingered through what was obviously the usual bag of wedding announcements, club minutes, recipe lists, feminist tracts, and fashion magazines and extracted an art postcard depicting Byron's death at Missolonghi. "I have mentioned before that we do not care to receive personal messages at the *Star-Leader*."

"Damn right," I said. "If you told me once, you told me a dozen times. Trouble is I don't even know the woman. Never heard of her. I'm a victim of mistaken identity. Go ahead and trash it. I don't want to have anything to do with it."

"Don't you want to read it?"

"Just give me an abstract. I'll take your word for it. Drop the rest of that junk on my desk when you leave."

Miss Lana stood her ground, glaring in a way that reminded me of something out of the Cretaceous epoch.

The postcards from Anne Delos were a second source of friction between us. This was the third in ten days. How Anne had found me I had no idea, unless she had hired detectives or worked through her husband's political connections. They all read about the same: honeyed reminders full of sweetness and trouble. Miss Lana thought they smelled of scandal; the idea filled her with passionate envy.

"Mr. Spandrell will hear about this!" she said in a voice as low as a whisper.

"Terrific," I said, offering her the city line. "You know where he is?"

"I know that he doesn't allow drinking in the newsroom, Mr. Elliot."

This was her trump. I glanced up sharply, half-expecting to see Barrett's ruddy face bobbing through the door, but in vain. Either Miss Lana was clairvoyant, or she had been eaves-dropping when I called the American. And either way she wasn't missing a chance to add alcohol abuse to her growing list of Elliot peccadilloes.

"He doesn't pay overtime either," I said. "You ever think of joining the Mounties, Miss Lana? They're looking for men like you."

No longer in a mood to play Mr. Personality with the company jade, I applied myself to the telephone again and got its little brother in Spandrell's house jangling an urgent summons. Then, cradling the receiver against my ear, I lit a cigarette, loaded a typewriter with scratch paper, and began to punch out headlines.

BERSERK COPY EDITOR/GARROTTES RECEPTIONIST
POLICE DISCOUNT SEX MOTIVE
NEWSROOM SLAYER AT LARGE
COPS GUN DOWN/MAD DOG/NEWSHOUND

"Who the hell is this?"

Spandrell came on the line, sounding like my air force drill instructor. Five feet away Miss Lana heard his voice and flinched.

"It's Precious, down at the paper," I said, using my working name to save time. "You know about the Oxley murder yet?"

"I got something on the car radio," he said guardedly.

"We're taking a shower on it, Chief. Ashcroft is at the scene losing his virginity. I can't raise Gratz. I thought you might want to spell me . . . Wait a minute." Miss Lana was straining forward in an effort to hear both sides of the conversation. "You want to talk to him or listen on the extension?"

Adept at petty office blackmail, the old bag knew enough not to blow her advantage by spilling her guts to Spandrell, especially when he was in a bad mood. She blushed hot pink and sulked toward the newsroom door, where she collided with

Ashcroft, who appeared out of nowhere, soaked up to his knees, a tear in his pants revealing a suit of paisley undershorts, and a gleam of triumph in his eyes.

"Check that," I said. "The kid's back."

"Are you guys crazy?" yelled Spandrell. "That's Wishty's story. Where's Wishty?"

"Home. Traffic court. I don't know. Wishty's got his head up Gratz's ass so far he can hardly breathe."

"I don't want to hear that shit," said Spandrell. "I talked to Gratz an hour ago. Wishty called him from the courthouse. He got a statement from the cops we can update in the morning."

"Doesn't sound like much," I said, watching Ashcroft pantomime the brutal murder of Kercheval's swivel chair. "The kid's been working a colour angle. He had the death house staked out all afternoon."

"Spike it!" said Spandrell. "That little snob's not getting any play off Wishty's beat while I run the damn paper. I hate poaching, Precious. No reporter of mine is going to cut another guy's throat for a crummy byline. Understand?"

"Right, Chief," I said. "You want me to leave a note for Gratz so at least we get the name and address straight?"

"Keep it up, Precious, and you'll make me a happy man," said Spandrell. "I'd just love to fire your butt."

He slammed his receiver down with a crack that nearly took my ear off. For a few seconds I listened to the purr of the dial tone. Miss Lana was hovering by the coat rack, torn between the kid's *tableau vivant* and her penchant for vicarious phone calls. Ashcroft shuffled his notes impatiently, looking ready to burst.

"Let's have it," I said finally, hanging up on dead air. "What have you got?"

"It's a real scoop, Precious. Wait till I tell you."

"Says who? Wishty already filed a police statement with Gratz. Canadian Press had the story two hours ago."

"Not just the murder," he said. "I beat everybody on the inside story. But you'll have to tell me how to handle it. Okay?"

"I guess I'm elected."

"Well, I did just what you said, Precious. I hung around with the radio guy."

"Name's Elliot, kid," I interrupted. "You two must have made the Bobbsey Twins look like grizzled veterans."

"Wait a second! This'll grab you," said Ashcroft, ignoring me while he flipped through his notes. "The tracker dog arrived a little after four o'clock. It jumped out a back window and headed straight into town through fields behind the house."

"You can never trust those dogs."

"No. No. He was following a trail."

"Sounds like a movie about some guy taking a Tennessee vacation with the posse hot on his heels," I said, nodding at his trousers. "Exactly how close did you follow this dog?"

"Aw, Precious. It seemed like a good idea. The cops wouldn't let me near the house, and there weren't any other leads. They couldn't stop me walking along the fencerows and watching. Anyway, it panned out, didn't it?"

I cocked an eyebrow and waited. Miss Lana had disappeared. No doubt she was back in her lair making the phone wires sing with her hot news flash about the murder.

"There's a rail line that runs through a deep cut next to the subdivisions on the east side of town. The dog found an abandoned footbridge over the tracks which led to a laneway between Winston Street and Redwood Place. As soon as I figured out where he was headed, I jogged back for my car and circled around to where Redwood dead ends against the rail cut. The cops didn't like it, but what could they do?"

"Good kid," I said. "So far you've earned a Pulitzer Prize for out-thinking police dogs and alienating the local fuzz."

"Damn, Precious. It's my first big story."

"Yeah. And you're going to blow it, especially if you keep calling me that and I don't help you get it in the newspaper."

Ashcroft flushed and went quiet for a moment or two. When he started talking again, his face wore one of those long-suffering expressions full of pity and resignation. I knew just how he felt.

"The cops reckon the killer came over the footbridge and maybe had a car parked in the laneway. By the time I arrived, they were going house to house asking people if they'd noticed anything."

"How do you know that?"

"I knocked on somebody's door after Renner left and asked."

"Amazing," I said, addressing a pneumatic tube canister Gratz had left on his desk. "You see, Trethgor, I told you the scanner indicated the presence of intelligent life forms on the planet. What happened next, kid?"

"Well, nothing really. I hung around watching Renner for an hour, and when I went back to my car the headlights were on. When I tried to start it the battery died. You think the cops would do something like that? Turning my headlights on, I mean? I had to take a cab."

"Ashcroft, I despair. You took all this time to tell me a dog ran across a bridge and your car broke down? Is this a news story or theatre of the absurd? Do I look —?"

"Just a minute!" he cried, snapping his fingers. "I hadn't pulled it all together before, but it fits, it fits!"

Ashcroft under the influence of an idea was a man possessed. His eyes glazed and focussed on a point about two yards behind my back, his speech patterns quickened and shaded into the breathless and exclamatory, and his hands punched ragged holes in the surrounding air.

"The driver!" he said. "He knew the old lady! He used to pick her up two nights a week for the Legion bingo. He told me for a fact she had plenty of cash stashed in the house. She hated banks. She used to pay cab fare out of a big wad of bills! The driver even warned her not to show that kind of money around town. But she never listened. Three years ago somebody mugged her where the city bus stops at the town end of the Blue Line, snatched her purse and knocked her on the head with a broken fence paling."

The kid stopped and shone at me with an expression that had *quod erat demonstrandum* spelled in neon all over it.

"So?" I said, and his face fell halfway to China.

"Well, it's cut-and-dried, isn't it? The killer had to be a local person, somebody who knew about the old footbridge and had heard Rose Oxley kept money hidden in her house. He walked out there from Redwood Place last night, knocked her over, set a fire to cover himself, and slipped back the way he came. All the cops have to do is watch for anybody spending a lot of money or trying to get out of town suddenly."

"Or maybe he'll just wander over to the police station and give himself up," I said. "Just because he's a killer, Ashcroft, it doesn't mean he's stupid. What if he just stays home and minds his own business?"

I propped my feet on the vinyl desktop and inspected the destruction of my European shoes. Poor lost soles in exile. My mind strayed to a bottle of Hennessy waiting like a friendly old lady in my hotel room. I lit a cigarette, fired the spent match at a gunmetal waste basket, and missed. The blue smoke was like mountain air to a healthy man. I watched it dissipate like a pleasant dream between me and the kid.

An elderly recluse had been murdered. It happened all the time. Like road accidents. Some wacko biker short on social inclinations heard she had a mattress stuffed with greenbacks and nailed her for it. It didn't matter if it was true about the money. It was a common rumour about old folks who lived alone. Some people thought they were witches. It wasn't much of a story unless they caught the Piltdown man who did it. And even then we would have to wait for courtroom testimony before satisfying the public's insatiable thirst for gory details.

But Ashcroft was on the scent. He had read too many books

about detectives, clues, motives, and logic. He didn't seem to realize that most convicted murderers either gave themselves up or got stumbled on accidentally by some lucky cop, usually on another case. Most killers got clean away. Murdering was probably a healthier profession than journalism.

While I was entertaining these negative thoughts, Ashcroft had been cooking up a succulent new lead.

"What about the daughter?" he exclaimed. "We could interview her! How she found the body, her feelings as she entered the death house."

"Very kinky, Ashcroft. But the cops have already told her to keep her mouth shut. You don't seem to understand the way things work. Let's call it a night. Wishty'll need all the help he can get in the morning."

"We could try," he said. The expression on his face reminded me of Uncle Dorsey's dog when she needed to pee.

"You can try. I'm bushed. I'm going to make like the trees and leave."

"Well, what should I do? I don't even know her name."

"Try Oxley."

"What if she's married?"

"Make the calls, kid. Don't make problems, make calls."

He started thumbing through a tattered phone book that looked like it dated from the time of the Dead Sea Scrolls. I headed for the coat rack, stopping by the women's desk to snag the postcard Miss Lana had dropped there along with the rest of my junk mail.

Ashcroft was getting on my nerves. I know a lot about human relations; they're like strips of flypaper. He just wanted a little professional advice, a mentor, a pal. And I just wanted to be left alone. All three of my marriages had begun with as little provocation. Anne Delos had wanted to borrow a coin so she could use the bathroom. You never knew where that sort of thing would end. And yet I'd always had a weakness for kids like Ashcroft, earnest kids who aspire to martyrdom and fame.

I trailed my coat back to the rim, dragged the city street directory out of its hiding place in Gratz's desk, and found Rose Oxley's address. Then I scrawled out a list of her three nearest neighbours. My second call unearthed a doctor who had a swarm of infants pounding and screaming in the background, who knew Mrs. Oxley and was, yes, shocked at the news of her murder. He had heard it on the radio. I said I was trying to locate the deceased person's daughter. And he said he thought the daughter's name was Ranger, though he had never met her.

I glanced at Ashcroft who was furiously tearing pages out of his notebook. His face was ashen, his eyes damp with embarrassment. Upper Canada College and the Left Bank weren't any help to him under the circumstances. The kid had no experience. He was starting from scratch. I tried to remember what it was like before I learned to trace a lead or think in double-decker headlines, but I'd learned all that from Uncle Dorsey. I felt sorry for Ashcroft. It seemed likely that he had never asked strangers dumb questions over the telephone before. And I realized he probably wasn't ready to talk to people of the lady-who-just-tripped-over-a-murdered-mother variety either.

There were two Rangers in the book. The first was a dud. An abrupt, officious female voice answered to the second number. I asked if this was the residence of Mrs. Ranger, daughter of Rose Oxley. The female voice said it was and what did I want. Mrs. Ranger did not wish to be disturbed.

I assumed a solemn editorial tone, full of gravity and Walter Cronkite, and told the female voice how sorry I felt about what had happened. Then I asked if it would be convenient for us (in emergencies, the first person plural always lends a note of dignity and authority) to come round and interview Mrs. Ranger. The voice humphed and said it certainly would not.

In the background I heard another female voice making forceful interrogative noises. My guess was that Mrs. Ranger didn't appreciate having decisions made for her by overzealous neighbours or relatives. I heard the receiver being handed over to another person, female voice number two, cool and strong but very weary.

"Yes. What do you want?"

I repeated the whole saga.

"Do you have to do this?" she asked with resignation.

"Well, it's the job, ma'am. I know it's not pleasant, but people like to know what happened, and a newspaper story sometimes helps in catching criminals; a reader sees the headline and remembers a car or a face that gives the police a lead."

It was a pretty good line. I almost believed it myself.

"I guess it would be all right," she said. "I'm a little tired right now. Could we make it later?"

"Certainly, Mrs. Ranger. Say eight o'clock?"

"Yes. That would be fine. Thank you."

I felt like a heel. Mrs. Ranger's voice had a pleasant forgiving timbre. I was sorry I had to string her along, sorry I was going to intrude on her private grief with the muddy workboots of the commercial press. At the best of times I was not sure we had right on our side, and in this case I could not regard the lady as an adversary.

I gave Ashcroft the lowdown. He seemed to regard a few quick phone calls as telepathic. I pointed him toward the door, sending him out to retrieve his car and check with the cops for an up-to-the-minute report. After wading through a leisurely dinner, I would meet him back at the newsroom and borrow his car for the Ranger interview, providing it would start. Later we could dovetail my sob story with his hard news lead, and even Spandrell wouldn't be able to spike the resulting soap opera.

5

It was eight-thirty p.m. when I finally coaxed Ashcroft's decade-old, rust-eaten Volkswagen to what threatened to be its last stop in front of a one-storey white clapboard cracker box festooned with strings of coloured lights. I was half an hour late. I had not eaten. I had not read my mail while sipping a post-prandial B&B at the Ritz bar. My chin ached where Barrett had socked me. My heart was practising scales on my rib cage after a near-collision at the foot of the *Star-Leader* parking ramp.

I drank from a brandy bottle fetched from the hotel in lieu of supper and did deep breathing to reduce my pulse rate. Trying to do both at once, I inhaled some of the brandy and had a coughing fit, tossing around the kid's front seat in imminent danger of asphyxiation. For as long as that took I forgot my chin and the small cut inside my mouth where a lower canine had punctured the flesh. What had gone wrong with Damon? A mystery for sure. By the time I reached the American he had drunk himself from Nirvana to hell and was squaring off against five tool-and-die apprentices about forty years younger than he was. I am all for letting the youth of the nation fight its own battles, but in this case I thought the boys were a bit overmatched by one smashed newsman. I was just telling Barrett to ease up and let them live when he punched me.

I was more surprised than hurt. Barrett and I blinked at each other for a moment or two and then the bastard started to cry, relieving me of responsibility for hitting him back. There was a waiter I had made friends with, a man who liked to bet me double or nothing on the size of my bar tab every night. The waiter and I dragged Barrett upstairs to my room, and I called a taxi to take him home. While we waited I poured a round of drinks in bathroom Dixie cups. The waiter diluted his with some of the stuff the municipality loosely called water and shook his head at the teary old man.

"He was watching the news on TV," he said. "Then all of sudden he starts cheering and whistling through his teeth like he's at a ball game or something. Wanted to buy drinks for the house on account of the old lady had been croaked. Never seen him like that before. Usually sits on his own and won't say boo. Somebody tells him to shut up and stop slandering the dead, and the next thing I know he's knocked over a table trying to get himself mutilated."

Barrett chose not to respond to this. He sat on the edge of my bed staring straight ahead, his hands resting primly on his knees, ignoring the brandy I had set out for him, a sure sign of insensibility in a man like that.

"Poor old guy," said the waiter, moved to pity and philosophy by the alcohol. "He got a snootful, that's for certain. People like him are worse than teenagers for holding their liquor. They're so mad that life crossed them up. I guess it's just lucky they're too feeble to do any damage."

He nodded omnisciently while I went through Barrett's pockets to pay his bill and make sure he had enough left to cover cab fare. When the driver arrived, I paid him in advance to see that Barrett got inside his house. Then I gave the waiter five dollars of my own for helping out. He wanted to toss me for it, double or nothing, but I was already late for my appointment with the murdered woman's daughter. I told him to cut the horseplay and not mention anything about the evening to Barrett. Then I hunched back across the city park, past the bandstand and the chamber of commerce banner, feeling bleak as the weather, seeing Barrett's ruby nose and streaming eyes, only sometimes it was Uncle Dorsey's face and sometimes it was mine.

Amy Ranger's house, to which I now directed my flat and reluctant feet, was about two miles from the *Star-Leader*, across a muddy river with an unpronounceable name that meant "cow

pie" in Ojibway, in a down-at-heel section of town called the
Rifle Range because it was once a militia drill ground. I took
comfort from the fact that this particular house, unlike its
neighbours, showed signs of recent repair. It was newly painted,
though the uneven trim and the paint pools on the porch
indicated it had not been a professional job. The card table-sized
lawn was clear of garbage and not presently in use as a mortuary
for car parts and children's toys. The aluminum storm door had
the initial *R* in italic script worked into its frame, and above the
R a real holly wreath gleamed under a coach lamp.

As soon as I rang the bell the front door cracked open enough
to reveal a sharp-eyed, sour-faced woman of about forty with
hair dyed black as soot. A lipstick-stained cigarette dangled from
her fingers. She glared at me malignantly.

"What do you want?"

It was the raspy voice of Mrs. Ranger's overzealous and self-
appointed guardian. Its owner frisked me with her eyes,
weighing this, bruising that, and then, after I told her who I was,
she stepped back to let me squeeze through into the house.

I found myself in a living room that resembled nothing so
much as a slice of Amazonian rain forest or a botanical garden
gone wild. Vines, tendrils, great rubbery leaves, and hungry-
looking blossoms ran riot over the walls and ceiling. I checked
the floor for protruding roots and runners; the floor was normal,
covered with a rattan carpet that looked dead. At the far end of
the room a couple of chairs and a sofa constructed of canvas and
chrome huddled like a last outpost of civilization around a glass
coffee table. On top of the table a fat goldfish blew bubbles and
swam idly around the perimeter of his bowl, awaiting developments.

"He's here," shouted the black-haired woman. "And don't say
I didn't warn you, Amy. You had a shock and shouldn't be talking
to the press."

I could hear someone rattling crockery in the kitchen. The
black-haired woman puffed irritably on her cigarette and frowned

at me. She reminded me of a junkyard guard dog; I just knew if I took a step off the welcome mat she would tear my leg off.

I had expected a carbon copy of the turnkey, but Mrs. Ranger was more like a positive to the first lady's negative. She belted out of the kitchen, hyperactive and childlike in leotard and jeans, wringing her hands, blowing a strand of hair out of her face, leaving a trail of nodding fronds in her wake. She was about thirty-five, scarecrow thin, and she flashed me a smile that could have bought her the state of Texas.

"I'm Amy Ranger," she said, shaking my hand. For an instant she peered into my face, frankly searching for character defects. She didn't jump to conclusions about people, at least not for the first thirty seconds or so. "I've just put on some coffee. It'll be ready in a minute. Why don't you take your coat off? Goodness! We're not very well, are we, Mr. Elliot? We shouldn't be walking around dressed like this."

Patting my coat sleeve, she examined me once more with an expression of stern sympathy, like a tree surgeon checking for leaf mould. The only person to expend anything approaching this amount of concern for my well-being since I came to Ockenden had been myself in a mirror.

"Now, Missy, I'm sure Mr. Elliot has a job to do like everyone else," she said, reverting to an earlier topic before I could get my mouth open.

"Slimy job!" said the black-haired woman.

"Missy, you're too-too-too suspicious. Don't you have to go somewhere now? I'm fine. Really, I'm fine. You've been more than helpful. But I think the crisis is over. Don't you have to cook dinner or something?"

Missy did a lizard imitation, staring me down through half-closed eyes, and shouldered herself into a chartreuse maxi-coat as old as Ashcroft's car. Then she eased out the door, throwing heartfelt good wishes and dramatic gestures back at Mrs. Ranger until the latch caught, nipping her in mid-lamentation. Her act was as phony as her hair colour.

Mrs. Ranger leaned backward against the door jamb as if to forestall Missy's re-entry and breathed a stagy sigh of relief.

"God, I'm glad you showed up. Why don't you sit down? I think she was ready to camp here all night just to find out about Rose. I've had it up to here with busybodies. Just toss your coat down anywhere. She's jealous because she thinks you are going to hear something she didn't. She's probably right. Oh, well. She's got a husband in the Collins Bay pen; that's why she hates newsmen. Missy Malchak's name gets plastered all over the court columns at least once a year and she does not think it's fair. You got any of that stuff left?"

"What?" I said, taken by surprise. I still hadn't unbuttoned my coat. I had barely moved from the doorway. Lulled by the frenetic pace of Mrs. Ranger's machine-gun monologue, I had begun to think I wouldn't have to say a word. Like the goldfish.

"Brandy, wasn't it?" she asked, wrinkling her nose. She brushed by me, stampeding toward the kitchen, talking over her shoulder. "My husband used to drink it. Said it helped his art. Don't ask me, though. Everything he painted looked like my bottomhole. He did that, too." She pointed to some foliage as she ducked a spider plant and disappeared into the next room. Behind the greenery I made out a framed black-and-white photograph of Mrs. Ranger dancing nude, arms and legs a blur.

"I could use a drink," she shouted. "If you want Scotch or beer, I've got both. I just didn't want to say anything in front of Missy. I'm a schoolteacher, you know."

She returned almost immediately, clattering a tray overflowing with mugs, sugar, milk, and shot glasses onto the table beside the fishbowl, grinning when I handed her the half-empty brandy bottle.

"It's okay," she said. "I'm used to newspaper people. Dad was a *Star-Leader* printer from the day he got out of the army till the day he died. My husband, Gil, drew cartoons and display advertising. You're the new women's editor, aren't you?"

She dropped back into one of the sling chairs, her eyes

darting with amusement. Holding her drink in one hand, she used the other to brush the unruly lock of hair from her face.

"Don't be surprised," she went on. "Ockenden's a small town. Rose knew about it the week you were hired. I remember because it was the first time she'd cracked a smile in years. I suppose I should thank you for brightening up her final days."

The last statement was meant as a joke, but Mrs. Ranger's voice hit a sour, bitter note.

"Rose knew everything that went on at the paper," she said. "She knew everything that went on in Ockenden for that matter. It was Rose who told me when Gil started fooling around with that woman in the classified ad department."

She stared coyly into her drink, rolling the glass between her palms, waiting for me to pick up the conversational ball and run with it. I kept quiet, suppressing a strong impulse to kick her ball off the field. Everything Mrs. Ranger said was loaded. The silence stretched before us like a long uphill road.

"Are you always this talkative?" she asked, sounding a little vexed.

"Hardly ever."

"You're cute," she said, knocking back the last of her brandy in one swallow. "I'm divorced. I can say things like that if I want." She fanned the air expansively with her left hand. For the first time I noticed the last two fingers were missing.

"Oh," she said, hiding the hand between her knees, peering at me self-consciously.

I was supposed to say something. Her bravura performance had been nothing but one lengthy compulsive introduction, and now it was my turn. I had driven there to interview Mrs. Ranger about her murdered mother, and instead she had tendered her unhappy history in code. This happens a lot to newsmen. Some take advantage of the situation, play father confessor or bedroom psychologist. That wasn't my line. I wanted to tell her the hand didn't bother me, but it wasn't any of my business. I wanted to tell her about my own mother's strawberry birthmark, or Uncle

Dorsey's eczema, or Rini's fat thighs which she hid in a dozen cunning ways, or Anne's shy lisp.

Instead there was a second patch of silence, ominous as a minefield that we both tiptoed through as gingerly as possible, watching the goldfish chase himself around the bowl stirring up clouds of grit.

6

She was a little Looncy Tunes after finding that body. But she was also pretty and her smile was like an anthology of TV toothpaste commercials, and what the hell, in this world you learned to trust people who let their quirks show; it's the so-called normal ones you have to watch out for. Feeling an uncharacteristic rush of humanitarianism, I decided I wanted to do Mrs. Ranger a favour. I decided to leave.

"You don't have to go through with this," I said, violating the sacred trust of every hard-nosed, rotten-livered journalist who had ever held up a bar or penned a news lead.

"No, no! I want to." She was adamant. "You'll have to forgive me. I'm a bit frazzled. I've had a shock." She hesitated over the word *shock*, fumbling for it as though she were acting in some cheap melodrama, not certain the word fit her experience but settling for it as a convenient tag for feelings she was afraid to describe more accurately.

"I'm not sad," she went on. "I'm shocked. I'd never seen Rose without her teeth before. Isn't that ridiculous? She wasn't my real mother and I hated her. I only looked after her because there was no one else in the world who would. God! I thought I'd feel wonderful, liberated, when she died, and now I don't know what to feel. I've been up and down all day since it happened, like two different people."

"Didn't the cops warn you not to talk to newsmen?" I asked.

"Sure," she said, with a shrug. "But I grew up with Billy Shaw; I don't do everything he tells me, even if he is the almighty police chief around here. Besides, they made me feel like dirt, like I'd committed an atrocity or something just finding the body. I'd dragged her out of the house, away from the smoke. I knew she was dead. I just did it. I tried to close her eyes and they wouldn't close. The way the police acted you'd think I'd killed her!"

What a long tale of woe is life, I thought, wishing I had stuck to editing recipes for peach cobbler and radish purée. Everything the lady said might be true, but it was too personal and complex to handle in a newspaper. Mrs. Ranger was dealing me facts I couldn't use, secrets I didn't want to hear.

"Perhaps you'd rather not go into it all again so soon," I said hopefully.

"Oh, no!" she said. "I want to talk. You don't mind, do you, Mr. Elliot?" She looked at me with sudden anxiety. "You don't think I'm foolish?"

"No," I said.

"Aren't you going to take notes?"

She looked disappointed. She wanted a real reporter with a real notebook and a pencil behind his ear. I flapped my hands over my pockets. I had nothing to write on but some cheque stubs, Anne's postcard, and a torn pay envelope. That was all I needed but I knew Mrs. Ranger would feel cheated. I had never gone to journalism school, never learned shorthand. It was Dorsey who taught me to listen, not write, while doing interviews. A man who always valued the spirit above the letter, Dorsey didn't believe in verbatim transcripts or tape recordings. "Posterity should never become the plastic garbage bag of the present," he said.

"I'll tell you what I told the police," she began.

Mrs. Ranger shoved her hands into her pockets and stretched her legs, watching her feet as she spoke. As if he could sense that he was no longer the centre of attention, the goldfish swam a couple of frantic laps upside down and stopped dead with his back to us.

"The last time I talked to Rose," she said, "was nine p.m. yesterday. She called to remind me to take her grocery shopping this afternoon after school. At eleven o'clock this morning I tried telephoning her to say I'd be late because of a staff meeting. I tried five or six times in half an hour. I even called the phone company, thinking a line might be down.

"It was about twelve-twenty when I arrived at the house. I left school as soon as I could. I remember hearing the noon bell as I left class to get my car. There wasn't anything unusual, no tire marks, no broken windows. Coming up the steps I smelled smoke. That's when I got scared. In a funny way I already knew she was dead. I banged on the storm door and yelled her name. I had a key but I was afraid to go in. I was afraid there might be someone inside waiting for me. I can't even remember whether the door was locked or not. The police got mad at me for not remembering. But I can't."

She looked as if she was going to cry then. I let her wander undisturbed for a moment or two in the private clutter of new and unusual memories. I felt like an intruder, but she seemed relieved to talk. She was calmer now, out of the manic phase I had walked in on. I could imagine the cops browbeating her for details, any detail at all, even if it didn't exist, that might fit into their notion of how a crime should be committed, making her feel guilty for not noticing if a door was locked, making her feel responsible for their own helplessness.

"I found Rose curled up in her nightgown and slippers, as if she'd fallen asleep on the dining room floor," said Mrs. Ranger finally. "Poor thing! She looked so peaceful. When I turned her face-up, she was dead, cold, not stiff. I thought they got stiff right away."

Instinct told me the lady was not asking for a lecture on rigor mortis, so I kept my mouth shut. Allowing another brief moment of discreet silence to pass, I nudged her back into the present with a performance of my ninety-nine-year-old cough. The goldfish was floating near the lip of his bowl, dejected.

"There was so much blood," she said. "When I turned her over, there was blood everywhere. She'd been stabbed with a pair of scissors, and one of the blades had broken off in her chest. I left her on the porch to call the fire department and waited in my car for the trucks to arrive. It was awful sitting in the car with Rose lying on the steps, but I couldn't think what else to do for her."

"Where was the fire?" I asked, breaking in to change the subject, surprised at the sound of my own voice. "Was it arson?"

"The police think so. The killer threw a match into a stack of old newspapers in my father's study. It should have worked, too. The room was full of dust and junk. I don't think Rose had been inside it since Dad died five years ago. But the door was shut and the papers packed too tightly to burn properly. Eventually the whole house would have gone up in flames; as it was, there was more smoke than anything else when the firemen broke in."

"Did she have any other relatives?"

"None. I was her stepdaughter. Dad married Rose after my real mother died nearly thirty years ago. She had a son of her own by a previous marriage; he died when I was ten. I don't know of anyone else."

"Do the police have any suspects?"

"Besides me?" She hesitated and reached up to smooth her hair. "That's a joke. I suppose I might as well tell you everything," she added, more to herself than to me.

I tried to look encouraging.

"This is off the record. I don't want you to print it."

I nodded.

"Rose had plenty of enemies. She was a malicious gossip. She spent more than half her days on the telephone spreading stories. It got so bad a few years ago that somebody tried to sue her. But people don't kill one another for telling tales, do they? I've been around her so long her stories and feuds kind of seem unreal."

"Who threatened the lawsuit?"

"A man named Rohovit. Wayne Rohovit. Rose caused some trouble between him and his fiancée's family. I have to admit she had guts. She hired a lawyer and told Rohovit she'd kick his ass in court. The suit never got that far, though. The lawyers wrote nasty letters back and forth for a year and Rohovit withdrew."

"Did the police ask about him?"

"I just mentioned his name as an example. There were plenty of others."

"Where does he live?"

"You should know that, Mr. Elliot." Her eyes flattened like nailheads. She spoke slowly and carefully, setting the words out like traps. "He still works at the *Star-Leader*. My father apprenticed him in the composing room. But I don't want you to go near him. Is that clear? If he thinks I told you about the lawsuit, he'll make me out worse than Rose. I have been trying all my life to be as unlike Rose as possible."

"What about the money?" I asked.

"What do you mean?"

"One of our reporters uncovered a rumour that Mrs. Oxley kept cash hidden in the house."

"That's a damn lie," she said. "Where do people get ideas like that?"

There was an edge to her voice. It could have been anger or it could have been surprise — I couldn't tell. The goldfish flicked his tail expectantly, watching us through the curved glass of his home.

"Rose was on the old-age pension. Anything else she had she got from me. That farm was worth a few thousand, but she wouldn't sell. She had offers, two last summer. It would have helped us both out. But she turned them down flat."

"You don't think she was getting money from someone else?"

Her eyes went up like little birds. Her knee kicked the table, slopping coffee onto the serviettes, the stain eating across the paper like the loss of innocence. She dabbed at the spill, stalling for time, trying to think of an answer.

"That's crazy," she said.

A little voice against the grain. Vulnerable as snow. I was sorry, sincerely sorry. But I knew certain feelings wouldn't survive the next day's headlines. Mrs. Ranger had been operating on the principle that bending a sympathetic ear can be therapeutic. But I was no analyst; someone else was picking up the tab. Her dark eyes slid away from mine, flashing betrayal.

"Blackmail," I said, trying not to sound like Ashcroft.

"Blackmail," she said.

She had to force the word out. It didn't sound nice in polite company. But once she spit it out she looked oddly relieved. I didn't like that. I had a feeling Mrs. Ranger's confessional style wasn't meant to reveal as much as it concealed.

"But that's ridiculous," she said, a grateful smile flooding her face. "After all, this is Canada, not Hollywood, Mr. Elliot."

I had to admit she was right. It did sound ridiculous. Babble, babble, babble. Who asked these questions anyway? I sneaked a peak at Mrs. Ranger dancing in her birthday suit. Dark hair. Slender legs. Would the spark never die?

"Forget it," I said quickly, checking my wristwatch.

Soon the movie theatres would shut up for the night, followed by the restaurants and bars, sending waves of stragglers to the subdivisions and to bed. I felt light-headed with embarrassment, starvation, and disease. The goldfish burrowed in his water, angling toward me for a better view. I wanted to tell him he was nothing but an orange carp.

And I wanted to say to her, "Tell me the truth, please. I don't want to hear anything else." But I am a man of sensibilities. I have read books, gone to concerts, talked to women over long candlelit dinners. The words might bruise her. I quelled myself. What did I know of life and death anyway? Give me three meals a day, a bottle of booze, and a companionable female, and that's life and death.

I stared, said nothing.

"More coffee?" she asked.

Angel eyes. Sipping coffee. Making small talk. While they autopsied Rose in some hospital basement. Yes, yes, yes, I thought. I didn't want to admit it was real either. And I didn't have to.

I shook my head as I got up to leave.

"Have you got a picture we could run with the story tomorrow?" I asked when I reached the door.

"Don't ask that. I thought you were being so nice. You could have asked all sorts of gruesome questions. I don't want her face splashed all over the newspaper. People despised her in this town. They'll only gloat. It's better to let it die down as fast as possible. Please?"

Her smile shimmered icily across the room.

I nodded assent. I didn't really care if we missed one mug shot of one murder victim. The presses would roll regardless. I wasn't a ghoul. The billions in China would never know the difference.

"Good night, Mrs. Ranger," I said.

"Good night, Mr. Elliot."

"Good night."

The words sounded like nails in the coffin of yet another might-have-been. "Never become a newsman and never fall in love." Did Dorsey mean to say the two activities were mutually exclusive? Or that each constituted an elemental pitfall in itself? Not for the first time it occurred to me that he had been talking about himself. Possibly under his green eyeshade he never suspected that everyone knew he and my mother were in love. I would have been happy to have him as a father; I had no particular loyalty toward the old one, since we had never had much to do with each other. But Dorsey was afraid to ask. And now it seemed sad and almost blasphemous to speculate on how things might have turned out if those two crabby, silent house ghosts had admitted their mutual interest.

I retreated through the alien cold to Ashcroft's car, aware of Missy's baleful gaze, her head like a black mushroom in the glare of a neighbouring window. The engine jerked into life, quivered spasmodically, rattling the frame. While it warmed up, I switched on the dash light and examined Anne's postcard.

Byron was still dying of fever at Missolonghi. A lesson in heroics. On the fragility of human aspiration. Or an allusion to my pneumonia.

"I should be boycotting you," she said, in a large looping script that reminded me of the largeness of her body, "not writing because I never hear from you — BUT here I am . . . I feel

COMPELLED to throw some words to that ghost of you out there with the thought that if I'm a good girl they will come back. Mr. Panadakis says to send you his hello. He seems fond of you or something. Honestly, you seem to jump into my mind at the ODDEST times. Love, Anne."

Mr. Panadakis was her notary. She had neglected to mention that if I was foolhardy enough to accept her invitation, her husband would have recourse to a system of justice less modern and more efficient than the police. I would be fertilizer for an olive tree. It was all there: the adolescent capitalizations, the coy promptings, the lack of remorse. Anne had never been good at imagining consequences. Her attention span extended no more than fifteen minutes forward or backward. She was one of those middle-aged women who call other middle-aged women "girls." She slept with a windup lion called Ed who played "You Are My Sunshine" while wagging his head from side to side. I knew I was being unjust, thinking of her like that. I liked Ed, too.

I thought of Amy Ranger: lonely, dutiful, vulnerable, and nervous. Shock was the watchword of the day. Three people had used it; no one seemed bereaved by Rose Oxley's passing, only shocked. Mrs. Ranger had talked of relief and hate. Someone had done the world a favour, snipping the old woman's mortal cord. Now the virtuous daughter, released from her stepmother's tyranny, only wanted to forget, to put it all behind her. She did not even seem concerned about catching the murderer. If I stretched, I could understand that. The dawn was here. A new day for Mrs. Ranger. She didn't want to play Cinderella one second longer. But she was scared, too. Change had come suddenly, cruelly, ambiguously. Or had I missed something?

I drove down the street; the left headlight blinked out. Later I would work up a philosophy. Now I wanted to sleep, dream. I hadn't the energy for moral complexity. Instead, I thought of Amy Ranger smiling like a traffic light in the jungle of a living room. Dancing naked. Glass bowl, tabletop, and vines climbing the walls. As if she had created it all.

7

Morning slipped up on me asleep on a sun-blanketed hillside, my head propped on a heap of clover, a half-consumed bottle of retsina cradled like a yearling in my arms, and some Greek shepherds quarrelling over a ewe nearby.

One of the shepherds prodded me in the ribs with his crook and said something I couldn't understand, which was strange because I spoke Greek reasonably well.

In reality it was Gratz, the city editor, and I was reclining on the green vinyl of the news desk with a stack of *Star-Leader*s under my head and a pneumatic canister held lovingly to my chest. Spandrell peered over Gratz's shoulder, his jaw hard set. I considered pretending to be unconscious, but they had already seen my eyes open. A stream of violent abuse was rattling like rain against my weathered brow.

I recalled driving back from Amy Ranger's botanical house and trudging up the newsroom stairs the night before to find Ashcroft, bleary-eyed and confused, trying to beat out the story of Rose Oxley's murder on a typewriter that refused to imprint the letter *o*. I had tactfully suggested he trade machines with any one of his absent colleagues, interpreted my notes, and directed him to wake me when he finished. I tried to guess why I was being yelled at if Ashcroft was still around.

Spandrell's meaty fist wafted a sheaf of copy paper under my nose as though it would bring me around faster.

"What the hell is this?" he demanded.

"Get offa that desk," piped up Gratz, bursting with righteous indignation.

I rolled gingerly until my feet touched the floor, catching my raincoat as it fell, attempting to assume an air of wounded delicacy. The effort was more than I could stand. Blood suddenly rushed through unaccustomed channels in my brain. The world diffused, blossomed into something opaque and fuchsia coloured. I grabbed at the rim to steady myself.

"He's drunk!" said Gratz.

"Get into my office," said Spandrell.

Was I drunk? I asked myself. Not obviously. I must have fallen asleep and that ace Ashcroft hadn't roused me in time. I draped my coat over a chair and wobbled after Spandrell. He was already seated, his habitual glare in place. Lips pinched to a knife edge. Eyes repeating unforgivable things. By the wall clock it was six-thirty. Outside, it was 7:18, eighty-two degrees, and snowing. Usually Gratz and the brain-damaged sports editor were the only bodies besides mine to haunt the building Saturday mornings. But Spandrell wasn't going to give me a chance to meditate upon the meaning of his unexpected presence.

"Did you have a hand in this?"

He tossed the loosely clipped sheets of paper at my belt buckle. They fluttered briefly like a shot pheasant before stalling into my outstretched hands. I read the slug line: "CITYOFFEAR/ba." It was Ashcroft's report.

"Well?"

I admitted nothing. He wanted an answer. I stared out the window. The sky was impending, like unpaid debts. The clock ticked like firecrackers. I thought of Saturday mornings at the dentist's when I was a kid, the drill whirring in the next room, children playing in the street, Dorsey shifting uneasily in the chair beside me in terror.

I read the story:

> In the newsrooms, homes, and marketplaces of the nation, the word is out: Ockenden is a City of Fear.
>
> First there was Jack the Ripper.
>
> Then came the Boston Strangler.
>
> In the small hours of the morning, Friday, the

Ockenden Slasher claimed his first victim, a sixty-eight-year-old widow named Rose Oxley.

Local police threw up barricades, called in tracker dogs, and organized house-to-house searches throughout the day in a vain attempt to net the vicious murderer.

Chief William Shaw issued a terse "no comment" last night when asked if he expected the Slasher to strike again.

In response to repeated questions from this reporter, Shaw warned the citizenry of Ockenden to "remain calm" and stay on the "alert" for clues while the crisis lasts.

Police have no immediate plans to institute a dusk-to-dawn curfew.

Meanwhile the Slasher is at large.

In an obvious attempt to lull the fiend into a false sense of security, police are playing their cards close to their chests.

Asked if he had any suspects, Chief Shaw muttered a laconic "no comment."

Constable Rick Myers, manning a police roadblock near the scene of the murder, claimed he had "no idea" who he was looking for but that he was prepared to shoot "if I have to."

All Ockenden policemen are equipped with .38-calibre "Specials."

This exciting real-life drama began at 12:27 p.m. yesterday when a "shocked" Amy Ranger, the victim's daughter, rang the police emergency number and said, "My mother's been killed."

Moments before, Mrs. Ranger had turned the fateful doorknob and entered the Oxley home, a sinister-looking two-storey brick farmhouse overgrown with ivy, to find her mother sprawled dead on the floor, viciously beaten and stabbed by an unknown assailant.

Due to a logistics mix-up, this reporter did not arrive at the scene until 2:45 p.m.

After spending several tense moments at the road-block, moments charged with the expectation of imminent violence, this reporter approached the murder house and questioned officers conducting the investigation.

While not permitted to enter the actual house, this reporter was allowed to roam freely in the front yard and examine such evidence as was available there.

Police refused to say whether they had discovered fingerprints belonging to the killer.

There had been a small fire near the back of the house; Chief Shaw was unwilling to speculate on whether the Slasher had set the fire to cover up his crime.

However, Shaw did confirm that the deceased had not been burned to death.

At 4:05 p.m. police tracker dog Norm arrived at the scene and immediately picked up a trail leading through a rear window and across some fields toward town.

This reporter traced tracker dog Norm to the edge of Ockenden at Redwood Place where police began a house-to-house search for leads.

Chief Shaw refused to confirm the searches, but this reporter was at the scene and was able to question a Redwood Place resident who said a plainclothes man had asked "if I seen anything funny on the street this morning."

The resident added that he works a night shift and had been asleep when the murder took place. This reporter had no way of checking his story.

In a startling twist to the Slasher drama, however, the *Star-Leader* was able to locate Amy Ranger and question her despite police efforts to withhold access.

In an exclusive interview with the *Star-Leader*, Mrs. Ranger admitted that she was "shocked" by her mother's death.

"I'd never seen Rose without her teeth before," said Mrs. Ranger.

The victim's daughter added, "I found Rose curled up in her nightgown and slippers as if she'd fallen asleep on the dining room floor.

"She'd been stabbed with a pair of scissors, and one of the blades had broken off in her chest."

Mrs Ranger made several off-the-record remarks which led this reporter to conclude that investigators have "plenty" of suspects.

She also alleged certain police insensitivity, bordering on brutality, when she was interrogated at the murder scene.

Her claims jibe with evidence of police harassment involving this reporter's automobile at the Redwood Place stakeout.

Chief Shaw remains tight-lipped on these as well as other key issues.

While rumours of mysterious money hoards and allegations of possible "blackmail" swirl, the City of Fear awaits.

Will the Slasher strike again? Will the police apprehend him before his bloodlust reawakens?

Asked if only a local man could have known the route across the fields from Oxley's house to Redwood Place, Shaw muttered a brief "no comment."

But the fact remains: he may pass you in the street, he may buy meat at your grocery store, he may be watching you as you read these lines.

In the City of Fear, the Slasher stalks.

Dawn hadn't showed between the slats of the blinds. The City of Fear nodded peacefully. I wanted to sleep more, and I needed a cigarette. Silence pressed in on us from the newsroom where Gratz sat frozen, pen poised, over a blank dummy pad. Spandrell stared at me, looking ready to copy edit my body with his bare hands.

"Ashcroft's canned," he began quietly, his voice rising in a crescendo as he spoke. "They can sue us for contempt of court, libel, slander, defamation of character, traducement, mis-representation —"

"But we haven't published it yet," I said reasonably. "I was going to read the copy before Gratz came to work. Ashcroft's green. He didn't do any harm."

"I told you to spike it. This is Wishty's beat."

"It's the kid's story. He earned it. Wishty was home all night beating off while Ashcroft was covering his ass."

"I don't pay you to argue," said Spandrell.

"Then you don't pay me enough."

I needed poise. Without poise this confrontation would have been impossible. Until I said the words, I had had no idea I was angry. Spandrell's rug was slightly askew; he cocked an eyebrow.

"What do you know about this Ranger interview?"

"I talked to her myself."

Spandrell's eyes blazed like accident flares. I wanted to jump on his face. I knew it was an evil impulse, but I have never been too proud to admit the baser aspects of my nature.

"Did she say all this stuff?"

"You're damn right."

"About suspects?"

"Off the record, she said Oxley had plenty of enemies. Ashcroft's only speculating about the cops. He'll have to cut the innuendo when he rewrites."

"Did she mention any names?"

"Not that I know of," I said, honouring Amy Ranger's request to keep Rohovit out of the limelight.

Spandrell looked as if he owned all the patents on meanness. His fist clenched, knuckles leaping like deer under his skin.

"No rewrites," he said. "Spike it. Tell Gratz to call in Wishty. I can't take a chance. I don't want some tight-ass police chief chewing me out for tampering with his witness. Wishty'll handle it."

"Tell Gratz yourself," I said. "I'll take a walk with the kid. I put him up to this."

The city editor's chair squealed like a puppy in the newsroom next door. I was too tired to care whether Spandrell fired me or ate me for breakfast. But I knew if I let him push me around, then he might as well have peed on my leg. I started for the door.

"Where do you think you're going?" he demanded.

"All you have to do," I said, turning, "is cut the cheap Sherlock Holmes and the melodrama, three takes tops, and you know as well as I do we'll have the best damned news story the *Star-Leader* has run in weeks, maybe months. Ashcroft's only problem was he tried too hard. In case you hadn't noticed — it wouldn't hurt if the other reporters around here caught the same disease. And if you're worried about us doing pirouettes around a bunch of country cops, then you're a damn sight less of an editor than you're cracked up to be."

Despite my wild compulsion to talk and Spandrell's momentary inability to respond, I shut up. The flame in his eyes guttered with confusion. I was on the side of the angels. He knew I was right. And what was more, he had put himself in an untenable position in front of Gratz and whoever else had entered the newsroom during the argument.

I asked myself what had happened to Dickie Bellfield's fire-eating investigative journalist. Maybe success was death to a newsman like Spandrell. He had parlayed an inheritance into ownership of the *Star-Leader*. A legman needed to stay lean and hungry; Spandrell had acquired a vested interest. I knew men like Uncle Dorsey, who could barely balance their cheque books let alone manage a daily paper, who had dogs' noses for news. They slept with their telephones in case a mayor farted or World War Three broke out while they dozed. Spandrell had become domesticated.

"Okay, okay, you write it," he said finally. "I don't want the kid messing in where he's not wanted anymore. Do a hard news lead and use that trash for a sidebar."

He choked the words out as though it took a superhuman effort to utter a sound, then swung around and started typing gibberish as a signal for me to get out.

Gratz was sucking a cigarette, doing his imitation of a real news editor. The sports editor was doing tiger stretches before an east-facing window as the sky turned to porridge. Ashcroft had returned and stood whey-faced beside his desk with a coffee and Danish clutched in his hands. He was working his lips like a drowning man. His eyes semaphored mute agony.

"You heard the boss," I said. "Give him two stories: one on the murder, one on the interview. Stick to the facts, cut the crap, and call the cops five minutes before deadline for an update."

Ignoring my speech, Ashcroft shoved the coffee and Danish toward me like burnt offerings.

"This is for you, Precious," he said. "I just got back. I worked all night. I only went out to get some coffee for you."

He looked played out, exhausted. His voice cracked with emotion.

"Come on, Ashcroft," I said, refusing to condescend in his moment of weakness, "if you can't stand the heat, get out of the kitchen. We don't give points for trying."

He stared at me incredulously. He had just heard me save his skin in Spandrell's office and now I was assaulting him with what seemed insane and exotic cruelty. But it was the best thing for him. He would either put his head down and do the job or realize he was cut out for some other line of work.

"But —," he said.

"No buts, Ashcroft. Don't kid yourself," I said. "You're young. You don't know. Things are never so bad they can't be worse. When I was your age —"

I stopped, for I saw that I was punchy and talking too much. Dangerous thing to tell people about yourself. They try to put you in a box.

"The ideal news lead has nine words and tells the reader who, where, what, why, and when," I said. "Remember that when you start rewriting. And remember the Kansas City milkman."

"The what?"

"That's the guy you're aiming at. Grade three education, semiliterate, Everyman. Soap operas, Monday night football, Johnny Carson. You've got to hook him and make him understand in the first paragraph. Come on, kid! The quick brown fox . . ."

If he had been smart, Ashcroft would have walked away from newspapers there and then. Instead, he gave me one of those my-head-is-bloodied-but-unbowed looks and wearily turned to his typewriter.

I set the coffee and Danish on my desk, grabbed my coat, and headed for the can. I retched into the toilet bowl for a while, getting more exercise than I had had in two weeks. The face that stared wild-eyed at me from the mirror above the sink bore all the earmarks of a first-class, end-of-the-road flame-out. I not only needed a shave and a haircut, I needed an undertaker to help repair the damage.

I threw water over the wreckage, rubbing it dry with a paper towel. I swallowed some of the stuff to quench the fire inside my body, but it didn't do any good.

And then I thought about Amy Ranger. There was something about her that made man's age-old longings respectable. Maybe it was the trouble she was going through that gave her dignity; maybe it was just her flashing eyes and slender legs. I wondered how I could be dying and yearning for a woman at the same moment.

Time flows through a newsroom like a restless wind, gusting at press time, declining into the doldrums of late afternoon. Back at my desk, I delivered myself up to the endlessly repeated ritual of pages and deadlines. Reporters drifted in off the street like derelicts to a soup kitchen. Damon Barrett called in sick. I tried to calculate how long it would take me to qualify for early retirement.

As each page was finished, I wandered into the composing room to check the forms before the printers locked them up and passed them on to the stereotyping department. Out of curiosity, I asked the foreman if Wayne Rohovit was on shift that morning. It turned out that Rohovit had fallen prey to the redundancy campaign launched when Spandrell took over the newspaper the year before. He had found a new job with a small outfit across town printing a community tab growing fat on pirated *Star-Leader* ad traffic. From the foreman's attitude, I guessed the firings were still a matter of hot debate in after-hours chapel meetings. Spandrell was not a popular man in the back shop either.

It was nearly noon. The first papers were just out on the street when the telephone rang. I should have been in my hotel room, but I hadn't wanted to give Spandrell and Gratz a chance to complain by leaving early. I had even managed to beat my deadlines for a change, hurdling every obstacle like the thorough-bred newsman I was.

The party on the other end of the line was Amy Ranger.

"Is this Mr. Elliot?"

I offered an affirmative conjecture.

The voice came back to me shy and hesitant, her telephone voice.

"I — I'm sorry to bother you. I know you must be busy. I wanted to thank you for the story in the paper. I was in a state last night. You could have made it very sensational."

Ashcroft's stories were sitting in proof in front of me. Gratz had buried them on inside local, ostensibly because he didn't have a picture to play with them on front.

"That's all right, Mrs. Ranger. Don't thank me."

"Some people get a kick out of that sort of thing."

"Sure. I know."

She hesitated. The way she was breathing made her sound nervous, afraid.

"I was wondering if you'd heard anything more. I mean more than what's in the paper."

"You should call the cops," I said.

"They're very abrupt with me, I'm afraid. I think they're mad because I talked to you."

"Bastards! They can't do that, you know."

"It's all right. But have you heard anything?"

"Not really," I said. "Ashcroft, the kid on the story, he heard they're looking for a hitchhiker somebody spotted on the highway shortly after noon. They're also checking on a car that may have been parked in the road opposite your mother's place. But nothing hangs together with the trail to Redwood Place. You realize that unless the cops catch a murderer right away it's usually a matter of sifting every little lead and hoping they get lucky."

"I guess so."

She seemed doubtful. There was a silence that seemed awkward and interminable.

"Mr. Elliot!" Her voice now was urgent. "I haven't anyone to help . . . you know. I'm a little lost. It was awful. I don't want to go back there alone."

"Well, can I do anything?"

"Would you? I mean, I just have to go inside and look around. I have to pick up some bank books and papers. It was a mess."

She trailed off almost absentmindedly. Her conversations

blew hot and cold, as though she were trying out for a part in a soap opera.

"Why don't you call for me in an hour?" I said. "We'll look things over together."

I said it fast and got her to hang up. I knew what she was thinking about and didn't want her to do too much of it. Ashcroft had filed an autopsy report from the cops. Rose Oxley's murderer had slammed those scissors into her hard enough to crush her rib cage. He had stabbed her seven times before the blade broke. It had not been a pretty sight.

8

"Rose said they call you Precious down at the paper. She said they think you're gay or something. You don't look gay to me. I mean I'm no expert. You just don't look gay to me. How come you're not married? Is that too personal? You don't have to say anything. I'll understand."

The afternoon sky was the colour of soggy newsprint; snowflakes speckled the grey streets like dandruff. Amy Ranger twittered away like a flock of swallows on a telephone wire as we drove through town to her mother's house. She was wearing jeans and a pea jacket. Her hair was done up at the back with a piece of leather and a wooden peg.

"Divorced," I said.

"Just like me," she said enthusiastically.

"Three times," I added. "A horse with my track record would have been shot."

She was driving a late model Datsun with the deliberation of a person who had learned to drive too late for it to become second nature. Her knuckles were white on the wheel, but I couldn't tell whether she was anxious about the car or revisiting the scene of the murder. Yet her composure startled me. The only other sign that she was under strain showed in the pencil-line arcs beneath her eyes. Sweating a little with fever, clutching my seat belt strap like a man on a subway, I looked much closer to the verge of nervous collapse than she did.

"Goodness, don't feel too badly," she said with a smile. "If it was all that easy, I'd have remarried long before this. Just look at the bright side. How many more mistakes can you make?"

Before I could formulate an adequate reply, she veered sharply and jammed on the brakes to avoid slicing my head off on the door of a *Star-Leader* delivery truck double parked by a corner box.

"Newspapers are tough on family life," she said, barely

pausing to correct the steering. "When we split, Gil said the glamour, the long hours, and the availability of the office girls were more than he could stand. I think that was a lot of bullshit, don't you? I mean if he'd wanted to stick with me, he would have. Do you have lots of girls, Mr. Elliot?"

She asked the question shyly, with a quick glance at me out of the corner of her eye. I noticed the slightly formal way she used the word "have" to denote something between the unequivocal "sleep with" and the ambiguous "date." It reminded me of Anne Delos, whose desire to avoid the topic of lust in conversation bordered on the pathological. Anne was forever feeling "agitated." And the question, "Why don't we take a nap, honey?" never had anything to do with sleep. My wife Rini, to her credit, had never been less than frank about sex. She would come right out and say "fuck." And when Rini said "fuck" the word had eighty-five syllables and left nothing to the imagination.

"More than I can handle," I said, sensing trouble.

She rolled her eyes and laughed, but I could see she was a little hurt. I wasn't in love with her, and whatever happened it wouldn't be fair to let her wake up one morning to find that I had moved on without a warning. It was better not to expect anything, need anything. There was no point in opening yourself up to that kind of pain.

She flexed her left hand and spread the remaining fingers to make the gaps more obvious, a gesture, I began to realize, she used when she was feeling sorry for herself and wanted sympathy.

"Does this bother you?" she asked.

"Not at all," I said. I had a feeling that Amy Ranger was a woman of more than ordinary warmth and dignity. She wanted me to like her but didn't want to ask. I suspected she would be just as happy to drop the whole pretense if I refused to play the game.

She waited. I didn't have anything else to add. I stared out the window, having a lot of fun worrying about smoking, drinking, and the sorry state of the dollar. We drove the last mile in silence.

After her phone call, I had puttered around the office for a while, stripping the wire for my time bank, sorting recipes, sweater patterns, and matrimonial announcements, editing the next week's Ann Landers columns — pretending to impose order on the universal chaos while inwardly asking myself unanswerable questions about Amy Ranger. When that was over, when I had finally odd-jobbed myself out of things to do and think about, I put on my raincoat and trudged downstairs to Payroll and Personnel.

The red-haired lady was still there. For all I knew, she never left the building. It was difficult to imagine her walking. She was still laughing at me. For some people I never lose my appeal.

"Remember those forms?" I said, slumping into a chair in front of her desk.

Her name was Nellie Shingles but everybody called her Red. She was shaking, and she was so big she gave you claustrophobia just being in the same room with her. What I had said was so funny she couldn't seem to get a word out in reply. I have always liked people with a sense of humour and an ability to appreciate the thundering ironies of life.

"Lost 'em," I said. "You got dupes?"

She shrieked as though I had driven a stake through her heart. For a second I thought she might be having an attack of something.

"Oh, honey," she said, folding her hands over her breasts as if they might try to escape. "Anything. Anything you want. When I heard about you and Spandrell this morning, I thought I'd died and gone to Hawaii. 'You don't pay me enough.' What a riot!"

"He'll fire me," I said grimly. "He'll find some excuse and boot my ass."

"Don't you believe it, Precious. He's stuck with you. I almost feel sorry for the bastard." She kicked open the filing cabinet. "See that? The guru of pucks won't last the month out. You're the only bona fide deskman Spandrell's got and he knows it. 'You don't pay me enough.' When I heard that I said to myself, 'Just ask me, Precious. Anything you want. Use and abuse me. My body is yours.'"

She threw her head back, and for a while her face disappeared behind her chins.

"I want to pick your brains about Gil Ranger and the broad he tangled with before his divorce," I said, as she subsided, wiping her eyes with a lace hanky that looked impossibly small in her vast, beringed hand.

Her eyes went opaque suddenly, pupils like spatters of molten lead. She hunched over the desk like a linebacker poised for a blitz. Her flesh stopped quaking. The stillness was awesome.

"I interviewed his ex about Rose Oxley's murder last night," I said. "She says Oxley blew the whistle on Ranger and his fancy lady. I thought you might know the story."

"You interested in Amy Ranger or the story?"

"Maybe both."

She had lie detector eyes.

"You came to the right person," she said warily. "I don't want you talking to anybody else about this. Least of all Alice."

"Who?"

"Alice Varney — she's the one got caught holding Gilbert's dick."

"The one with the clap?"

"You got a great memory, Precious. Only she hasn't got the clap. I just said that because you're so damn good-looking."

Nellie's lips tightened like elastic bands over her teeth in a travesty of her usual smile. I had the sudden feeling I was about to hear something I had never wanted to know. That was the price I paid for turning forty and still not being able to mind my own business.

"Gil Ranger broke Alice's heart," she said, taking a line from the afternoon soaps. "She was fresh from the farm, like eggs, and he broke her. He primed her with all kinds of talk about leaving Amy and moving to Montreal or Vancouver and getting married. When Rose Oxley put the word out, he denied everything. The story got around that Alice was a home wrecker and a slut, that was Gil's excuse. Amy was smart. She never believed him. In the end he left town, and the rest of us had to stay put and live it down."

"The way she talks, Rose Oxley was to blame for the whole crack-up," I said.

"That's her privilege, honey. Amy's a sweet thing, but she always had a tendency to ignore unpleasantness. She knew Gil was fooling around; she'd have let it go but for that stepmother of hers. Everybody blamed Rose because she upset the status quo, but the status quo stank. You understand? Rose just waited until she could do the maximum amount of damage before she took the lid off."

"You think Ranger wanted to kill her?"

"He had a motive all right, but he wouldn't have had the guts to kill a roach. Gil made messes and left them for other people to deal with. The last I heard he was out west doing layouts for some oil magazine. The police'll find him. And if you think Alice had anything to do with it, you're dead wrong. She's got an alibi as tight as a deacon's asshole."

"Maybe I should talk to her," I said.

"You stay away from Alice, honey. You stay away if you know what's good for you. Just take my word for it. Alice is a good girl. She was tucked up in bed all that night."

"How do you know?" I asked, feeling like a pig in a packing plant.

"I was with her."

"I see."

A hoarse rumbling sound bubbled up from deep in the fat lady's throat. Her chest began to heave as if a couple of cats had gotten into a fight inside her blouse.

"Oh, Precious! Oh, honey!" she cried, laughing now, trying not to suffocate herself. "If you could see the look on your face! Oh, honey! Welcome to the big bad world. What a sweetheart! You act so tough."

*　*　*

I hadn't mentioned any of this during the drive across town because Mrs. Ranger hated snoops and because she seemed bent on avoiding the topic of her stepmother's murder. It was almost sunset when she pointed ahead to a house that stood stark against the skyline, staring over the fields like an Easter Island statue. The front porch had all but lost a battle with gravity and age. The brickwork needed repointing. Someone had kept the lawn trimmed until first frost, but in back the disused farm buildings, grey and decrepit, were disappearing in a jungle of weed and vines.

"It's all mine," said Mrs. Ranger ruefully, as we entered the driveway. "I hate it. I called the real estate people this morning, but they can't put it on the market until the will is probated."

I took her key and let myself in through the front door in case the police had left any nasty reminders for her to trip over. Aside from a dark stain like a Rorschach inkblot on the threadbare carpet, there was nothing to indicate a murder had taken place.

At first she wouldn't budge from the door, eyes nailed to the spot, hands fluttering over her face like wings as she tried to shut out the horror.

"Let's find what we need and get out of here," I said, breaking the spell.

Her eyes flew up to me, grateful.

"Yes! You're right," she said, leading the way toward the back of the house. "I'm not going to fall apart. It was such a shock with the smoke and everything. But the worst of it was I was almost relieved she was dead."

The rooms were dark, cramped, and cluttered with heavy old furniture, badly finished and ugly. A couple of easy chairs and a faded sofa, shrouded in antimacassars and doilies, grazed like elephants in the living room. Over the mantelpiece hung a glass case filled with stuffed songbirds, their tiny feet glued to branches. ("I wish I could let them all go," she said.) Wherever I looked, there were rows and rows of ancient family photographs, someone's stern and hawk-faced ancestors, all witnesses to the crime.

"No relation," said Mrs. Ranger, reading my mind. "Not even to Rose. We lost everything in a fire when I was ten, including my stepbrother. For four years Rose went around to every auction in the county buying up old pictures. As if she was trying to replace what she had lost. It was Brian, her son, who did this," she added quickly, holding up her maimed hand. "For telling tales when I was eight."

I had to force open the study door with my shoulder. The firemen had brought a hose through the window, and the floor was inches deep in ash and glass. A scorched rolltop desk stood in a corner, its slats cracked and twisted. A trestle table ran along the opposite wall, covered with ash, the remains of cardboard boxes, and smoke-damaged bundles of yellowing *Star-Leaders*. Next to the door, there was a glass-front bookcase, its panes smashed out, bursting with mounds of rank, blackened newspapers.

"I know," she said, catching my grimace of distaste. "It was an obsession. Daddy was only a pack rat; he brought the papers home and stored them. But Rose spent all her spare time sifting the pages, clipping and filing the juicy bits — over there in boxes — gloating. There's a hell of a lot of dirt you can dig out of old news stories."

"Is that what happened with Rohovit?"

She was sorting amid the ruins of the desk, prying scraps of paper out of pigeonholes with the handle of a broken magnifying glass. I moved around the room, kicking piles of ash, turning things over with my shoe.

"You don't give up, do you?" she said at last, but without rancour. She had decided to trust me. "Wayne started out a delinquent. He stole cars, got a girl pregnant, went to reform school. On his nineteenth birthday he got drunk and killed a hitchhiker with a stolen car. He served two years for manslaughter and found religion. After that, he straightened right out, and since the kid he killed wasn't anyone local, the people around here were inclined to let the past bury itself. Except for Rose. Wayne met some out-of-town girl at a Baptist crusade and announced he was going to marry her. A week later, her family got a collection of press clippings in the mail."

"And you don't think he bore a grudge?" I asked.

"I don't think Wayne gave a good goddamn in the end. The whole thing turned into a fiasco, and after the dust settled, the girl's father decided he liked Wayne all the better because he'd let Jesus Christ make such a big difference in his life. The only one who got burned was Rose. If anything, she bore a grudge against him."

"Look at this," I exclaimed.

Turning over a stack of charred *Star-Leader*s dating from the late 1950s, I had discovered an old zinc halftone cut, the mainstay of picture reproduction before newspapers switched to cold type and photo processing. I hadn't seen one in years, and it brought back sunny memories of Uncle Dorsey's home printing shop *cum* bolt hole. The cut had been scorched and bent by the fire, its image all but obliterated.

"Oh those," she said, glancing across the room. "I told you Dad worked in the composing room. He used to drag odds and ends like that home for me to play with. I used to think I was born with ink on my hands."

"Did you know that Rohovit had been fired?" I asked.

"No. Does it matter?"

She looked at me blankly and rubbed her nose as though it tickled, a gesture I recognized as a signal that I was trespassing. Like a lot of people with a fondness for volunteering information, Amy Ranger resented being cross-examined or pinned down.

"Do you smell smoke?" she asked, her voice choked and dry.

I shook my head. The atmosphere was getting to me, too. But there was no smoke, only soot everywhere. Everything we touched left a grubby deposit on our hands and clothes.

"Strange things are going on in my head," she said. "I feel like I'm a little girl and it's all happening again. I know it sounds crazy. The fire, the voices. I can feel it all around me." She looked at her hands. "I've got to wash this off. I've got to."

"Why do you think she was killed?" I snapped. It occurred to me that her dithering helplessness was a screen, conscious or not I couldn't tell.

"I've been wondering," she said, her voice returning to its normal tone, "if the murderer took that rumour about her money seriously. Remember?"

I nodded encouragement.

"Maybe it started out as a burglary, only the burglar panicked when Rose caught him going through her things. That's what I think, anyway," she said briskly. "And I hope they don't catch whoever did it because I don't want anyone else to suffer for Rose and because I don't want this to drag on. I'm free now. I just want to forget about it as quickly as possible. Do you think I'm awful for talking like this?"

"Do you want a character reference?"

"Go to hell!"

I smiled. And she smiled. She had a lot of heat banked behind those handsome eyes. But her story was pat, a cop's story; it came off the rack, and if you didn't mind a couple of loose threads, it fitted the facts pretty well. Unlike Ashcroft's blood-chilling extravaganza, this was a story you could pull over your head at night like a security blanket. Rose Oxley's killer wasn't really a killer. He was an accident-prone B and E man. Until I heard the words from Amy Ranger's lips, it had been my story, too. Now I wasn't so sure.

"Come with me," she said, suddenly abandoning her search through the debris. "I want to show you something."

I pocketed the zinc cut for good luck, since I wasn't likely to see another outside a museum, and followed her upstairs to the master bedroom. There was a double bed with a centre sag like the Grand Canyon, a dresser littered with dusty cosmetic jars dating from the last twenty-five years and festooned with strings of cheap beads, and a wing table groaning under a regiment of ancestral photographs and a leather-bound album. Amy handed me a snapshot of a soldier clad in British Army kit circa 1943, a small wiry man with a trim moustache and tiny fanatical eyes.

"My father," she said, leafing nervously through the album. "The rest are fake. There used to be one of Brian but I don't see it." Her voice trailed off. A frame fell to the floor, its glass shattered. "Damn!" she said. But she seemed preoccupied.

"Is it important?" I asked.

"I just wanted to show you what he looked like," she said. "Maybe it's in the other bedroom."

She disappeared into the hall; I could hear her shoes on the hardwood planks, crossing and recrossing the next room. Presently she left the bedroom and her footsteps receded down the hall.

"Come here," she called.

She was waiting by the bathroom door.

"Light a match," she said breathlessly. "The switch is broken."

I struck a match on the wall, revealing an old porcelain suite, glowing orange. She pointed to the medicine shelf above the sink.

There was a man's shaving brush, straight razor, a cake of shaving soap, a worn toothbrush, a bit of stained white thread, a comb, its tines choked with grey hair and dandruff, and a dirty drinking glass. Before I could guess the implications of all that junk, the match flame bit into my thumb and Amy Ranger was falling and I was half-dragging, half-carrying her down the grim stairs to the open door.

Leaning her against the porch rail, I ran back into the house to turn off the lights and lock the doors. I was afraid she would

faint dead away or gag. Her jaw was set, eyes faraway. A tiny
rime of sweat had formed on her upper lip. I put my arm around
her and helped her to the car.

"That was my father," she said. "Dead five years and she
hadn't touched a thing. Rose never let anything go. She lived in
the past. It strangled her. Ever since we came to live with her, I've
been afraid I'd end up the same. And now she's gone, and I'll sell
everything and start fresh."

Suddenly there were tears like tiny planets in her eyes, and
she pounded the steering wheel with her fists.

"It doesn't make sense. I'm so afraid this is all a dream, that
she'll keep coming back and coming back. It makes me sick to
think about."

"What doesn't make sense?" I asked.

"That someone would want to kill her. Who could do it?
Why?"

She broke into a convulsing sob, choked. More than anything
else she seemed afraid, afraid of a world where killers strike
without motive, where brothers mutilate sisters, where mothers
thrive on hate and little girls grow up in loneliness. I reached for
her across the seat. There was nothing else I could do. I felt sure
the Kansas City milkman would approve.

For a moment she clung to me, then suddenly she was
straddling my legs, weeping, and kissing me. She moaned, and
I could feel the release of pent-up passion and fear and
loneliness. And I did not try to stop her.

9

We drove slowly back to Amy's house, cautiously threading the maze of wintry streets, neither of us saying anything. From time to time I caught her sneaking shy, happy little glances in my direction. Rose Oxley's corpse had been buried, at least temporarily, in the past and forgotten.

I staggered into the living room, feeling like Johnny Weissmuller on a Tarzan set, and Amy immediately took a proprietary attitude toward my body. She hung my raincoat in the bedroom closet and pushed me down on the couch beside the goldfish bowl. The television emitted inane commentary while she fixed me a drink. The sensations were almost painful as I began to relax. I had another drink to anaesthetize myself from my own good feelings.

About twenty minutes after we arrived, the phone rang. Amy took it in the bedroom and returned looking relieved and triumphant. The real estate agent had called back. He had been calling while she was out. When Amy told him she was interested in selling her mother's farm, he had checked his card index and found the number of a Toronto lawyer named Quincy Liggett who had tried to buy Rose out over the summer. Liggett still wanted the property, wanted it so much he was willing to ante up five thousand dollars in option money pending approval of the Oxley will in probate court.

"What's even better," enthused Amy, dipping a finger into the fish water and tickling the occupant's ribs, "is that Liggett's company specializes in suburban development. They'll probably tear the house down to clear the land. It can't happen soon enough," she added. "Out of sight, out of mind."

I could barely keep my own eyes open, let alone attend to what she was saying. When I finally understood, I got so excited that I dozed off, waking fitfully to be aware of the drone of the TV and my hostess doing domestic things in the kitchen.

Outside, it was black as a nun's habit and cold as a meat locker; inside, the plants and I were putting out new roots.

Around eight o'clock she roused me gently to sit up and take dinner: crab meat, salad, chilled white wine, and strong coffee. I couldn't do it justice. Before the coffee arrived to revive my flagging corpuscles, I had slumped onto my side and drifted once more into unconsciousness.

I came to the surface briefly to find her tugging at my trousers. I was in the bedroom. She was putting me to bed. I made no objection. For a while I lay under the covers, toasty as a marshmallow, unable to fall back to sleep because of the residual ache in my body. In the bathroom I could hear her taking a bath. Then she was beside me again, warm and soft and damp. I was a perfect gentleman and fell asleep right away.

The cold slate afternoon sky was visible through the net curtains of the bedroom window when I awoke. I awoke because she was watching me. She was standing in the doorway, leaning on the jamb, her hands in the pockets of her jeans, a stray wisp of hair drifting over her forehead. As a prize for not dying, I got coffee, two Sunday papers from Toronto, more coffee with brandy, and a poached egg. After which I went back to sleep.

Night. I woke up to find her fast asleep, lying on her side with her back and bum pressed against me. She was wearing a blue nightgown that had rucked up over her ass. I crept from the bed and beat a path through the undergrowth to the kitchen to make myself a sandwich. I had the sandwich and a glass of milk and a nip or two from what was left of the Hennessy in the living room with the goldfish, who was terrific company. When I crawled back into bed, Amy was awake, and together we did things which were not strictly in the interests of my health.

In the morning she put her feet in the small of my back and pushed until I got up. She gave me coffee in the bathtub, brought my cigarettes, pouted when I wouldn't eat breakfast, and called a cab to take me to work. With all the rest I had had, I was feeling sharp and brittle, as though there were two of me.

The one with all the sleep, food, and loving had just been born again, and the world looked fresh and clean to him.

At the top of the newsroom stairs, I collided with Gratz on his way out of the can. He stiffened like a setter, then pounced. Where had I been all weekend? That was about the last thing I would consider telling Gratz. He trod on my heels. I could smell soap from the men's room. Just where the hell had I been? He'd called the American; he had scoured the bars. I turned wearily to face him, and he started to walk up my legs.

"Let me guess," I said. "Something fishy about the tuna meringue teacake recipe? Or did we miss Lana Deptford's annual X-rated Tupperware bash?"

"You're starting in sports this morning," he said.

"Did Krishna quit?" I asked. Nothing surprised me in that place. Barrett had said he was about the worst sports editor the *Star-Leader* had ever had because his mind was always on the *Rig-Veda, Upanishads*, and *Mahabharata*.

"Spandrell gave him the air Saturday," said Gratz, in awe. "He flipped out after you left. Called the chief a servant of Siva, the Destroyer."

"That's the way it is nowadays," I said. "Everybody's a critic."

"I almost hadda restrain him."

"The guy was on a short fuse, Gratz. What do you suppose set him off?"

"The chief was cutting his copy."

"There is no place in an organization of this calibre," I said, "for a man who cannot submit to editorial control."

Gratz eyed me suspiciously as I skipped into the sports department cubicle. Hanging from the ceiling was a large hand-painted sign that read "SPROTS." My predecessor had taped the hoary Zen koan, "What is the sound of one hand clapping?" above the keys of the typewriter. There was another on the desk blotter: "What you see fluttering up there on the staff is *not* the wind, *not* your mind . . . (whereupon eight monks attained satori)." In the desk drawer, I found copies of *An Autobiography of a Yogi* and *On the Road*. Apparently, in that ethereal atmosphere there had been no need for telephone directories. I checked the filing cabinets. They contained nothing but an eighty-page typescript entitled *Tantric Ice Hockey*.

The departmental staff consisted of one Rudiger Kunow, an intensely enthusiastic ex-jock with a trick knee and a neck brace. During the course of the morning, Spandrell spiked Wishty's latest batch of erroneous court notices and reassigned him to me as part of "a rebuilding program." Kunow and Wishty hit it off like Kahlúa and Coke at a disco joint. They initiated me with an extempore trivia quiz in which I got twenty out of twenty wrong answers.

The big news we couldn't print for lack of hard evidence was the story of how the Ockenden Oaks had just returned from an exhibition series in Europe with a sixty percent incidence of VD. On the other hand, Spandrell was a snowmobile fanatic, and we were running a story a day on the chamber of commerce winter carnival that wouldn't take place for another three weeks. Kunow was sitting on a six-para tale about a fifteen-year-old Oaks goalie fined by his coach for wandering into the team hotel stoned after curfew. I banked the day's carnival advance and played the goalie story under a three-column file shot of the coach signing an autograph for an adoring fan.

Half an hour after the press run began, Kunow was strutting through the newsroom as though he had just won the National Midget Hockey Sportswriter of the Year Award. He was laughing and telling a Damon Barrett story. Barrett had come to work drunk and had gone home again in a cab after storming out of the women's bathroom, demanding to know why the urinals had been removed from the wall. I told Kunow to shut up or I would stick my grease pencil in his ass and kick him till it came out his navel.

It was a few minutes after noon when Lana Deptford and

Blythe Ashcroft converged at the gap in the wallboard dividers that otherwise served to protect the rest of the newsroom from contamination by mixed metaphors, pernicious hyperbole, galloping clichés, and other departmental diseases. They held a brief staring match; Miss Lana won, three falls to nil. She dropped a stack of mail on my desk without a word. But as she left, she couldn't resist flashing me one of those exultant I-told-you-so looks, as if to say she had known all along that a man of my insufficiencies would never cut it as women's editor.

"Precious?" said Ashcroft.

"He's not in," I said.

I began leafing through my windfall of hockey calendars, handwritten minor league scores, curling announcements, Oaks programs, pigeon-racing flyers. At the bottom of the pile was a plain manila envelope addressed to Moss C. Elliot, Esq., personally, no return address. Unencumbered by scruple or courtesy, Miss Lana had savaged the envelope in her frenzy to get at the contents.

Bright-eyed, cocky, sweating in a brand new down coat, Ashcroft draped himself over my desk like an Eskimo pinup and cleared his throat.

"Precious is not in," I said. "He must have seen you coming."

"I've got another scoop," he said, unassailed.

"Precious absolutely refuses to talk about murders, cops, clues, and cover-ups," I said. "He told me to tell you that if he wanted excitement, he'd take up skydiving."

"It's not the Oxley murder," said Ashcroft, looking disappointed. "That's a bust anyway. I can't get a word out of the police. Gratz says it's a stand-by story," he added with a laugh, "stand by the phone until something happens."

"Makes you want to eat your hands, doesn't it?" I said, shaking my head at the ordinary eternal inadequacy of existence. "Killer won't cooperate. Police won't cooperate. I won't cooperate! What the hell are we doing here?"

"I just want to be a newsman," said the kid virtuously.

"Sure you do. Everybody does once. But it's rarely terminal and they mostly get over it, like acne and hives. Now why don't you go back to school and learn to do something useful with yourself?"

Ashcroft retreated from my desk to a chair by the window. From the side pocket of his parka he produced a pipe, a pouch, a packet of cleaners, and a box of wooden matches, which he arranged neatly on the ledge beside him.

"The trouble with you, Precious," he said at length, his voice emanating like an oracle from inside a cloud of blue smoke, "is that you're old-fashioned. Gratz is right. Television has changed the shape of modern journalism. Reporting is a young man's business these days. You've got to move with the flow."

I wanted to jump on his knees. I had to tell myself it wasn't his fault; he was young; it would pass. Suddenly, the world was his clam shell; it existed for the sole purpose of inspiring news copy. It had ceased to matter that Rose Oxley had actually died so that his byline might live a day in print. And as for Moss Elliot, he was just another jaded hack, a seedy anachronism with the crabgrass of life sprouting from his ears.

While he was talking, Ashcroft's pipe had gone out. A dozen spent matches lay at his feet like the bodies of dead soldiers with their heads pointing toward the enemy. I used the respite to check the contents of my mutilated envelope. On top, typed under an embossed letterhead, was a note from someone who signed himself Otto Kleppinger, Wildlife Artist and Private Investigator. The letterhead bore the images of a duck on the wing and a smoking revolver. The return address was a downtown Toronto post office box. The note read:

> Re: Emerald pendant. Description: Family heirloom.
> Insured value: $45,000 U.S. Property of Mrs. Anne
> Delos, Athens, Greece.

Mr. Moss Claude Elliot, aka Precious.

Pursuant to our investigation of the theft of an emerald pendant in October of this year, and on behalf of our client, Mrs. Anne Delos, and her attorney, Mr. Ari Panadakis, we have been authorized to contact Mr. Moss Claude Elliot, aka Precious, and solicit his cooperation in the matter at hand.

I.e.: Insofar as the subject has refused to acknowledge our client's repeated requests for information dealing with the theft and disposition of said emerald pendant, we have been authorized to bring pressure to bear locally in order to facilitate recovery of said item, or, should recovery be deemed impractical, quick settlement of outstanding insurance claims.

To this end we enclose an affidavit form in triplicate for the subject's convenience. The subject is advised that the affidavit is for insurance purposes only and that he will not be liable to charges stemming from the theft of the pendant outside the State of Greece.

> Respectfully,
> Otto Kleppinger
> Wildlife Artist &
> Private Investigator
> enc. Affidavit form (3)

Either this was a bad joke, I thought, or Anne Delos was blackmailing me into answering her damn postcards. Somehow neither alternative made sense. Between the lines, I detected the crabbed and wily intellect of Ari Panadakis, the notary, a con artist for whom truth was merely an excuse for baroque invention. The whole thing even had a kind of hapless logic. Emerald gone, Precious gone. *Ergo,* Precious stole emerald!

What made it worse was that the Greeks had already expelled me under suspicious circumstances. Who would ever believe my side of the story? Suddenly I saw my face on a thousand post office bulletin boards: Moss Claude Elliot, aka Precious, international jewel thief, agent provocateur, gigolo. Worst of all was the remote possibility that Anne had forgotten about hocking the gem in the first place.

She was a big awkward woman, what Uncle Dorsey in his cups would have called "a real looker," with a childlike ingenuousness that made you want to weep and dark lustrous eyes that made you want to go out and buy a suit of white armour. All Panadakis had to do was convince her to hire some clumsy private detective to trace me — that explained how she got my address — then shake me down for a false confession and pocket the insurance money.

I had a feeling one quick phone call would put paid to Ari's scheme, but I was worried about the consequences. And phone calls to women like Anne Delos always have consequences. On the whole it seemed wiser to stand pat and call the little notary's bluff. And who the hell was this guy Kleppinger anyway?

Ashcroft wouldn't know; unconscious of my personal crisis, he was in full flight, explaining the ins and outs of his new scoop, showering himself with sparks in his excitement. I hadn't been paying much attention. The city reporter had called in sick; Gratz had assigned Ashcroft to cover the municipal council meeting at eight o'clock that evening. The kid had spent all morning nosing around city hall for signs of graft and corruption. Why, then, had he mentioned the name Liggett? Liggett . . . Liggett! The name rolled around in my head like a rock in an oil drum for several seconds before I remembered Amy's phone call from the real estate agent two days earlier. But Ashcroft had already left it far behind, baying after other game.

"What are you talking about?" I asked.

"Dawkins," he said. "Dawkins is straight. I tell you. I don't think he'd —"

"Liggett, kid. Who's Liggett?"

"He's the lawyer for Barryknoll Developments. Liggett, Triggers, and Follansbee."

"Who is Barryknoll?"

"That's what I've been trying to tell you."

"Who is Dawkins?"

"My source. He's the one —"

"Start from the beginning, kid. But spare me the melo-drama."

Ashcroft gave me his long-suffering look. I temporarily forgot about Otto Kleppinger and the emerald pendant caper. An idea had struck without preamble or argument. The next instant it was gone, like all my best ideas, flipping its tail in the murky river of my subconscious.

"Barryknoll is an investment group represented legally by Liggett, Triggers, and Follansbee, a Toronto corporate law firm," said Ashcroft, the soul of patience. "Max Dawkins sits for the east ward on city council."

"That's very good, Ashers," I said. "It sounds almost like English."

"Barryknoll, Liggett, and some members of council, including the mayor, are pushing a zoning amendment for the east side," he went on, enunciating slowly and carefully so that I could understand. "They're going to railroad it through council tonight because it's the last meeting before the winter carnival recess and several key councillors will be absent. The amendment was only placed on the agenda this morning. Apparently, there was an ad hoc meeting of the planning committee at the mayor's house Saturday night to approve the draft amendment. Dawkins is on the planning committee, but somehow he didn't get the invitation."

"Civics I," I said. "Wait till your opponent goes to the bathroom and outvote him. That's modern democracy. We did it to the Russians over Korea; they were out of practice. Did Dawkins spill all that?" I asked.

"That's right," said Ashcroft, sucking his pipe, looking wise. "Things were pretty tense at city hall this morning. When I got there, Dawkins and the mayor had been locked in the mayor's chambers for an hour yelling at each other. When Dawkins came out, he headed straight for the parking lot. I tried to talk to him; he didn't even want to be seen standing near me. All I got was a very loud 'No comment!'

"But when I left to come back to the newsroom, he was waiting outside. I mean I didn't really know who he was even then. He blinked his headlights a couple of times up a back street and made me drive to the waterfront with him where no one would see us before he'd say anything."

"Hell hath no fury like a politician scorned," I said. "He give you all this stuff for the record?"

"I don't think so," said Ashcroft uncertainly. "He asked if I could use a tip without letting anyone know where I got it. He made me swear to it, said he'd have my balls for dog food if I told. You're not going to tell, are you?" he asked, suddenly worried.

"Nuts, kid. Between you and me, Dawkins is Deep Throat from now on. Suit you?"

"Well . . ."

"Listen, Ashcroft," I said. "You've got nothing. This isn't *Newsweek* or the *Washington Post*. We can't afford to print uncorroborated tips from unnamed sources. You think Dawkins is honest?"

"I guess so," he answered, his pipe beginning to droop.

"Then why is he spilling his guts off the record? I want to know what his angle is. What's he afraid of? Put in some legwork and you might have a story. A bit of a comedown from the Ockenden Slasher, but a story. What makes you think this whole flap isn't about some penny-ante subdivision or apartment building?"

"It's not!" said Ashcroft. "It's big! Hundreds, maybe thousands of acres."

"You'll need to know exactly. Go back up against Dawkins. There must be a draft plan that goes with the rezoning application. Sounds like you won't get one officially, but he might let you have a copy. Poke around a bit on your own. I'd check the registry office, roust out some of the title histories for land out there; you can get names and addresses from the city directory the way I did to find Rose Oxley's daughter. You'll have to get the legal descriptions from city hall."

Ashcroft was straining forward in his chair, pipe clenched at attention, eyes like pearl buttons.

"What do you think it all means?" he asked breathlessly.

"I don't know, kid," I said. "Barryknoll might be speculating. But who'd speculate on a dump like Ockenden? Unless somebody knows something."

"Like what?"

"Beats me. Maybe it's a boondoggle. Maybe Dawkins is exaggerating. Maybe it's just a bunch of local pols wrangling over municipal turf. That's what you're going to find out. Right?"

"Right!" said Ashcroft, giving a surprised nod, knocking his ashes onto the floor. "I mean sure. I won't say anything about it. I'll just work on it secretly until I put it all together."

"Sure thing, kid. Now why don't you ease out the back way so no one will know you were here."

"I don't think it matters if — oh, I see."

He nodded his way back to the newsroom, thinking about his scoop, not really noticing anything else. I headed for the food machines and bought a cup of coffee and tried to read the future in the dregs. They looked pretty much like all the other coffee dregs I had seen. Before leaving the office, I filed Kleppinger in my one file folder, marked *Hockey, Tantric*. Then I hurried off to hold Amy's hand while they buried her stepmother.

10

The following night the Ockenden Oaks collided with the Bytown Badgers in a dusty concrete boot box called the Cedric Palliser Terrence O'Malley Memorial Arena. According to a plaque embedded in the lobby tiles, O'Malley had been an Irish hod carrier from County Clare who slaved for ten years in the mid-1800s to save steerage fare for the Atlantic crossing, was quarantined off Saint John on a cholera ship and mugged in Quebec City, walked from Montreal to Ockenden, and died a week later of gangrene toe. Some people were just born to trouble.

The weather was grim. The isobars were dipping down from James Bay like amoebae questing for food. Kunow was covering the game, and I would have preferred to spend the evening in Amy's kitchen. But as sports editor, I was expected to hold court in the press box above the ice, drink beer, and bat sage witticisms back and forth with the radio crew, scouts, minor league coaches, and injured Oaks.

At eight p.m. I shouldered my way past the ticket queues, palmed my press pass to the attendant, and slipped upstairs past the concession booths to the gondola. Below, the teams wheeled menacingly at opposite ends of the rink, staring into each others' faces like boxers at a weigh-in, taking impudent swipes with their sticks in the other team's territory. The evening promised prolonged fisticuffs, a little hockey, and plenty of blood on the ice.

In the stands the fans were hiving like bees to watch the carnage. There were hordes of youngsters in nylon jackets festooned with crests and lettered names like Brad and Jackie. Boys yelled at players on the ice and pelted each other with popcorn. Girls eddied and swirled in the aisles, watching the boys. The rest, loosely referred to as adults, wandered around comparing seat numbers with ticket stubs, eating hot dogs, and arguing sporting dogma with their neighbours.

I knocked the top off a bottle of beer and wondered why Cedric Palliser Terrence O'Malley had had his heart set on Ockenden. It seemed like a pretty eccentric choice to me. I wondered what Ashcroft had found out about Liggett and Barryknoll, if anything. The kid had disappeared mysteriously after deadline without letting anyone know where he was going. I was just beginning to wonder about Amy, the strange sadness that knotted her insides, the darting beauty of her eyes, when my first interruption wedged his way through the pressbox door.

Bernie Tassio, owner of a riding stable on the edge of town, was a chubby little man in his late thirties with a high-pitched voice and wispy blond hair. His pale blue eyes were sensitive and opaque. He wore an out-of-season pastel-coloured leisure suit and patent-leather loafers, and his cheeks were as red as a hydrant.

"What'd they do to your hair, Bernie?" I asked, exhibiting sportsmanlike bonhomie.

"You like it, Precious? Had it styled in Toronto. You know, change my image."

"What'd they do? Give you a blow job?"

Bernie's sensitive eyes began to water. He got that hunted look he wore every time he dashed through the newsroom on his way to the sports department with a handful of free passes or a printed circular. He was always on the make for free publicity. Lately, he had gotten hooked in with a school for retarded children and was bussing them to the stable afternoons to gulp microwaved hot dogs and pet the horses. I had already told him once I wouldn't touch it. I wasn't listening to him.

Fumbling for change, I came across the lucky zinc cut I had rescued from Rose Oxley's gossip bin. I rubbed its grainy surface with my thumb and wished for Bernie Tassio to vanish. It didn't work. I thought of Amy. The funeral had made her blue. Afterward, we sat in the sling chairs, drinking brandy like grape juice, smoking, and talking. She asked me about my past and told me the melancholy saga of her own divorce. We put blankets down on the rattan rug and made love. When she came, she shouted, and it was like that first time in the car in her step-mother's driveway, all passion and trying to forget.

"I just loathe horses," Bernie was saying, "loathe them! And the stable hands — you know they never get rid of the smell! But it's not settled, so you can't print the story yet. Expect my call in a couple of days."

"Print what?" I asked.

I had the cut in my hand and was playing with it, running it across my knuckles like a coin. I was concentrating on that and the picture of Amy, naked beneath the plants, when the little red-faced man, suddenly vehement, slopped his beer on the floor beside my foot. I glanced up.

"You think you're too damn good for this town, don't you?" he said, looking venomous.

It was true, I thought. I couldn't disagree with him. But I tried to look torn up about it so as not to cause further offence. The spilled beer was soaking into the floorboards like blood in a butcher shop.

"I'm doing you a favour," said Bernie. "This'll start you off in sports with a blockbuster. Not a soul in Ockenden knows about the track changing hands."

"Not for lack of interest, I'll bet," I said. "Who's the sucker?"

"Outtatown guy," said Bernie. "Don't ask me anything about it because I don't know. He works through a lawyer in Toronto. But I don't care where the money comes from just as long as it buys me a ticket out of Ockenden."

"I know what you mean," I said, "not much culture. Do the names Liggett and Barryknoll mean anything to you, Bern?"

His face went flabby as though he had just been caught walking the streets in nothing but an overcoat and rubber boots.

"How did you know?" he squealed. "I made that boy at the radio station promise not to breath a word. It must be all over town."

Bernie had his hand on my elbow. He did a little dance of vexation.

The first period was over, and I had drunk my way from hangover to sobriety and was starting to get potted again. I caught sight of Ashcroft. He was struggling against a tide of humanity pressing toward the refreshment booths, waving his arms to attract my attention, trout-eyed, cheeks pink with cold, clad in a parka, mukluks, and a fur hat. It took him five minutes to find his way to the press box.

"Am I bothering you?" he asked, puffing and sighing like a lady in a delivery room.

"Bernie and I were just discussing Chapman's Homer," I said. "I think Bernie prefers the Pope translation. Park your sled and have a beer and don't, whatever you do, don't mention you-know-what in front of you-know-who."

I nodded at Bernie. The two of them looked at each other suspiciously, a meeting of truly great minds. The fans roared below us, shaking the gondola, raising dust. There was blood on the blue line. Two players were undressing each other at centre ice. A spectator had been smacked with a puck and required medical attention.

"What?" shouted Ashcroft above the commotion. "Don't mention what? Listen, I found out what Liggett's up to on the east side."

Bernie made a lunge at the kid. For a second I thought they might go over onto the ice together. Bernie was shaking his arm, shouting at him. Ashcroft looked alarmed.

"What's going on? What are you talking about?" yelled Bernie. He was drunk. I don't think he had much capacity. "Is it big? Liggett's been telling me I'm a jerk for holding on to the old fire trap. He talks like he's a fucking philanthropist just making an offer. If you guys know something, you gotta tell me!"

"Were you really discussing Homer?" cried Ashcroft.

In the stands the uproar was subsiding. We no longer had to

scream at one another. Bernie had released his stranglehold on Ashcroft's wrist and was reading our lips, his mouth agape.

"What happened at the council meeting?" I asked. Conversations with Ashcroft often fell just short of being surreal. Until I filled in the blanks, nothing he had to say would make sense to Bernie. I stopped listening and remembered getting cross-eyed after we made love on the blankets. Amy dancing by herself to the radio, looking like the photograph on the wall. The rug rustling beneath our bodies. The philodendron tickling my ass and Amy, laughing, sweating, moaning, absolutely driven out of herself by the funeral and the booze.

"It passed," said Ashcroft, glancing warily at Bernie. "At least, I think it did. The agenda read: 'Parcel redesignated I-1.' That's planning code for heavy industrial. Can you beat that? It passed on a show of hands. No debate. Dawkins abstained. I drove up and down the concessions all afternoon before I found somebody who'd talk. All the owners are scared to let out a peep. Liggett's been telling them the slightest publicity will queer the deal."

"That's what he told me!" cried Bernie, looking ready to burst. "That's what he told me!"

"Not another word, Ashcroft," I said, winking at him over my beer bottle. "What say, Bernie? You got anything we could use? Want to trade?"

His eyes narrowed shrewdly, flicked furtively from side to side. He licked his lips, started to say something, then thought better of it.

"What have you got?" he asked. "How do I know it'll do me any good?"

"It's a bomb, isn't it, kid?" I said. Ashcroft eyes shone with sudden comprehension. He nodded enthusiastically. "It'll buy you a ticket anywhere you want to go, Bern."

Bernie's body trembled with anticipation.

"You know about the Oaks' slush fund?" he asked. "The money they set aside to pay under-the-table bonuses at the end of the season?"

"Not good enough," I said. "Every team in the league's got an illegal kitty."

Ashcroft looked aghast. He had grown up sheltered. The ordinary, everyday, run-of-the-mill perfidy of human nature had never touched him, except on TV.

Bernie's eyes appealed to Ashcroft. Ashcroft looked to me for guidance. I shook my head.

"I heard a rumour," Bernie said, his voice lowering to a whisper. "I heard a rumour that last year the board of directors voted five thousand dollars from the slush fund to help finance Mayor Warren's re-election campaign."

"Keep going," I said. "Now you're cooking."

"The city owns the hockey team, Precious. Council appoints the board. Billy Shaw, the chief of police, is chairman. Then there's Warren, Whitaker Brubacher, the Ford dealer and boss of the police commission, and Felix Playfair, the city solicitor. They backed their own candidate with the taxpayer's money!"

"They'll never make it into a movie," I said. Ashcroft's mouth was opening and closing. "How come nobody's sniffed all this out before now?"

"It's true!" squealed Bernie. "It's true! A lot of people knew about the slush fund. But the newspaper wouldn't go after the story because the damn publisher had backed Warren's re-election. You guys would have looked dumb with shit all over your faces."

Bernie was quivering with rage and anxiety. He didn't like getting pushed around any more than I did. He'd had a lot of practise, but he still didn't like it.

"Tell him, kid," I said, cracking another beer.

Before he could get a word out, the sports fans exploded, nearly blowing the roof off O'Malley's arena. The Oaks had recently traded off a couple of Swiss cheese goaltenders for a fire plug Indian called Duke, with a devastating left uppercut and knuckles like razors. Duke had just obliged the management by knocking the front teeth out of a couple of Badger forwards and was chasing a third into the bleachers.

"I finally did find someone who would talk!" Ashcroft shouted, when he realized the ruckus wasn't going to die down. "A cat lady!"

"A what?" I yelled back.

"You know, a lady with cats. She must have had fifty or more."

"Crazy?" I shouted.

"I think she likes cats! She has goats, too," he added, turning to Bernie with an expression of wonderment. "She's kind of a hippy and she doesn't want to leave. Liggett's making her mad. A couple of weeks ago she ripped her phone off the wall. She's quite pretty, really."

Bernie groaned. He was rocking in agony. The crowd was screaming for blood. Ashcroft had fallen in love with a cat lady and we were never going to hear the end of it. The kid seemed to sense the onset of despair; he made an effort to get back on track.

"Her name is Susan!" he yelled.

We were all drunk except for the kid who was never straight anyway. Some of the fans were down on the ice, scooting around after Badger players who hadn't already retreated to the dressing rooms.

"Please, Precious," wailed Bernie piteously. "Please!"

"Why'd she rip the phone off the wall?" I asked Ashcroft. "What did Liggett want her to do?"

"I was coming to that," said the kid, staring down at the riot. "Liggett and Barryknoll are laying out cash for cheap six-month options, renewable at the discretion of the purchaser. They're offering better than market for the land. Those old farmers are jumping at the chance to retire. And they figure the option money is gravy."

"But if the land were to suddenly jump in value," I said, "Barryknoll would make a killing flogging the options."

"I never thought of that," said Ashcroft.

Bernie was in shock. His eyes glazed over. His Adam's apple worked up and down his throat without making a sound.

"Satisfied?" I asked.

He stared at me without understanding.

"They acted like they were doing me a favour," he said finally. "Like they were doing me a favour."

"You talk to Dawkins yet?" I asked Ashcroft, who was leaning far out over the ice to see under the press box.

"Not yet," he cried. "Spandrell put me on special assignment this morning. I don't know what it is yet, but I'm not going to have much time for zoning stories."

"You tell him about Dawkins?"

"I said I wanted to do a follow on the council wrap-up, but he told me to drop it. Not my beat. I got a raise."

"Wonderful. Are you going to call Dawkins?" I asked.

"I guess so. I guess it doesn't take long to make a call."

"You got it, kid."

"I need a lawyer. I shouldn't try to handle this myself," said Bernie Tassio. He had spilled beer down the front of his leisure suit. "Liggett said I was a jerk for not selling."

"Listen, Ashcroft," I said. He had pulled his head into the press box again. He was starting to sweat inside his parka and mukluks. Downstairs, police and security guards were clearing the ice so that the game could continue. "It's tough to chase down a boring rezoning story. It's fun to be on special assignment and get raises. What's more, if you do get the goods on Liggett and Barryknoll, nobody around here will love you. If they can make a profit on the deal, the good people of Ockenden won't want the world to know a single slimy detail. But it's the job, kid. Somebody's got to do the honest-to-God legwork. If you don't want it, then someone will, because that's how newsmen are made."

Ashcroft blinked his eyes at me a couple of times but didn't say anything. He was stung. I shouldn't have been making speeches, drunk as I was. I always got carried away and made journalism sound like joining the Marines. That was the way Uncle Dorsey had talked. Whenever I got drunk, I sounded like Uncle Dorsey.

Whistles shrilled on the ice surface. The two centres had started pummelling each other in the faceoff circle, and the rest of the players were standing around, leaning on their sticks, taking bets on the winner. While I was watching them, the kid slipped away, leaving his beer half-finished. I drank what was left before heading for the dressing rooms and the post-game interviews.

I finally left the arena through a side exit, past a chain-link fence into the parking lot. A bus was rumbling a few yards away, warming up to take the wounded home. There were a few cars left. By the street exit a dark Buick emitted clouds of exhaust, its occupants hidden by the shadows.

I had to walk that way. My head was down, trying to keep my feet from fouling in the crusted ruts left by the cars after the game. I paid no attention to the Buick. Lots of people ran their engines before driving in the winter. I was thinking of Amy, looking forward to sitting in her kitchen, drinking coffee. I didn't love her, but I had strong feelings at that moment about sitting in her kitchen. I heard the chunk of the car doors, the quick rush of feet over the snow. And then, before I could turn around, something hit me on the back of my skull.

The stars went out. The streetlights went out. I went out. Then I woke slightly to feel meaty hands hooking me under the armpits, dragging my body to the Buick. Someone bundled me into the back seat. I hit the opposite door with my head. I felt sick to my stomach. My head lolled gracelessly. I couldn't think.

11

The world had shown itself to be a cruel and irrational place. It was morally the equivalent of Mars, barely fit for the existence of simple life forms like slugs and fungus.

I lay in the corner of the Buick's back seat, feigning unconsciousness. This seemed like a good idea, since I was already pretty close to the real thing, and I reasoned that most people are sensible enough not to hit an unconscious man. Which only shows how wrong you can be.

The car did a drag-strip acceleration out of the parking lot. I felt the rear wheels slide away as we turned onto the street too fast. Then it slowed to join traffic on Acorn Avenue as we headed toward the centre of town away from the lakefront. I could tell there was someone sitting beside me on the back seat. That meant there were at least two of these bozos. The guy beside me lit a cigarette. Nobody said a word.

The pain gathered itself like a large animal at the base of my skull and charged forward to batter the inside of my forehead, again and again. It was difficult to pay attention to anything else. Each time it butted the front of my brain box, I would shiver and choke with nausea.

I tried to think of a reason why anyone would want to sandbag me in the O'Malley parking lot, manhandle me into the back seat of a waiting car like a piece of left luggage, and then chauffeur my insentient corpse around the back streets of Ockenden. A certain amount of resentment began to accrue in my battered cortex. These bozos had to be mistaken. I was a victim of erroneous assault. I was about to lodge a protest. And then the guy next to me leaned over and placed the tip of his cigarette against the inside of my wrist.

A new pain snaked up my arm and into my brain, getting into a fight with the old pain. Suddenly the two of them were having a field day at my expense.

I opened my eyes, which was what the thug had intended me to do. And then I puked on the seat between us, which he hadn't. He recoiled in disgust. I glared at him, burping ominously.

"That's terrible," said a raspy, adenoidal voice in the front seat. "Look what you did to my car." It was Jerry Mennenga.

Through the red mist of pain, I distinguished the bulky outline of Marty, Jerry's enforcer, beside me. He was wearing an alpaca overcoat. The whole car smelled like a goat. I leaned over and tried to puke on his sleeve. He punched me back into the corner where I lay quietly, moaning to myself.

Jerry slowed for a stoplight at the edge of the chamber of commerce park. I grabbed the door handle and tried to let myself out. The door was locked. I yanked the release button, but nothing happened.

"I got one o' them, you know, kiddy locks," said Jerry in the front seat. "I take the grandchildren to the zoo or sumpin, I don't want them falling outta the car. You should treat other people's property with more respect."

"What the hell are you doing?" I screamed. "Are you crazy?"

"I told you you shouldn't get involved in business."

"I paid you," I cried. "I sent you the cheque a month ago. We're quits. I don't owe you a cent!"

"Not that business," said Jerry. "You're a very popular guy around Toronto these days."

I didn't know what he was talking about. Streetlights flashed by like gunshots. I made a lunge for Jerry in the front seat and Marty caught me in the throat with his elbow. I couldn't speak. There was a stone in my glottis. Marty explained to me in quaint monosyllabic Italo-Canadian that he was going to tie a knot in my fingers if I forgot my manners again. I chuckled weakly; it was a very funny thing to say. He reached for my hand and slipped the glove off. I yelled. He looked at me quizzically. I said I would cooperate. Anything Jerry wanted he could have. He twisted my little finger. I screamed.

Jerry pulled into the *Star-Leader* parking lot. The building was dark. He craned his neck and advised Marty not to damage me. Marty said he was only kidding. Was I hurt? I wasn't hurt. Sure I knew he was only kidding. Jerry and I were friends. Marty and I were friends. We were all buddies. It was like being in the Lions Club. Marty opened the window to air out the back seat. I tried to squeeze out the window.

"Are you going to be quiet?" asked Jerry.

I was doubled over on the car floor, massaging the back of my knee where Marty's karate chop had landed.

"What'd you sap me for?" I asked. I couldn't raise my voice above a whisper.

"Aw, Marty wasn't going to hurt you," he said. "It's like them wild animals, you know. When they catch them, they give 'em a little sumpin to knock 'em out, so they don't hurt themselves trying to get away. Marty just didn't want you to hurt yourself. It's very humane."

"Humane! Are you crazy?"

Jerry shrugged. He had a lot of philosophy. He had a week-old copy of the *Daily Racing Form* on the seat beside him. He perched a pair of bifocals on the bridge of his nose and began to read the paper by the dash light. I took this as a signal that he was about to get to the point. I massaged my leg, wondering if I would ever again feel anything from the knee down.

"A pal of yours by the name of Kleppinger has been coming around the bar," he said finally. "You know this Kleppinger?"

"Never heard of him," I said. "Must have been after some other guy. Can I go now?"

"The first time he came around he was just looking for you, you know. Said he was a private dick. Said you were missing. I knew you wasn't missing. But I wasn't going to tell Kleppinger that. Your buddy Bellfield told him."

"Terrific," I said. "Did he get his thirty pieces of silver, too?"

"I don't know nothin about that," said Jerry. "But Kleppinger was back last week asking if you'd been trying to fence some hot jewels around town. Somebody must have told him I was in business. Maybe it was that creep Bellfield."

My throat felt as if someone had hacked through my vocal cords with a dull saw. Jerry handed me a flask from inside his coat pocket. It bit like a dog; it was Hennessy. Jerry had a long memory when it came to his regulars.

"Maybe you'd know this guy if you saw him," he said, trying to encourage me. "Fat guy in a trench coat and sunglasses. He wears a leather hat from Austria with a feather in it. And he's a abalone."

"Abalone?"

"Yeah, you know. All white like a rabbit. Pink eyes. You know him, Precious?"

Jerry made rabbit ears with his fingers and stared at me sadly over the rims of his bifocals. I shook my head. The brandy still had its teeth in my windpipe. My eyes were streaming.

"I'm disappointed," said Jerry. "You should have come to me for advice. If I'd known you had something to sell, you could have hit me for a hell of a lot more than a couple of hundred bucks."

I shook my head again. I took another shot from the brandy flask. The first swallow had beaten my neurons into insensibility. The pain had reached a tolerable level. I was trying to understand what had happened. Marty was staring out the window, keeping his eye on the parking lot, humming.

"It was very intelligent, Precious, to lay low like this," said Jerry, his voice an asthmatic drone. "Nobody had you pegged for anything but a dumb newspaperman. When the heat's off, we can get you maybe twenty, twenty-five grand for the emerald."

"I didn't steal the fucking emerald," I said.

"I know. I know," said Jerry, with a chuckle. "Listen, Precious, you can level with me. We've known each other for years. You tell me you didn't steal no emerald and I'll believe you."

"I didn't steal it," I said.

"That's very smart, Precious. Don't admit anything. I was the same when I was your age. Stop singing, Marty! Maybe you would like to take a walk, Precious."

Jerry nodded at the dumpster next to the loading bay. I finished the brandy. Marty had his glove on the door handle. I wasn't afraid. The Hennessy had given me a vision. My thoughts went on wings. I waited until Marty was halfway out of the car.

"What about Kleppinger?" I asked.

Jerry gave me one of those long, slow looks. I could see his opinion of Moss Elliot was changing. His sad eyes grew sadder. I had never met a man for whom making money was such a melancholy proceeding. He should have stuck to modelling or tending bars. He folded his newspaper and carefully placed his glasses on top of it on the passenger seat.

"Kleppinger's a fruitcake," he said finally. "The first thing he did was flash me a card with a bird on it. Said he knew you. I pointed to Marty and he walked over and started shooting off his mouth about this emerald. He didn't know you from his asshole."

"I already got a client who's interested in the rock," I said. I needed elbow room. Jerry was ready to believe anything except the truth. And I couldn't explain about Anne Delos and her nefarious notary while eating Marty's knuckle sandwich.

Jerry suddenly looked very old. He looked as though his car had just died, or his daughter had eloped with a knife thrower in a circus. I don't know how he had managed to survive doing business this way all his life.

"Who is this person?" he asked. "Is he healthy?"

"His name is Quincy Liggett," I said. "He's a lawyer in T-O."

"Liggett!" Jerry gave a low whistle. "That's very bad, Precious. I should be asking about your health."

"You know him?" I asked.

"Yeah, I know him," said Jerry. "He's a three-piece suit, a whatchamacallit bagman for the Conservatives, but he does legit work for some mobs, especially the Volpone family. Why do you wanna get mixed up with a shark like that when there are plenty of decent, reputable people to do business with?"

Jerry was in his fifties. His eyes were haggard, his face pitted and runnelled like a badlands. His breath came and went like a hundred tin whistles. He switched on the car heater and lit the squashed butt of an old Havana he had been saving on the dashboard.

"Have you shook hands with Liggett?" he asked. "Have you talked money?"

I shook my head. He looked relieved. I was nailing down the lid of my own coffin. I had to talk to Anne Delos. I had to get Otto Kleppinger off my back. Jerry had an envelope in his hand. He was tapping it against the steering wheel, thinking. Marty was staring at the parking lot. Maybe he was a connoisseur of parking lots, I thought. Maybe he liked to compare the way the lines were painted. He was humming something familiar but unrecognizable.

"I take forty per off the top," Jerry said. "I got a grand here. Earnest money. Which I want you to have. I always had a feeling you were crooked, Precious. I just didn't think it would be jewels. Bad cheques, stock fraud, maybe." He shrugged. "Jewels is pretty high class."

"What if Liggett wants the emerald?" I said, pushing away Jerry's hand with the envelope.

"I would be very disappointed that you had violated a sacred trust for fiscal considerations," said Jerry, looking sorrowful and perplexed. "Marty, Precious's mitt isn't working too good."

Marty reached over and closed my fingers around the thousand dollars, squeezing them until the blood ran out of my hand. I sat there with my hand on my lap, shaking my head. I was going crazy. I wanted to shove Jerry's cigar up his nose. I wanted to lower Marty up to his hips in a lead pot. But I couldn't move. My limbs had turned to broccoli.

"We don't have to deal right away," Jerry was saying, his voice coming out of his nose like a muted French horn. "We'll stonewall Kleppinger until he gets tired of pissing up the wrong tree. That'll make you look clean. Then we'll fence the rock in another town."

My knee buckled when they let me out of the car. The Buick launched itself into the street like a torpedo. I watched it go. "Stay away from Quincy Liggett," Jerry had said. "He's a bad man, Precious. He's a amoral." I looked in the envelope. There was a thousand dollars, staring back at me like sliced bacon. When things got straightened out, Jerry would want it returned. I had to be careful. I limped upstairs to the newsroom and cleaned myself up in the bathroom. Then I borrowed five dollars from the envelope for cab fare to Amy's house.

I had telephoned from the arena, telling her not to wait up. She had coffee and sandwiches waiting by the fishbowl when I came through the door. It had started to snow; I brushed the flakes from my eyes and saw her curled up on the sofa with a flannel nightgown wrapped round her body. Her hair was down and she was reading a book by the corner lamp. Everything smelled of moist earth and coffee grounds. I felt like a stranger.

She knew right away something was wrong. I was pale and shaky, coughing again, and there was small cut where Marty had sapped me. I had hoped she would be asleep so that I could conceal the damage until morning, when it would be less obvious. Yet she didn't berate me, didn't ask questions. She didn't stake any claims; she was a woman who knew how to respect privacy.

She ran to me, skinned my coat off over my hands, and dragged me down on the couch. She brought brandy for the coffee and aspirin for my head. Accidentally she brushed my wound. She rushed to the kitchen for ice. Her eyes were wide with strangeness.

She was beautiful like that. Her nipples tipping the flannel cloth like acorns. She shivered when I touched her. She was still afraid of me. Her husband hadn't been much in the sexual line, despite all the talk and conquests. She had allowed me everything already. When I was away from her, I would visualize her soft private parts. My desire for her was constant. With me, she could let herself go. It was a drunkenness of arms and legs and lips and eyes. But I had something even love couldn't cure.

I was separate. I was a sojourner. Yet her face was already dear to me. I liked the tiny pencil lines under her eyes. The strands of hair that never stayed in place. But when I looked at her I thought of my mother and Uncle Dorsey, sharing the same house all those years yet remaining strangers, sleeping in separate beds. I was not a stayer. I was destined to spend my days with the Damon Barretts and Jerry Mennengas of the world, in bars, in rented rooms. Most of the time that was all right. I wasn't in love with Amy Ranger. But when I looked at her, sometimes, it tore my heart out. I wanted to curl up between her legs and sleep with my nose pressed against her sex.

12

The next night after we had gone to bed she read me poetry from a book. It was Thomas Wyatt.

And she me took in her arms long and small
And there withal did me sweetly kiss
And said, Dear heart, how like you this?

I had read it before, but when Amy said the words I was eaten up with wanting to get inside her skin. We had had our first argument. It was about the past as much as the future. She wanted me to leave my room at the American House and move in with her. She was thirty-five and hungered after a child. I was a good man, even if I drank too much and fought in bars.

It didn't seem strange to be talking about marriage so abruptly. I had stayed in her bed four nights. I was starting to wake up early each morning so I could watch her face before it woke to the consciousness of sin. She had Anne Delos and Rini and all the rest beaten to dust. Yet I knew I would be nothing but trouble and care to her.

Earlier that evening, Ashcroft had called; he wouldn't say why, except that he was saving a table at Boot Hill's, a hotel bar near the waterfront where the band played country swing and the management sponsored lady wrestlers Saturday afternoons.

"I love new ideas," I said, and hung up.

My body had more bruises than a pound of hamburger. I wanted to sit home with Amy and the goldfish. But Amy wanted to be out and about. She had never been to the Boot; she had to meet Ashcroft. She even volunteered to drive.

We arrived a little after nine o'clock. There were more than thirty cars in the lot. The kid's Volkswagen crouched alone and leprous in a corner.

"This is my favourite part of town," she said, locking her door.

The air was so thick with flurries I wanted to sneeze. I supposed she meant the old port area. Across the street were the blackened ruins of a warehouse block, torched the previous year by an insurance ring interested in do-it-yourself urban renewal. Boot Hill's had the distinction of being the only downtown business with an unrestricted view of the lake.

We found ourselves in a smelly barnboard seraglio, eye-deep in cowboys and girls who hadn't seen a range since they left their mothers' kitchens. The band performed behind a split-rail fence studded with strobes and coloured floodlights. There were a couple of dozen barrel-top tables, a tile dance floor, a mechanical bull, and a long Victorian bar presided over by Boot Hill himself, a hoarse fat man with a face like a shoe and a live microphone clipped to his Roy Rogers shirt.

Ashcroft sat by the computer games with a stunning blond woman, over six feet tall, dressed in an embroidered sheepskin coat, jeans, and a T-shirt. He had a bottle of beer and a club sandwich on the table in front of him. He was eyeing the sandwich suspiciously, as though he expected the chicken to get up and make a run for it. Amy held my hand. I pointed to Ashcroft's bottle and signalled the bartender to bring two more. "Flasher in the raincoat wants a coupla beers," came the bartender's voice, booming over the public address system. "Free drink for the lucky lady if he keeps it buttoned."

The blond was Susan, the cat lady. The kid shoved a quarter of the sandwich into his face before shaking hands with Amy. He nodded at me enthusiastically, chewing the lump in his cheek, but said nothing.

"This is Ashcroft," I said. "He's a rough diamond."

"He hasn't eaten all day," said the cat lady.

His eyes were red rimmed and sleepy, his skin the colour of oysters. He hadn't shaved; his beard was sending a skirmishing line of slim reddish hairs through his chin. The skin around his nose was blistered and raw from too much blowing.

He hadn't shown up at the office that morning. After deadline, I had run a misdirected page proof through to the city desk myself in order to ask Gratz what had happened to his ace legman.

"Kid's on special assignment," he had said, with a lewd wink. "If you ask me, he's goldbricking. He met some broad and he's out there getting his pencil sharpened."

I had warned Gratz to get his mind out of the gutter. We had bylaws against public littering.

"You call that a beard?" I said, as Ashcroft swallowed.

"Geez, Precious, I've been shaving since I was fourteen."

"Sure, and nicked yourself both times."

The cat lady glared at me. I had her pegged for one of the bird and bunny crowd. She had that crazed look, as if she was ready to give her life for brown rice and bean curd. The kid's voice sounded like air in a rusty pipe.

"Umph. Umph," he said. He had just thrown a second helping of club sandwich after its brother. The skin around his eyes crinkled, his head bobbed up and down, and he sniffed wetly through his nose. I interpreted this grotesque display as laughter.

"Ashcroft has a mind as scattered as winds on a runway," I said.

"This is boring," said Susan. "Can you dance swing?" She was asking Amy; it took us both by surprise. She stood up and dropped her coat; her boobs quivered underneath her T-shirt like rabbits in a snowdrift. Amy was impressed. She had a mischievous glint in her eye. There was a tent of silence around the table.

"Love to," said my girl.

"Too bad, Flasher," boomed the voice of Boot Hill. It was a

shock. He was standing over me with the beer on a tray. "She's a better man than you, buddy."

I wanted to fix his sex life with that microphone. Amy was grinning. The cat lady looked smug. Ashcroft had paused in mid-chew to observe developments. Now his eyes crinkled up and he laughed some more, shaking his head from side to side, marvelling at the ironies of life.

I nearly lost my composure. Amy gave my hand a light-hearted squeeze and said, "Don't worry, sweetheart. It's only a dance." The two women loped toward the dance floor like deer. A hundred eyes followed them like periscopes. I grabbed Amy's coat and started to go after her. Ashcroft held my wrist, made me sit down again. I was weak with rage.

"Couple gay boys by the Space Invaders," said Boot Hill, safe behind the bar.

The kid hooked up the third section of his sandwich in one hand and signalled me with the index finger of the other.

"She's something else, isn't she?" he said.

"Right, kid. I don't think they've even got a name for it yet."

"She's a lawyer, too."

"I see," I said.

Boot Hill was at the other end of the bar picking on a woman with a club foot. I found a waitress and ordered a triple Hennessy. Amy and Susan had disappeared into the frantic melee on the dance floor. Ashcroft snagged a spiral notebook out of his parka pocket and tossed it on the table like a fish fillet.

"We spent all day in Toronto, running back and forth between Queen's Park and the Department of Industrial and Corporate Affairs. We dug up a file on Barryknoll. Then Susan had an idea that we might be looking at a whole web of interlocking companies, at least, that's the way these developers operate, especially if there's anything shady. So, working on that angle, we got the department to give us a list of all the companies incorporated the same year as Barryknoll. It's all in the notes."

Ashcroft had been using his sandwich for punctuation. He

put what was left in his mouth and blew his nose on a paper serviette.

The kid's writing was very neat. He was the sort of kid who got As for deportment, grooming, and attitude all through grammar school and so grew to have an exaggerated sense of the role these things played in later life.

The first page was headed Barryknoll Developments, Ltd., care of Liggett, Triggers, and Follansbee, at an Adelaide Street Station postal box. There were three company directors: Daisy Mathews, 48 Ardmore Terrace, Toronto; Katherine Terry, 289 De Grassi Street, Toronto; and Diana Barryhill, 116A Jarvis Street, Toronto. The next two pages dealt with Bar-Hi Construction, Ltd., and Barrybrae Holdings, Ltd., both care of Liggett's mailbox number. The directors' names varied, except for Diana Barryhill, who showed up on every list.

Turning to the fourth page, I got a rude shock. Ashcroft had titled this section Bar-Tor Holdings, Ltd. The last time I had heard that name was talking to Dickie Bellfield in Mennenga's bar the month before; Bar-Tor was Spandrell's company, the company that owned the *Star-Leader*. According to Ashcroft, Bar-Tor's address was identical with the rest. There was no mention of the newspaper. Spandrell did not appear in the list of directors, but the Barryhill broad did.

I had so many ideas at once I couldn't lay hands on them as they stampeded by. I knocked back the brandy to steady my nerves. Susan and Amy emanated from the dance floor to the bar, laughing like angels. An urgent "umph, umph" across the table told me Ashcroft was ready to talk. I glanced up just in time to see the Everest in his cheek disappear down his gullet. He poured the rest of his beer after it and wiped his mouth with the back of his hand.

"That's not all," he said. "I haven't had a wink of sleep thinking about this story. I keep asking myself, 'What would Precious do next? What would he want to know?'"

"Thanks," I said, "but why me?"

"You're the only real newsman I know."

"Not me, Ashcroft. I'm not a newsman. I never was a newsman. I've been faking it all my life."

"Sure, sure," said Ashcroft. "Listen, I copied the letters patent for each of the companies." He retrieved his notebook and flipped to the back pages. "Barrybrae does property management. Bar-Hi was incorporated 'to carry on the business of builders and contractors for the purpose of building, erecting, altering, repairing, or doing any other work in connection with any and all classes of building.' Barryknoll and Bar-Tor are holding companies. They invest money in other businesses, stocks, bonds, and debentures."

"Never mind the Harvard Business School stuff," I said. "What about this Barryhill woman? You got addresses here. Did you check any of them out?"

"I knew you were going to say that! I made a bet with Susan," said Ashcroft triumphantly. "Take Barryknoll: Daisy Mathews and Katherine Terry are secretaries in Liggett's office. Daisy Mathews is a married woman; she comes up a second time as D. R. Rosicki on the Bar-Hi list. That's her maiden name. The other directors are a former mail boy, a commissionaire, and another Liggett typist."

"That still leaves Barryhill," I said.

I was barely listening. Ashcroft didn't know about the Bar-Tor connection with Spandrell and the *Star-Leader*. I could understand that; the kid was green and Bar-Tor wasn't listed on the masthead. As Bernie Tassio had said, the *Star-Leader* had supported Jake Warren for mayor in the last election. Warren was a wealthy evangelical minister with his own TV show in Toronto. He owned a flashy ranch-style home in the subdivisions with a religious grotto made of cinder blocks and seashells in his front yard. Liggett had Warren in his pocket. Warren had the chief of police, the city solicitor, various aldermen, and sundry solid citizens in *his* pocket. It was a cosy arrangement and it smelled bad enough to kill flies.

"Who the hell is Diana Barryhill?" I asked.

"Exactly," said Ashcroft, pounding the table with his fist. "I don't know."

"Well, how did you find out about Mathews and the others?"

"That was easy," he said, acting nonchalant. "I photocopied the annual reports and barged into her apartment asking questions. I talked to Daisy Mathews just after she got home from work. She's separated from her husband and lives alone. I told her I was an agent with the Department of Industrial and Corporate Affairs, investigations branch, checking the authenticity of signatures and addresses. Right away she was frightened. I waved the papers in front of her face, and she bought it. Liggett has her sign Bar-Tor, Barrybrae, Bar-Hi, and Barryknoll documents as a matter of course She doesn't even get paid extra for being a company director. Susan says it's standard practice for lawyers to keep shelf companies ready for their clients to use in emergencies. They can nominate anyone as a director."

"This is all very gratifying, Ashcroft," I said. "You've got what we Anglicans call chutzpah. But what about Barryhill?"

"That's what queers the pattern," he said, a little mystified. "Mathews doesn't know anything about Diana Barryhill. She's never seen her, never talked on the phone with her. The signature is either already there when Mathews signs, or a blank space is left to be filled in later. I drove to the Jarvis Street address to talk to this woman myself, but I ran out of luck. It was a dummy address."

"What do you mean?"

"It's an old convent converted into a boarding house, real skid row joint and all. The caretaker is a Portuguese gentleman in his mid-thirties who can hardly speak English. Barryhill's name isn't on the mailbox, and when I asked about her the guy yelled incomprehensible things until I left. You know, I got the feeling he knew who she was."

"Maybe it's a mail drop, or maybe Barryhill's a false name," I said.

"She's also an exotic dancer," said Ashcroft, breaking the conversation like a tackle and reversing field with the ball. He was watching Susan proceed toward us, her legs moving like a pair of greyhounds on a leash. Amy was perched on a bar stool, talking to a young man with curly black hair and an earring. "She wrestles here sometimes," he added, "but the management won't let her fight every week because she put a couple of girls in the hospital."

"Did you show him the map?" she asked, her hand pressing the back of Ashcroft's neck. She looked like something you'd see in *Vogue* with a snake draped over her shoulders and blood dripping from her fingernails. "I like your old lady, Precious. She's a hoot! She says you're not too smart, but you fuck like a stallion."

"She said that?" I asked. I wondered if Ashcroft understood what he was getting into. I had a feeling I knew why she kept goats instead of, say, hamsters.

"Not really. It was just a joke. She only said you weren't too bright."

Amy was laughing with the man at the bar and looking at us. I was worrying about her and thinking about Liggett and Barryknoll and the strange greed that had Ockenden wound up like a ball of yarn. Even if I disliked Spandrell, I hated to discover a fellow newspaperman on the take. But he was beginning to look a lot like a child with his hand in the cookie jar. Someone had fronted him money for the *Star-Leader*. Bellfield had said the cash came from his dead wife's estate. But chances were Spandrell's dead wife was a Sicilian businessman with a string of pizza parlours and laundromats as a cover for something more lucrative and less legal.

I didn't love Amy. I wasn't jealous. But I was getting hot. The noise seemed to rise a few hundred decibels. All the faces in the bar looked like sallow moons. I started to take off my coat.

"Not in here, Flasher!" yelled Boot Hill over the microphone. He'd been waiting. "Save it for the schoolyard! We all seen it before!"

"Did you show him the map?" asked Susan, laughing, rubbing Ashcroft's scalp affectionately.

"Holy cow!" he said. "I almost forgot."

He rummaged momentarily in his parka and came up with a stack of soiled photocopies that looked as though they had been used to pack a lunch.

"Who's that guy Amy's talking to?" I asked, feeling a little uncomfortable. He was whispering in her ear now, making her double over with laughter.

"Jealous?" asked Susan.

"I thought he might be a witness," I said.

"A witness to what?"

"The murder I'm about to commit."

Ashcroft shoved the Xerox of a hand-drawn map under my nose. He was a good kid, would have been better if he'd had someone walking around with him, holding a gun to his head. The map showed Ockenden and the lakefront and a large rectangular patch of cross-hatching, almost as large again as the city, to the east. Ashcroft stabbed the map with his finger, leaving a new grease mark.

"That's Tassio's riding stable!" he said. "That's Susan's farm! And see that road? That's the Blue Line — the scissors murder. You don't think she was holding out on them, and they killed her for the land?"

Susan was tickling his chin. She was delighted with everything he said, no matter how inane. Of course, the thought had crossed my mind, too. But as soon as Ashcroft said the words, I discounted them. His eyes were bulging with all the excitement and attention.

"Nuts, Ashers," I said. "Why don't you ask Liggett? The only time people get killed over real estate is during wars and gold rushes. I think it's safe to say we have no gold in Ockenden, and the last time I looked the city was not at war."

"But —"

"Forget it, kid," I said. Susan sulked, patting the kid's

shoulder to make him feel better. "The cops would laugh you onto the street and Liggett would drive over you with a lawsuit. You'd better stick to finding Barryhill."

There were better angles, but not for Ashcroft. The story was getting too murky for an inexperienced kid like that. As I had said, nobody would thank him for plowing up all this corruption. And there wasn't any point in getting his nose punched in for putting it where it didn't belong.

On the other hand Amy was planning to chaperone her theatre class to a matinee at the O'Keefe Centre the next afternoon. I had an idea that if she hustled in the morning, she could meet Bellfield for lunch, telling him she had spotted his ad in the Yellow Pages and wanted her students to see what it took to be a professional writer. Flattery was the only way to make Dickie Bellfield do tricks, and it worked every time. Over lunch, she could casually pick his brains about Spandrell, without letting on that she knew me. If Bellfield dreamed we were out to nail his client, it would take sodium pentothal or torture to make him talk. But he would turn into Aunt Blabby, gossiping with a pretty woman he didn't know.

"But how?" asked the kid, a frail anchor in a sea of confusion. Amy was pushing her way toward the table, the guy with the earring clasping her elbow. Susan's eyes sparkled with anticipation. I wasn't jealous. I pointed to the nearest phone.

"Kid, I'd like to introduce you to a handy little device that lets you into the homes and hearts of the nation at a very small cost and minimal outlay of energy. It is called the —"

"I get it," said Ashcroft heavily. He was hurt again. He thought he had cracked the case when he had only made it more complicated.

I could hear Amy's laughter.

The guy with the earring looked at me and said to her, "Baby, you can do better than that!" Amy gave him a playful shove.

I wasn't jealous, but I was giddy. I took a swing at his face, nicked his chin, and fell on the floor. Amy screamed. I stood up and tried to tear the man's lungs out for whispering secrets in her ear. He caught me over the eye with a haymaker, and I was down again, bleeding. He was getting ready to put the boots to me when Susan sat on him. She could have gone to the Olympics with that hold. He was turning blue when the bouncers finally pulled him free. She wasn't even breathing hard.

Amy was embarrassed, but she was excited, too. Her eyes shone as she drove out of the parking lot. I wanted to lick my wounds at the American; I was tired of the world and yearned for solitude. She took me to her house and put ice on my forehead. She was crazy; I wanted to walk away from her. She sulked in the bedroom, came out wearing her hair; and we made love on the floor.

My ribs felt like hot blades. She said she would do anything, anything. I asked her to meet Bellfield for me; she read me the poem. Later, just before the alarm went off summoning me to work, I slept a little. When I woke up, she was watching me. I told her I just hated to depend on another human being that much.

13

Outside, it was still black as a pit pony. The streets were littered with snowflakes, big as goose feathers. More were zooming down every second, crash-landing with an eerie lapping sound like waves on a lake.

Barrett was nodding at his desk, looking like an alcohol abuse ad, when I climbed the newsroom steps. He was shaky and at pains to excuse himself for coming to work three hours early. His alarm clock had had a fatal seizure, he explained, leaving him wide awake like a whale beached on a reef in an ocean of night.

My company acted on him like a tonic. He was after me like a terrier. Could I do him a big favour? No, I said. Spandrell wanted a column on ice fishing for the weekend edition. Barrett had all the facts; he just couldn't seem to assemble them into sentences anymore. I said I couldn't help unless he thought the publisher would be interested in a long think piece on Tantric ice hockey. Barrett shook his head doubtfully. Then I told him he could nap on the spare desk in the sports department, and I would wake him when it was time to start flagellating his type-writer keys in earnest.

An hour later Barrett was snoring tragically, and Wishty drifted in with a story written in what he considered to be the best contemporary sports-reporting mode. I couldn't even figure out what game the teams were playing. "Even Dostoevsky had to give the score," I said. Then I put in a vivid half hour jigging the copy into shape for deadline.

At nine a.m. I put the last of my pages to bed, pointed Barrett toward the newsroom, and dealt Wishty and Kunow their night assignments. Gratz still had two hours before the compositors locked up front and local. So the clatter of typewriters and the thump and whoosh of pneumatic tubes continued beyond the office dividers long after I had propped my feet on the desk and lit a meditative cigarette.

My mother had died at fifty-nine. The first time. She was technically dead after inhaling the pop-top from a beer can when an alert nurse noticed her heart was still beating. It took her eight more years to do the thing properly, in bed with the lights out, as in making love, and so quietly no one knew until morning. Uncle Dorsey had collapsed in the press room when he was seventy-two, a testament to the medicinal properties of rye whisky and Cuban cigars.

Seeing Damon Barrett reminded me of the ends of things: ends of worlds, ends of lives, ends of relationships. I harboured no exalted ambitions. I wanted them to be able to write my life story on an aerogram form. But I was suffering from an inability to keep things the way they were, which I found discouraging. Dorsey would have understood what ailed me. Before dying, he had visited one of the new computerized newsrooms in Toronto and returned home puzzled at the alteration in what, for him, had been a way of life. "It was too damn quiet," he had told me, shaking his head. "There was no shouting, no laughter."

Thinking about the past, I was plotting the future. I had left Amy in her bathrobe, looking like a Christmas tree angel under the porch light. She smiled bravely, her hands at her throat, showing me the stubs of her missing fingers. She was all love. It made me sweat to see her like that. I wanted to fly in the face of instinct, break the pattern of evasion and loss, confess my immoderate lusts. But I hesitated; it wouldn't be easy to change; it would be a bitch.

Just then Ashcroft appeared from the newsroom, parka'd up to his chapped nostrils, already unlimbering his pipe like field artillery.

"I found her," he said, sniffing wetly, blowing his nose on a swampy monogrammed handkerchief. "I've got a cold."

"I don't want to hear about it," I said. It was distressing. Ashcroft was on a streak. He couldn't go to the bathroom without stumbling over a clue. He had the newsman's disease all right, acute inability to mind his own business.

"She was right here in Ockenden all the time," he said, incapable of taking a hint, puffing into his pipe and sprinkling ashes over my shoes. "In the cemetery, dead, for twenty-five years."

"I knew it," I said. "Nothing simple, right? I'd rather drink rat poison than hear a word from you about another dead broad. You know, kid, there are lots of people who grow up without ever thinking of becoming novelists or newsmen. Many are able to lead normal productive lives. You could be a schoolteacher and take holidays three months every year. I had a friend, a mechanic in the air force, who started building toilet floats in his garage. Before you could say Jack Robinson, he had a factory popping out toilet floats by the millions. He had a charming wife, built like a church, half a dozen infant geniuses in braces, a dog with bad breath, and a mistress in the city. I ask you —"

"It might not be the same woman," he said, paying no attention to me whatsoever. "But she was the only Diana Barryhill I could find."

"With that and a quarter," I said, "you could buy yourself a cup of coffee."

"Do you want me to tell you what happened or not?" he asked, gouging irritably at the bowl of his pipe with a pocket-knife.

"No," I said.

The phone rang. It was a hockey mother, Cleta Keneally by name, whose son I had viciously maligned the day before by failing to mention his exploits in a banner headline. Mrs. K. herself was a writer with stories in *Animal Lovers' Magazine, Marriage and Family Living*, and the *Pentecostal Evangel*, so she spoke with authority when she accused me of arrogant and slapdash journalism. Lately, she had detected a conspiracy to hold Ockenden and its inhabitants up to ridicule in the sports section of the *Star-Leader*. Her lawyer thought she ought to sue. With a name like Precious, was I gay or something? I hung up. Ashcroft had snapped his pipestem in two. He surveyed the remains mournfully.

"All right," I said. "What happened?"

"Susan helped," he said, brightening up. "She remembered seeing the name Barryhill in the Ockenden phone book. I made up a cover story. I said I worked at the library and had found a book belonging to Diana Barryhill in the stacks. I said it looked as though it might be valuable as a keepsake, and I wanted to return it."

"That should get you two-to-five," I said. "Impersonating a public official is a criminal offence."

"She'll never remember," said Ashcroft. "She's a little bats."

"Who?"

"The old auntie. Juanita Barryhill. They're moving her into the county home for the aged before the end of the month. She's had three house fires in the last six weeks, and the police think she started them all."

"Who told you that?"

"She did. She thinks it's a big joke. She said there's nothing like discovering a hidden character defect to make life worth living again. When I left, she wanted to know if I'd spotted any suspicious behaviour patterns. I had a Latin teacher like that in school, a spinster with white hair in a net."

"Is white hair a clue, or am I just dumb?" I asked. He was waxing enthusiastic again, racing up blind alleys like a puppy on a spree.

"I'm establishing character," he said primly. "It turned out she really used to teach Latin. What do you think of that?"

"Amazing," I said. I cocked an eyebrow and waited.

Ashcroft had driven to Juanita Barryhill's house first thing in the morning with his librarian cover story. The old lady had found him amusing. But Diana Barryhill was ancient history. Ashcroft had been shocked. Juanita found this even more amusing. Over tea and scones, they had exchanged notions on the topic of mortality. At the time, Diana's death had been a great tragedy. Her immediate family had moved to Toronto following the funeral to escape the weight of memory. Now it was all but forgotten. Juanita had asked for Diana's book. Ashcroft had promised to mail it.

"Ashcroft," I said, "you have no conscience."

Outside it was so dark that the city had left the streetlights on. Inside, baseboard heaters cracked like hammers. Ashcroft was triumphant. He interpreted my remark as praise. He was so smug about finding Diana Barryhill, he had failed to realize that a dead woman is a dead end.

"It's a dead end," I said lighting a cigarette. "Too bad, kid. You lose. Go home and get some sleep."

An idea was growing like ragweed in the compost of my ignorance. I tried to root it out; it had sunk its tendrils into my brain. This was an idea that wanted to live.

"But what about the story?" Ashcroft asked.

I knew how he felt. His Barryknoll scoop was going the way of the scissors murder, into oblivion. His best efforts had left him sitting on his hands awaiting a revelation.

"I'm stumped," I said. "We need a fresh angle. If Liggett's going long on land, it's a cinch it's not on spec. But we don't know the principals and we don't know what they're holding for leverage."

"Maybe I could call him," said the kid, tapping the telephone with a piece of pipestem, his eyes greedy.

"Nix that," I said. "You want to tip your hand? You want Liggett to talk, you have to deal with him. Right now all you can say is 'pretty please.' It's time to punch the clock and wait for him to make the next move."

Ashcroft didn't like it. Precious was showing the white feather. He had feet of clay up to his armpits. I nodded at Damon Barrett, concentrating like a bloodhound over his typewriter, pecking at the keys with his index fingers just like a real newsman.

"Barrett's been on a toot," I said. "He needs a ghostwriter. Why don't you give me a break and hyperactivate next to him for a change. While you're at it, put on your thinking cap. Maybe you'll crack the coconut."

Ashcroft sulked. He hadn't believed a word I'd said. He was learning to hate condescension. He slunk off looking like a martyr waiting for the stones to strike. I calculated it would take him about fifteen minutes to decide to call Liggett anyway.

At first, Miss Lana would barely admit that she knew me. I wanted the key to the microfilm machine in the morgue. She handed me a postcard instead. It bore the familiar duck and pistol logo. It read: "I found you. I can lose you. And I mean *lose*."

"It's a gag," I said. "I know a store in Toronto where they sell them by the gross."

Spandrell, she said, had barred the morgue to outsiders. They upset the intricate filing system. I stopped Gratz on his way back from the bathroom. Had I been fired? Was I not a fully paid up member of the Printers' Bowling and Athletic Association? Gratz looked hunted but admitted as much. Miss Lana sniffed as if to say this would be an anomaly of mercifully brief duration. She turned over the key.

In the morgue I sorted through a dozen drawers containing tapes of old *Star-Leader*s and Ockenden *Adviser*s, a predecessor. Miss Lana's intricate filing system had been invented by a chimpanzee with an unusually low IQ. It took me half an hour to assemble the three half-inch tapes for 1958. Ashcroft had said twenty-five years; that made 1958 the year of Diana Barryhill's death.

After an hour of threading and rethreading microfilms through the reader, I had a headache and nothing to show for it. No obit. No death notice. No memorial ad. I had seen the movie twice; it was a snorer. In 1958 nothing important had happened. No Beatles. No trips to the moon. No oil crisis. Men wore crewcuts; women wore bras. Rebecca Pinckney had offered to pose nude for the boys in my class if we all chipped in a dollar. My mother, an early advocate of sex education, had offered to do it free, scaring me away from little girls at least until 1959.

I scrolled through the year once more, reading a story here, a cutline there, trying to get a sense of the flow of events in a small Ontario city. In January the biggest news appeared on the sports pages. The league-leading Oaks were being touted as champions. The town heroes, a brace of defencemen called Brian Oxley and Aaron Raftis, were eating up the opposition. Recognizing Oxley's name, I looked around for a photo, but the local shutterbugs let me down. I found nothing but wire shots of National Hockey League goalies and art pictures of ten-year-old figure skaters.

In February the Oaks hit a slump. For some reason, which I failed to catch, they started to bump down the standings like a ball on a staircase. Lulled by the ruck of meaningless stories, my curiosity took several minutes to rouse itself. Something was missing. Something nibbled like minnows at the bare toes of my unconscious. I rolled the tape back slowly, then forward again. Unreeling a few turns from the spool, I held the tape up to the light and ran my fingertips over its surface. The microfilm had been cut and spliced, carefully, expertly.

I tapped my foot on the tiles and kept my head. Yes, yes, I thought, getting a little excited as I always did when I felt a story beginning to break. I had something there. I replaced the tape on its spool and ran it through the reader again, keeping track of the pagination as I went. Gaps showed up in the sports section first. There was no pattern; one or two pages a week had been snipped out. In early February pages began to disappear helter-skelter throughout the newspaper. A half-dozen front pages in a row vanished without a trace. By the end of March the cutting had stopped. Whatever needed covering up had fallen from public scrutiny.

I had theories, all right, but none of them took me anywhere.

I needed a map. I was flying blind. I checked the bound copies; the same mad revisionist historian had razored them. I had a year, and a name, and a bunch of blank cheques I couldn't cash without some answers from the past. Then I remembered Rose Oxley's study, its horde of scorched and soggy newspapers.

I patted my jacket pockets until I found the zinc cut I had saved from the study floor the day after her murder. For a good luck piece, it wasn't doing me any good at all. I stared at the scorched image for a while. It stared back at me. There should have been a date stamp but the fire had licked it clean. Maybe I had a clue, I thought; maybe I had a lump of zinc alloy worth less than a nickel. Whatever I had, I was starting to sound like Ashcroft again.

I heard the latch give on the morgue door. Spandrell was standing there, looking extraterrestrial in a snowmobile suit, backlit and silhouetted by the newsroom lights.

"What the hell are you doing in here?" he snarled. His cheeks were rare as beef from the wind.

My heart did laps up and down my ribs. The zinc cut fell to the floor with a clang like a dinner bell. I stooped to retrieve it.

"The Oaks," I said. "I'm checking their roots. Get it? Oaks . . . roots? It's my beat," I added.

"I hate wisecracks," he said. "Maybe you'd like to deliver papers instead of edit them."

Spandrell's tone was raw and peremptory. His wig was askew. Behind his glasses his eyes said things too crude for syntax. The newsroom behind him was so quiet you could have heard flies landing on the desktops.

14

The American was like a swamp, its floors awash with melting snow tracked in by the customers. Its ancient heating system kicked in every time the door opened, giving the place an atmosphere more congenial to plants than humans. And the combination of steam rising from the stainless steel bins of roast beef, mashed potatoes, and peas and cigarette smoke whirling beneath the flyspecked ceiling meant you could either die or get a nourishing meal just breathing the air.

It was early evening. The boys from the plants had come off shift. Sly, the tavern recreational vehicle, was making her way from table to table, looking for an invitation or a friendly pat on the rump. Mrs. Miniver, the cook, was shuffling stale decks of white bread for her hot sandwiches. At one end of the room a four-piece band was arranging sound equipment on a temporary stage made of rough planks. I recognized Alice Varney, Gil Ranger's paramour from classified, talking nervously to one of the musicians. Nellie Shingles sat alone at a nearby table, looking dejected. Both of the women sported cowboy boots and hats and rayon-rhinestone western shirts.

I threaded my way to a free table in a corner by the door to the washrooms. Outside, it was bleak and stormy. The snow that had begun to sift down that morning had continued all day. In the streets, snowplows made weird ceremonies, flashing their blue and amber lamps. Wind-whipped dry flakes danced like dervishes under the streetlights. There was tension in the bar, as though we were all straining against the cold and the long dreary nights ahead.

"Hey, Precious, have a drink!" Nellie shouted, tugging Alice by the elbow, docking next to me. "Isn't it awful? You could cut the air in here with a stomach pump. You come for the show? Alice is making her debut. I told her I'd get the paper to send someone."

Nellie was huge and awkward in all that fringe. Alice seemed thinner and paler than in the office. She could have taken a bath in her Texas hat. While Nellie bantered, Alice's washed-out eyes traced the false grain of the formica tabletop.

"Isn't he adorable, sweetheart?" said Nellie. "My God. Precious is the only man at the *Star-Leader* who doesn't try to make me every time he catches me behind a desk. What are you drinking, Precious? Give me a chaste kiss!"

Laughing gaily, she presented her plump wattles. She was playing up to me for Alice's benefit, but everything she said rang flat because of some trouble between the two of them. When the waiter arrived, prancing like a faun, I ordered a double Hennessy and a beer. My chest ached from the weather. My knee gimped where Marty had chopped the tendons. What I needed, I decided, was a little do-it-yourself chemotherapy.

"Shit!" Alice exploded. "Cut the crap. What are you going to do now? Get your cheek bronzed? He didn't come to hear me sing."

When she got a little colour in her face, Alice was no bow-wow. She pounded the table with her fist and flounced off toward the jukebox. Nellie apologized. Her friend was nervous about the singing. She wanted to go on the road with the band, and Nellie wouldn't let her because she was afraid of the competition. They had compromised on a local gig. If Alice proved herself in front of the hometown crowd, Nellie was going to be her manager. Alice was playing Johnny Cash on the juke-box, swaying in time to the music, her pale eyes far away. Excusing herself, the red-haired lady hurried over to protect her budding star from stage door Don Juans.

"Thought I'd find you here," said a husky voice at my shoulder, familiar yet unfriendly.

It was Damon Barrett, wearing a down coat and an olive drab balaclava out of which poked his horn-rimmed glasses. He had slipped in through the back door in the corridor leading to the toilets.

"Where's your dog team, Barrett?" I asked. I was feeling jumpy, tired of people sneaking up on me.

It was the wrong thing to say. Barrett had left his sense of humour in a snowbank. He stood still, glaring at me for a moment or two. And when he spoke, his voice sounded like furniture being dragged across a concrete floor.

"That's a good one, Precious," he said. "Remind me to cut your grass some time."

The old man had me worried. Somewhere he had taken a U-turn and was driving against traffic. It had started the day Rose Oxley was murdered, when he slugged me and I stuffed him in a cab to keep him out of trouble. Now he reminded me of Uncle Dorsey near the end, errant, fragile. I could have pushed him over with a finger.

He skinned the face mask over his head, securing his glasses with his free hand, lurching off balance. I reached out to steady his arm; he jerked angrily away.

"Where is she?" he snarled. The thick air wafted toward me the stale, fruity smell of the homemade wine he kept in his cellar to poison guests.

"Don't play me for an idiot," he said. "That fucking kid tipped me off."

"Ashcroft? You've got me punching in a dark room, Damon," I said. "Why don't you sit down?"

"This is punching in a dark room," cried Barrett, as he took a wild swing at my chin. I ducked and grabbed his wrists, forcing him into the chair opposite. Being attacked by Barrett was a little like being savaged by a dead sheep.

His hands twitched like crabs on a beach. His face was cracked and scarred, skin hanging like a tent over the bones. I offered him the last of the brandy, and he launched it shakily toward his lips. The liquor acted as a tranquilizer. But when he turned to me, his irises shimmered like glass.

"He needed me to make a call. He wanted to talk to some lawyer in Toronto, but the receptionist was wise to him and kept him on hold. I had to make out I was a farmer from the east side to get this guy Liggett on the line."

"Ashcroft watches too much TV," I said.

"But I heard him say her name," interrupted Barrett, the ugliness of his relief-map face animated by pain or greed or desire, some pent-up obsession that made his jaundiced eyes glitter.

"Whose name?"

"Diana Barryhill."

He leaned forward on his knuckles, repeating the name, as if the sound of the name alone had a soothing quality.

For a moment or two I watched the traffic pass to and from the can, motley and grotesque. Chaucer could have written a book about it. Next to the jukebox, Nellie and Alice were having an altercation. Nellie spat words into her friend's face. Alice continued to sway to the music, her eyelids closed. Nellie tried to put her arms around her. Alice went limp, so that the fat lady had to hold her knees up off the floor. Nellie was nonplussed. Alice seemed to know how to get around her, at least in public.

"She's dead," I said finally.

"The hell she is!" Barrett had waited hungrily for me to speak. Now his anger flared up again. "Who told you that?"

"Her aunt," I said, a little unnerved by the old man's fierceness. "An old woman in town. Ashcroft talked to her. I am strictly advisory, like the Green Berets."

"She's lying."

I wasn't used to that kind of directness from Barrett. He was a drunk, a hack, and a liar. Yet I have always admired people with the courage of their illusions. Barrett thought he was putting on a good front. But his act was as transparent as plastic pants. The news copy he wrote read as if he had tossed a couple of hundred words into a hat and picked them out at random. Most of the time, he gleaned considerable inspiration from the local Andrew Carnegie franchise.

"I always knew she wasn't dead," he said, calming down, his

moods changing like the weather. "She just went away. After a while they all said she was dead. But no one knew that for certain. They just wanted to keep it quiet."

"Who wanted to keep it quiet?" I asked. Barrett was crazy. It didn't surprise me much that we were having this conversation. Damon was Ockenden born and bred. He probably knew what the missing news pages contained.

"Them! The family," he shot back irritably. "She wasn't a bad girl, you know. They made her out that way in the paper. I reckon Rose Oxley blackened her name forever. But she wasn't a tramp. It was mostly lies. You got an address?" he asked, veering out of the fog.

"Barrett," I said, "they've done studies. Trying to understand people like you has been found to cause tumours in rats. Take it from the top. Once upon a time . . ."

In fact, I realized I was getting excited again. First the spliced microfilm, now Barrett. I didn't know what I had. It was like catching ghosts. Something made me want to abandon the old man, walk away and leave him alone with his private miseries. But the story lust was on me, and I was afraid. I was a newsman; I had no kinship, obligation, or loyalty, except to the story. It was something Dorsey had known; after a while you had to disregard people.

Barrett looked at me sharply.

"Why do you want to know?"

"Jesus, it's a story!"

"Not that. That happened too long ago."

"I mean Liggett," I said, "the land promotion, the politics. The Barryhill woman's an angle. Tell me about her and I can crack Ashcroft's story."

"Oh," he grunted.

Barrett fished a pack of cigarettes out of his coat pocket. He tried to light two in succession, dropping them both on the floor before the flame caught. Leaning over to retrieve them, he nearly fell on his face. I snatched the pack away from him, treated myself, and set fire to another for Barrett. But he dropped it as well.

"It's all in the papers," he said absentmindedly, waving a hand in the direction of the *Star-Leader*.

Alice was singing to herself, rehearsing, as the band tuned its instruments. Mobs of people were weaving and moiling, and Alice danced alone on the stage. A fit of unrest was on Nellie. Her hair, which looked as though it had been soaked in red ink, framed her fat white face under the Stetson. She was rooted like a stump, pinned to the floor near the jukebox, her flesh quaking, her eyes roving anxiously from her friend to the bar crowd.

"It *was* there!" I said. "Somebody doctored the files, as in amputate. It's as if whatever happened was erased from history. Diana Barryhill didn't disappear — she never existed. How does that grab you?"

Barrett's eyes narrowed shrewdly.

"It wasn't me, if that's what you're thinking," he said.

"The thought had crossed my mind," I said.

"I tried to forget," he went on. "I wouldn't have come back if I hadn't forgotten a whole hell of a lot already. I had it capped, too, until somebody murdered Rose Oxley. Since then, I've been all twisted, remembering . . ."

"I don't get it," I said. "What's got you so fired up?"

In the time it took me to say the words, Barrett's voice rose from a whisper to a rant. His face was red and pockmarked, lined with broken blood vessels and thin blue veins. He stared myopically over his bulbous nose, his eyes like two grey stones.

"Lies!" he cried. "Talk! This town drove her out! Rose Oxley got what she deserved! I was glad. I only wished I had done it myself. I wish it had been me who killed her!"

"Give me a break," I said. Barrett blinked. "Ashcroft's not as dumb as he looks. He found Barryhill's name on some incorporation papers. He's even got an address. You come clean with me, and I'll fill you in. If you keep acting like some overpaid ham, I'm going to take a hike."

Barrett gulped beer from the bottle. He had the shakes so bad he couldn't handle a glass. He worked his throat muscles, choking something back. His face wore the expression of a man trying to absorb some momentous and unforeseen piece of news.

The noise the band was making behind Alice suddenly came together and swelled into the opening bars of "Faithless Love." Alice, her eyes shut tight, crooned the words into a hand mike, her thin voice quavering with intensity and emotion. *Faithless love like a river flowing / Raindrops falling on a broken* . . . Her song was lost in the crowd din. Her hair hung in strings beneath the cowboy hat. "Alice is really beautiful," Nellie said, as she brushed by, waddling toward the stage.

"They said she ran off with a man," said Barrett. "A boy-friend. It was a lie!" His voice trailed off as he re-examined the consequences of her exit. "She was a good girl, Precious."

I wanted to drag Barrett outside into the snow, wake him to life, and make him give me answers. He knew something all right, but it was so real to him he didn't think it needed explaining. Instead, he talked around and around.

"Jesus, Damon, somebody elect you guardian angel, lord protector of the young and the innocent?" I asked, but the irony was lost on him.

"It was a small town," he said.

"That's when you used to work on the *Star-Leader*."

"That's right," said Barrett, brightening a little. "It was about the time I left Ockenden. They were holding a job for me in Toronto. In those days, I could just about write my own ticket."

"What was the boyfriend's name?"

"I don't remember." He wouldn't look me in the face.

Down in some valley where nobody goes/ The night rolls in like a cold dark wind/ Faithless love like a river flows . . . Alice was still singing but losing heart fast. Some lint-brained youth in a hard hat stood on a chair and hung a moon toward the stage. Somebody else started flipping cardboard coasters at her hat like Frisbees.

"Damn!" I said. "I just forgot that address Ashcroft gave me. I've got a terrific memory, too. It's a shame it's so short."

"It was Raftis," said Barrett. "A kid named Raftis."

"And now she's returned like General MacArthur," I said, "ready to drop the bomb on Ockenden."

"What are you talking about?" asked Barrett.

"Those papers Ashcroft turned up — if they're real, this Diana has got her mitts on most of the east side of town. It's nothing simple. I'm not sure how she fits in. She may even own the damn newspaper. Does this mean anything to you?"

I palmed the zinc cut and showed it to him like a detective flashing his badge. The old man was staring at me, his mouth ajar.

Just then, a commotion broke out in front of the stage. The general uproar had been rising steadily. The band squeaked and twanged to a halt. Alice, wide-eyed, her lips twisted like elastic bands, was screaming at Nellie. A boy with his shirt-tail out ran up and attempted to waltz her off the planks. Alice clouted him with the mike. Feedback burned the air. Alice was blaming Nellie for the crowd. Nellie was silent, mortified.

Barrett was looking at the cut, his eyes boring at the soft metal like gimlets. I knew the image itself was too damaged to offer any hope of casual identification, but I had a hunch there was someone in Ockenden who had seen the original photo and who wouldn't need more than a hint or nudge to put a name to the silhouette.

Barrett was not my man, or so he said.

"It's nobody," he mumbled. "It's just a face. I don't recognize it." His voice was garbled as though a dentist had just shot his jaw full of Novocaine.

Alice and Nellie were having a shoving match. Alice had the red-haired woman by her lapels and was trying to give her a shake. Nellie stood like a rock, her face a storm of freckles. Amid shouts of "El-Fatso" and "Rip her clothes off!" two waiters tossed their towels and check pads behind the bar and converged on the struggling women. Barrett stroked his temples, lost in a deep angry silence.

I watched the waiters herd Alice and Nellie through the street door. I looked around, and Barrett was gone. Suddenly galvanized, the old man had dashed out, squeezing by the women, his parka billowing like a sheet in a gale.

Plunging through the melee in front of the stage, I tried to catch up. But the mob was restive. Seeing the women maul each other had made the boys tense and sensitive to offence. They slowed me down as I made my way across the room. Bouncing like a featherweight, the little man who had attempted to dance with Alice took a punch at the back of my head.

By the time I reached the sidewalk, Barrett had vanished. A car hovered at a nearby stoplight; it might have been his. In an alley next to the American, I could hear a woman sobbing, another making comforting sounds in a child's voice. I walked the other way, not wishing to intrude. I was left hanging, a dumb guy in the snow, with his mouth open and a one-way ticket to Nowhere.

15

I walked across the park, past the bandstand and the chamber of commerce banner, to the *Star-Leader*, where I telephoned for a cab to drive me out to the Rifle Range. Amy's porch light beckoned. And when I finally arrived, the reception committee waxed enthusiastic.

She had returned from the Toronto field trip laden with gifts: bottles of liquor unavailable at the local government outlet, a mohair scarf long enough to strangle an elephant, cartons of Quebec cigarettes, pigskin gloves, a windup duck, a dozen organic candy canes, and a heart-shaped notepad for those sweaty locker-room interviews. There was enough plunder to open a corner variety store.

Amy was cheerfully anxious, gauging my reactions with a wary eye. When I was done opening parcels, she gave me a hug and a kiss that nearly led to something serious, then dashed into the kitchen to save dinner. We were eating Japanese, her house specialty. Sashimi, tempura, and teriyaki. For the pièce de résistance, she had bought a quart of saki. She wanted to know if I was hungry; I said I was hungry enough to eat my teeth.

As a prelude I undressed in the bathroom and sank into Amy's tub with a cigarette and a B&B. The water was hot enough to cook eggs. On the counter beside the sink, a transistor radio delivered the CBC news; they could have been transmitting from Timbuctoo for all it mattered to me. Outside, a north wind rattled the storm windows in staccato gusts. I could hear Amy humming over the stove and the clatter of pans. I tasted my drink and felt the heat race through my veins.

"Hurry up," she called, at length. "You'll turn all wrinkled and shrivelled."

I had been thinking of Diana Barryhill, the zinc cut, the spliced microfilm, and Damon looking second hand and depressed in the American House. The sound of Amy's voice broke the spell.

Suddenly, every theory, every clue I had began to look like pure fiction, made of something lighter than air.

"You want to come in here and straighten me out?" I asked. The bathroom door was ajar. We didn't have to shout.

"Not on your life," she said, laughing. "This dinner depends on pinpoint timing and I'm not letting you sidetrack it."

She sounded carefree and cheerful. I remembered her stepbrother's name scattered like a bad omen through old *Star-Leader*s. Amy had been ten when it all happened. Perhaps that was too young to have noticed anything useful. But, as the locals kept telling me, Ockenden was a small town; it had been a lot smaller twenty-five yeas ago.

"What did you find out from Dickie Bellfield?" I asked.

"Darling, is that man really a friend of yours?"

"Not exactly," I said. "Call him a former colleague. We have a working relationship founded on mutual disrespect. It usually stops working about thirty seconds after we shake hands. But we get along very well when we're apart."

"I thought he was going to grope me in the restaurant!"

"He has a difficult time relating to women."

"You should have warned me," she said. "Over the phone, he mistook me for someone else, a girl in a massage parlour who apparently found him irresistible. Then he refused to go out for lunch until I mentioned that all my students were female. I must say when he finally saw them I could barely hold him back."

"Loves young people," I said. "Prince of a man."

"He seems to be very successful at what he does," she said. "He told us all about it. We nearly missed the opening act at the O'Keefe."

"He's a great kidder," I said. "Dickie adds a zero to his net after every rye and ginger. On a good day."

"What makes you so humorous tonight?" she asked.

"Just giddy. Did he talk about Spandrell?"

"Well, I casually dropped the name the way you said I should. I just mentioned that we had this wonderful new publisher at the local paper. Mr. Bellfield sniggered. You know I never actually knew what a snigger was before. He seemed to think it was terribly funny, me gushing over Spandrell like that. He can be so condescending. I felt like clouting him. And he had his hand on Mitzi Radaemaker's knee!"

"Great affection for children and dogs," I said.

"Moss, you're incorrigible!"

She came pushing through the bathroom door to shoo me out of the tub and into some clothes. She was in a fine mood, clowning a little the way women do when they feel safe with a man. I rose from the water like a legendary kraken, shrivelled and wrinkled. She cocked an eyebrow and sat on the toilet seat to watch me dress.

"It must have been a disappointment when he didn't follow through," I said. "The tragedy of Dickie Bellfield's life is that he's absolutely harmless. He's the sort of person who would have a hard time committing a car accident."

"Well, he's a great gossip, once you get him primed," she said archly. "That seems to be a characteristic of you media types."

"Sticks and stones . . ."

Wind shrieked in the eaves. Laughing, Amy stripped my towel away. Steam swirled around us like snakes. We were lovers, yet we barely knew each other. Outside, the world froze and contracted under a shroud of snow. I reached for a shirt to keep me warm.

"There was quite a scandal," she said. I had to think before I remembered she was talking about Spandrell. "But even before that the Toronto press crowd had him pegged for a rotten apple. He'd worked on Fleet Street all right, but not for any respectable paper. Where a story was concerned, he had the ethics of a rat. He would buy information, practise trade-offs . . ."

"Blackmail, you mean."

"Well, not exactly. He was good at digging dirt. Bellfield said he had a modus operandi that worked like a chain letter. He'd get something on one man and suppress it in exchange for a bigger story on the next until he hit the jackpot. Then he would publish. The public thought he was some kind of crusader. His editors knew about the stuff he swept under the carpet, but, officially, they ignored it. The stories he gave them were sensational. I guess newspapers can be just as slimy as the rest of us!"

"True, too true," I said, reaching out to give her a comforting pat on the head.

"Oh, Moss, don't mock me!"

"What about the scandal?" I asked. "It must have been pretty raw. Or did Spandrell's habitual low and dirty ways just finally prove too embarrassing to live with?"

"Bellfield hedged," said Amy, "but it sounds as if he really did blackmail somebody in the end. Spandrell hushed up a lead turned in by one of his staff. The reporter got suspicious when his story didn't appear in the *Daily News* and kicked up a big stink about it. The *Daily News* kept it quiet. There was some sort of in-house investigation, after which Spandrell took a leave of absence and then quit. He was never fired. Everybody got out with their public images intact."

"Any idea what it was he covered up?" I asked.

"Darling, I'm good, but not that good," she said, her eyes full of mischief. "Your friend tends to become uncomfortable off the topic of himself. He did ask me if I'd run into an old buddy of his called Precious Elliot. I said, why no! And he told me all the sordid details: the unhappy childhood, the life of sin, the drinking, the tragic inability to stay faithful to your wives."

"Bellfield's an unreliable witness," I said. "Nothing he says would stand up in court. Did he tell you how women keep mistaking him for Paul Newman on the subway?"

"Noooo, he didn't tell me that," she said. "But he did say one nice thing, though he didn't mean it that way. According to Mr. Bellfield, you're the last of the old-time newsmen; a dinosaur, he said. You'd straighten out fast if you'd only stop chasing fire engines. That is rather nice, isn't it? You're almost a romantic hero."

"Close, but you get no cigar," I said. "My Uncle Dorsey Elliot was the last newsman, the end of the breed. They cracked the mould after Dorsey."

"If I can't have a cigar, can I have that?"

I was dried off and red as a lobster. Amy looked happy and beautiful, perched like a bird on the edge of the toilet seat. Desire for her suddenly gripped me by the throat. I was choked with wanting to touch her. We gasped in unison and kissed. Slapping me playfully across the buns, she ducked away to the kitchen, laughing.

"Now, now, too many hands spoil the cook!"

I started pulling on my trousers and socks.

"What does this man Spandrell look like?" she asked.

"The way he sounds," I said. "Big and mean. He wears a rug."

"A what?"

"A toupee. It's the ugliest one I ever saw. Have you ever heard of a broad named Diana Barryhill?" I asked.

There was no answer; in the kitchen, the clatter of dinner dishes ceased.

"Hello, out there!" I called. "Amy?"

Her silence was ominous; it ended with the crash of falling crockery like ice cracking on a pond.

"Are you all right?" I asked as soon as I reached the kitchen.

She was standing like a pillar in the centre of dinner, which radiated like blast debris from Ground Zero. To her left was the teriyaki; to her right, tempura. Her eyes were huge and resembled the sashimi rolls that had herded together like sheep grazing under the table. She was pale as dishwater. She gazed at the mess with an air of vague perplexity.

"All right?" she said, her voice an echo of mine.

I suddenly discovered that I was tired. Not sleepy, just tired of life. She was gone right out of herself. And until she said the words, I hadn't realized how helpless and anxious I felt.

I flicked my cigarette into the sink and circled an arm around her shoulders. I didn't love her. What had I done? I pushed her

down in a chair before she fell down. She got right up and put a
foot in the teriyaki. I poured saki into a shot glass; she took it like
medicine. "What do you want?" she asked. "What do you want?"

I said nothing. What was there to say? She looked at her feet.
With exaggerated self-possession she bent over and took off her
soiled shoes. Then she stepped carefully into the living room.
Seconds later she was back, framed in the doorway.

"What do you know about Diana Barryhill?" she asked angrily.

"Nothing. Her name came up. That's all."

"Is she in Ockenden?"

"Not that I know of."

Amy considered this for a moment. "I told you not to pry. I
told you when Rose died I was finished with my past." The hand
with the missing fingers toyed coyly with the shirt buttons at her
throat. "You startled me," she added, her eyes on the floor. "I'm
sorry about dinner. I had it on a tray."

She had aroused my curiosity with her histrionics. But that
hand was a No Trespassing sign. Until now, Amy's past had
been an easy topic to avoid. We talked about my stellar career, the
taste of booze, which of her breasts was bigger, deep things. She
had not wanted the police to catch her stepmother's killer
because that would have meant plowing up old ground. At first,
I had construed this as evidence of a rational and ultimately
healthy fatalism. Now I wasn't so sure.

"What was she to you?" I asked, almost choking on my own
misgivings.

"Nothing to me, Moss. She was my brother's friend. To be
specific, they fucked. Are you going to quote me? You should
have warned me your interest was strictly professional. I'd have
made it worth my while." Her voice had jumped an octave due
to incipient hysteria.

"What happened to her?"

"You bastard. You don't know when to quit, do you?" Her
tone suddenly dropped again. Anger had given her a shot of self-
control. "Diana was smart. After Brian died, she left town for

good. She went so far no one could bring her back. No one could touch her. That's what I should have done. Now if you'll excuse me, this tacky conversation is at an end."

Amy turned and disappeared. I followed, reaching the bathroom door just as the lock snapped shut. For a couple of minutes I stood there feeling about as foolish as I looked, listening to the shower running. Then I hurried back to the kitchen and poured myself a stiff drink. I was on my third when I heard the bathroom door reopen and the bedroom door slam shut. I began to clean up the dinner mess.

In the next room, I told myself, brushing dust off the sashimi and popping them into my mouth, in the next room was a woman who was a person. It was stupid, this idea that you knew someone better because you shared a bed. Although I knew what Amy whispered in moments of great ecstasy, that did not mean I knew her. Far from it. When I looked at her, it was like looking at pictures in a gallery — every time there was something new.

After I finished the dishes, I sat in the unlit living room awhile, taking counsel from a brandy bottle, fronds nodding, the goldfish fanning the water like a hedonist. When I went to bed, she rolled away from my touch to stare at the wall. She was making such a racket with her eyes that I got up and started to dress again.

"What are you doing?" she asked.

"I'm going back to the American."

"No you're not. I want you to stay."

Her voice had an edge to it. I took off my pants again and crawled in beside her. She had her back to me. When I touched it, her skin was damp and clammy.

"Bastard," she hissed.

I started to get up, but she grabbed my wrist, her nails digging me like talons. I stayed where I was. She obviously didn't know her own mind. It was going to be a long night.

16

It was six-twenty when I trudged up to the drab newsroom the next morning. The clock-thermometer read 7:18 and eighty-two degrees. Just outside the front door, a municipal snowplow had stalled in the gutter, drifted in up to its headlights. A not-yet-risen sun hung fire below the horizon. Fresh snow squeaked like chalk under my shoes.

Ashcroft's mukluks sprawled like dead jackrabbits on a day-old issue of the *Star-Leader* next to the darkroom entrance, as if he expected room service to come up and currycomb them overnight. I pushed the door open a crack and spied him stretched on the counter beside the sink, the trays, chemical bottles, and enlarger pushed to one end to give him room. He slept like a babe in arms.

Kicking his boots inside, I latched the door before hitting the overhead light. The kid sat straight up and started talking as though he hadn't been sleeping at all.

"Hey, Precious. I thought you'd read the signal."

"So would anybody else coming up the stairs," I said. "You're lucky I'm not Gratz or Spandrell. Anyway, since when did this place enter the low-rent district? You and Barrett would do better at the Sally Ann. They've got beds."

"I was hiding out," he said.

"The hell you were!"

He had that excited look in his eyes, as if he'd just discovered boys were different from girls and why. Every time he got that look, it meant trouble.

"I went to Toronto last night to find Liggett," he said breathlessly. "He wouldn't say boo over the phone, but I thought he might be different in person."

"Damn it!" I said. "I told you to lay off Liggett. The man is bent. You haven't got the slightest idea what you're getting into."

I tried to sound indignant; the kid only smirked and nodded his head.

"I already know all about that," he said. "I knew I'd heard his name before. A couple of years ago he was agent for Hal Riggins, the linebacker. Riggins got caught pushing cocaine across the border and somebody broke his legs to keep his mouth shut while Liggett eased out the back door. Riggins is still doing time. It was in the papers."

"If you knew that," I said, "and still went after him, you're dumber than I thought."

Ashcroft ate insults like candy. His mouth widened into a grin, showing enough teeth to choke a horse.

"I tailed him from the lobby of his building on Bay Street to a parking garage on Adelaide," he said. "Then I lost him."

"You mean he got into his car and drove away?"

"Well, yes, more or less. It was rush hour. I couldn't flag a cab. I don't know how the hell those guys do it on TV. But that's not the point. Somebody was tailing me!" He said this as if getting mugged for a story was an honour, like winning the Victoria Cross. "I didn't notice till I got back to my car and hit the highway driving back to Ockenden. Whoever it was, they were pretty good. They stayed behind till Oshawa, then drove by and front-tailed me to the Burger King exit. They were right on my bumper when I crossed the city limits."

"Who?" I asked.

"Whoever was following me."

"Listen, Einstein, you think I've got giblets for brains? What kind of car were they driving?"

"A big one. It was snowing. I couldn't tell what make."

"At least tell me what colour it was?"

"Black."

"Are you sure?"

"No."

"This is crazy," I said. Talking to Ashcroft was a war of

nerves. He blinked anxiously. His eyes peeked out at me like field mice. "How come they didn't get you? How come I have all the bad luck?"

"I backdoored them," he said looking smug. "Oldest trick in the book. I parked in front of the American, went in and had a few beers, then slid out the rear exit and walked over here through the alleys."

"I guess that means you're tied one-all with the opposition," I said. "Remind me not to stick around for the rubber match."

"I'm not worried."

"Well, I am, Ashers, and I've been around a lot more cut-rate hoods than you have."

"But don't you see, Precious? It means we're really onto something."

"Don't call me that, kid," I said. "Sure, we'll just follow the trail of broken arms and heads to Diana Barryhill's house, these being but trivial occupational hazards of inquisitive newsmen. We haven't got a damn thing on this crowd, Ashcroft. But you're right. It's dirtier than we thought. Must be, or Liggett and his syndicate friends wouldn't bother to put a carload of heavies on your trail. But all you're doing is making them irritable for no good reason. Believe me, you don't want to get these guys irritated. Frankly, I don't think Canadian literature could stand the loss."

Ashcroft deflated. He was disappointed in me, puzzled.

"Now, don't get that way," I said. "I'm not saying forget it. I'm only saying you've put them on the alert, and you didn't want to do that. We've got to lay low for a while, lull them. Understand?"

"Sure. I guess."

"Take a holiday," I said. "Take a trip up the Amazon."

"What? Oh, Susan, you mean?" His eyes popped like Ping-Pong balls. "That reminds me! She had an idea about Barryknoll."

"Never mind," I said. "I don't want to hear it."

"The names," he said. "The names: Barryknoll, Bar-Tor, Bar-Hi, and Barrybrae; they're all variations on the woman's surname. I mean Diana Barryhill!"

"Great, kid. Somebody's a poet. A for effort. How about lending me your vehicle tonight? I've got a heavy date with a light lady."

"What? What about Amy?"

"Grow up, kid."

"Okay, anything you say," he muttered, without looking at me. The way he said them made the words mean something else. "The car is in the lot across the street from the American. I won't need it today."

He handed me the keys.

"Have it for you in the morning," I said airily. "Now get your ass out of here before Gratz arrives. When you come back for work, try to act normally. I know it's a strain."

That morning I missed every deadline by ten minutes, thinking about Ashcroft's story. A Mrs. Rintoul telephoned me to discuss the non-delivery of her newspaper the previous day. I averred that it was probably under a foot of snow in her front yard. She accused me of impertinence and disrespect toward a subscriber. I told her she was an old fart. She said she would call the publisher and have me terminated. I gave her Spandrell's extension number.

A child of indeterminate sex telephoned to find out what time it was.

My stringer in Trenton had filed eighteen inches about an annual grad-teacher hockey match at the local high school. The score was "the same as last year's," he reported. I phoned the misguided young man. He said he didn't know the score; he had lifted the story from a Trenton radio station. They didn't have the score, either. I terminated him.

Wishty suffered a gas attack of such an offensive nature as to bring the sports desk to a grinding halt for several seconds.

"Sorry, Precious," he said. "I guess it was something I ate."

"Wishty," I said, "that was nothing you ate. That was something that crawled up your leg and died!"

I discovered Otto Kleppinger's postcard on my dead copy spike. I put a call through to an operator in Athens; the operator put me on hold. For twenty minutes I held, listening to satellite static over Bimini. I hung up on the operator.

The phone rang.

The hermaphroditic voice of the kid who had called earlier was asking me why his and/or her school bus was late. I gave him and/or her Spandrell's extension number.

The phone rang again.

"Elliot!" I shouted. "What is it this time?"

"Precious, it's Damon."

"Who?"

"Damon. I've got to see you. I've got to talk."

His voice was breathless and urgent. I craned my neck to look through the sports department door into the newsroom. He was seated at his desk near the coat rack, hunched over the receiver, with his back toward me. He had his coat on.

"What's up, Barrett?"

"I can't talk over the phone."

"Is everybody nuts around here?"

"Can you be at my place by noon?"

"Sure, if that's what —"

Barrett replaced the receiver and hurried through the newsroom door to the stairwell, scattering scraps of copy paper in his slipstream. No one seemed to notice his departure, but silence hung like a proclamation over the office. For a change, everyone seemed to be working.

At eleven-thirty I walked over to the American for my mail and caught a cab to Barrett's house.

A nondescript frame building with white stucco siding and a tin roof that needed paint, it was located on the west side of town between the fairgrounds and a bow in the river where willows crowded the banks and wept on the residents' backyards. The city had cut down all the trees along the street and replaced them with seedlings in need of assertiveness training.

Barrett's battered Cutlass was tethered in the driveway in front of the garage. The storm door at the side swung open in the wind. The front door was closed permanently and shrouded in translucent plastic that billowed and snapped. Twice before, Barrett had had me in to talk about old times and sample his cellar: raspberry wine, carrot wine, loganberry wine — I forget the rest.

I knocked at the side door, but there was no answer. I knocked again and shouted Barrett's name. I tried the doorknob. It wasn't locked. Before walking in unannounced, I checked the street for witnesses. An old man in galoshes, houndstooth overcoat, and earmuffs was shovelling his sidewalk across the pavement. He dipped gingerly into the snow with his shovel, so that only a fraction of the blade was covered, and then dropped most of the load as he tried to carry it to a pile in the gutter. He wasn't watching me.

The kitchen light was burning. Open bottles of Alberta vodka and Amaretto stood at attention on the countertop. I shuddered a little; there was no accounting for taste. The rest of the room was neat and clean. Like many men, Barrett was a good housekeeper. He had been married twice, at least; he had pointed out his latest ex in the American one night. She was his type, I suppose, brassy blond with a pair of knockers that would hang to her knees if they weren't battened down and bolstered up. She drank draft beer and sat with a barrel-bellied line foreman from a cable factory. It looked to me as though she had traded down in the deal, but women see these things differently. Perhaps she had grown tired of Barrett's petty vanities and old stories.

The dining and living rooms were much the same, shabby but clean, free of dust-collecting knickknacks, fashion magazines, and pets. Barrett had hung sporting pictures on the wood-panelled walls. The coffee table held a rack with his prize Dunhills and a jar of tobacco. The bookshelves were full of how-to books, hunting and fishing works from the days when he used to get them gratis from the publishers, and mystery novels. It was a man's pad but with the difference that this man had reached the age of wisdom and no longer decorated for the purpose of attracting women.

In the bedroom, I found Barrett.

Somewhere I had read that the body cools after death at a steady rate of one-and-a-half degrees an hour. I put my hand inside his shirt; he was still warm. I lifted an arm and let it drop. There was no stiffening of the muscles. The blood around the hole in his temple had barely begun to congeal.

He was lying between the bed and a card table desk facing a window. He was on his back in an attitude that suggested he had been thrown there by the force of the shot. There was a snub-nosed revolver, the make of which I didn't recognize, cradled in the palm of his open right hand. His face wore a look of mild astonishment, a look more intelligent than any he had recently displayed in life.

There was a cheap Sears portable typewriter on the green baize tabletop, with a sheet of yellow newsprint wound in the carriage. I leaned over Barrett to read it.

> I can't go on. There is nothing left. I didn't mean to do anything wrong.

It was unsigned, possibly unfinished, but patently suicidal.

Sitting on the bed, I examined the fishing photos Barrett had plastered around the room. They certainly helped his wallpaper. In some of them, he looked happy, though ill at ease in front of a camera. It seemed to me a touch high-handed, not to mention inconsiderate, to call me across town this way and then kill himself before I arrived. I wasn't mad at him, but I wasn't enthusiastic about it either.

I was meditating on Barrett's poor manners, perhaps my mind was wandering, when I heard the closet door groan behind me. Quite suddenly, it occurred to me that Damon had been dead so short a time that it was odd I had seen no sign of his murderer, no getaway car, no hurrying figure. There was the old man shovelling his walk. I made a mental note to talk to the man in the houndstooth coat.

I was thinking this through in the time it took to wrench myself around to face whoever was moving on the other side of the bed. I was just a little late. Once more my head became the target of extreme physical aggression. I wondered why, as a taxpayer of a month's standing, I was not being adequately protected by the police. This was rude and illegal, not to mention unpleasant and aggravating. I wanted to lodge a protest. I raised my fist.

And found myself adrift in a houndstooth Milky Way.

17

When I came to, the law was all around. They were on the floor with rubber pinky teasers, tape measures, and magnifying glasses. They were darting up and down with old-fashioned Graflex cameras, photographing the bodies, mine and Barrett's. Two of them, dressed in peaked caps and polyester coats with fur collars, stood guard at the bedroom door in case either of us tried to make a run for it. One silver-haired relic took notes while a detective dictated.

The detective was wearing what the police mistakenly refer to as plain clothes: checked pants, checked jacket, wine shirt, and a white tie with a knot as big as a fist. His face had been sculpted with a spade; he combed his hair in a ducktail. He was scanning the room, sighting down a ballpoint pen, and muttering an inventory to the grey-haired steno.

I wondered who had slugged me. I wondered this with uncanny clarity for a man in my condition. Had I met Rose Oxley's killer? Or had the cops done it? Briefly, I had a vision of six policemen huddled like orphans in the closet while I entered and mused over Barrett's body. But if the cops had been waiting in the house to play paddleball with my head, they would have realized I wasn't responsible for the old man's death. And I was distinctly aware of an atmosphere of crude suspicion, all directed at me.

The more I thought about this, the worse I felt. That man Lazarus had been a fool to want to rise from the dead. Eventually, some idiot waved a phial of ammonium carbonate under my nose to bring me around. My stomach tried to get out through my mouth, and I groaned. The detective leaned over and scowled.

"You kill Barrett?" he asked, his voice strangling on suppressed rage. He was one of those shallow men who confuse loudness with authority. It was clear he didn't want to hear my side of the story.

"You bet," I said. "And then I put the gun in his hand, typed a suicide note, kicked myself in the head, and cunningly hid on the floor where the cops wouldn't find me."

The detective snorted. He had probably grown up wanting nothing more than to become a bully and a lout. I could imagine him giving his wife the third degree every night before they went to bed. "Who left the top off the toothpaste? Fess up, Marge. Talk now or I'll break your face!" He was the type of guy who made you dream that once, just once, you would stumble on him, trussed up like a turkey in a dark alley, and you happened to be holding a baseball bat with a spike in the fat end.

"You got it wrong, buddy," he said. "The gun was in your hand. There was no suicide note. And maybe Barrett hit you just as he was shot. You know, like in a struggle."

I stayed down on the floor, thinking this over awhile.

"I guess you're right," I said. "Now that I look back, I believe that's the way it happened."

"Your name Moss Elliot?" he asked. Torquemada wasn't used to irony. He felt safe working on the self-evident. He flipped open my wallet, comparing an old press card photo with my remains on the floor.

I slipped a hand into my coat pocket. The cops froze.

"You didn't, by any chance, find a thin metal plate about the size of a silver dollar," I said, "while you were helping yourself to my goods and chattels?"

"I'll do the asking. You do the talking," said the detective. He jerked me off the floor by my lapels and dropped me onto a captain's chair by the wall. "Keep your fucking hands out of your pockets and don't get funny."

I was thinking about the zinc cut, which had disappeared while I was unconscious. A little kid inside my head was throwing rocks at my eyeballs. I felt a draught and noticed that the window wasn't closed properly. A set of footprints led from the window to a stand of willows by the river. The police had spotted them, too. A burly constable was out there to make sure they didn't get away.

"What were doing here, Elliot?" asked the detective.

I told him about Barrett's telephone call.

"What do you think he was going to tell you?" he asked.

"If I'd known that, I wouldn't be here."

"Tough guy, Elliot. Tell me a story and make it a good one. I got enough to put you in stir for the night. And once I get you there, I got ways of making you talk."

He was a big man, and I was sure he spoke the truth. He flexed his biceps. His cheeks pumped as though his heart had moved up there from his chest. On the whole, it was not comforting to find myself observing the Canadian system of justice at such close range. In the U.S. cops were shackled by the Miranda precedent and the Bill of Rights. In Canada you didn't have the right to remain silent, call a lawyer, or otherwise fox the police the way they did on television.

I thought fast; it hurt less that way. I didn't know whether to laugh in the detective's face or lose my temper. I suspected everyone, including the Ockenden police force, of conniving with Liggett and Barryknoll. I remembered Bernie Tassio's story about Chief Shaw and the Oaks' slush fund. For all I knew, I was the last honest man in town.

Buying time, I advised the man in the checked suit to go and commit first-degree sexual assault on a duck. His eyes flared dangerously. I was about to become a human punching bag.

I told him to stop fucking with me when he had a fucking murder to solve. I demanded to see the fucking chief of police. I shouted Rose Oxley's name three or four times. I called into question the detective's masculinity, implying that he was a victim of the condition known as undescended testicles. The cops shifted uneasily. In the mirror over Barrett's dresser I could see my face, black with rage, a trickle of blood hanging like string from my ear. The detective made as if to gut-punch me, and I screamed.

"I'm Chief Shaw," said a calm, quiet voice in the background.

I swivelled to glare at the speaker. He was one of the uniformed policemen guarding the door, a stone-jawed bulldog of a man with a melancholy face under his peaked cap. His eyes glittered shrewdly.

"All right, Renner, you can get out," he said, addressing the detective. "Take the boys with you. Wait outside, mind! And be careful with that!"

The last was snapped at the stenographer, who had begun to wander toward the door with the murder gun suspended at the end of his ballpoint by its trigger guard. Shaw eyed me as the other men filed out and the door was shut. Renner was the last to leave. He threw a wicked glance at the back of the police chief's head, then slammed the door, leaving us alone with Barrett's body. Shaw sat on the bed, then stretched out wearily, pulling his cap over his eyes.

Besides the slush fund perfidy, I had heard Shaw hated newsmen, this after a young man, a disgrace to the calling, was caught trading sex in the courthouse men's room in return for keeping defendants' names out of the *Star-Leader* police file. A year later the newspaper had wreaked vengeance when Shaw's own men arrested his wife in a routine raid on a pyramid game in the suburbs. But he was also a hero, a bona fide Sir Isaac Brock, having talked a demented sniper into giving himself up over the barrel of a war-surplus Mauser.

"You're the guy who shacked up with Amy Ranger," he said finally, pushing his cap back on his forehead with an index finger.

I must have looked surprised.

"I'm psychic," he said.

"They got a cure for that nowadays," I said.

"It's a small town," he said, with a shrug. "Want a smoke?"

He offered me a package of Exports, pulled out a lighter, and did the honours for both of us. Then he turned Chinese again, quiet and inscrutable. The cigarette was soothing. The smoke got into my veins, tasted like the proof of God. My body shook like a beaten dog.

"What do you think happened to Barrett?" asked Shaw.

"He's dead," I said, "as in not walking around anymore, seeing things, breathing."

"I mean how do you make all this, Elliot?" he asked again, not the least impatient with me.

I slumped in the captain's chair with more knobs on my head than a bull elk. I knew this was a sucker ploy; Renner had softened me up, all unreason and brutality, and now Shaw was being pally, asking my opinion, dealing blunt questions, without rancour or bluff. I was supposed to be so scared and disoriented I would jump at the chance to be friends and tell him everything he wanted to know. I looked at Barrett and decided I owed it to him to fight a skirmishing retreat.

"This is a setup," I said. "Who called you guys? How did you get here so fast? You must have been on your way when I got clubbed."

"Old man down the street saw you sneaking in the side door," said Shaw, with a dry unenthusiastic chuckle. "He didn't figure Barrett was home at this time of day. He said you looked real guilty."

"What about the footprints?" I asked.

"That's the way he went all right. Killer finds his way around town pretty well. Not many know the old towpath behind the trees down there."

"You mean, you don't think I killed Barrett?" I asked.

"Hell's bells, Elliot, how dumb do I look? Renner's hot for my job, that's all. I like to let him make a fool of himself once in a while. Kind of takes the pressure off. Now why'd you pick this afternoon to visit old Damon here?"

"I had an invitation," I said.

"Okay," said Shaw philosophically. "I'll talk; you listen. As soon as we found you, I called Gratz at the paper office to put a lid on the story. And he was willing because the case involved two employees, and his corporate conscience told him the *Star-Leader* didn't need the publicity. Besides, he was feeling guilty."

"What's that supposed to mean?" I asked, staring moodily out the window, where Renner was supervising the taking of plaster moulds.

"Why, they fired Damon this morning," said Shaw. "I thought you'd know that."

"Hell, no!" I said.

"It seems he was copying stories word for word out of magazines. Beats me why you journalists would be so touchy about a thing like that. I didn't know you had ethics."

"So they fired him?" I said. Shaw had said the word "journalist" as if it were something that spent most of its time under rocks. But I didn't like cops, either, so we were even.

"That new publisher did it," he said. "Right bugger, isn't he?"

"Spandrell?"

"That's him. Anyway, if you get the drift, that makes your suicide note sound pretty plausible. You're sure there was one?"

"I was here in the room, wide awake and sentient, when I saw it," I said. "But the note was a plant."

"Let's just shoot our groundhogs one at a time," he said. "You say there was a note and now there isn't. You say you didn't know Barrett was fired. Would a man kill himself over something like that?"

"Some might," I said. "Barrett was fighting an uphill slope. He drank and couldn't write worth a damn any longer. This was a dead-end job. I don't think he could have found another."

"So he called you over here just after he'd been canned from the last job on earth he could probably hold and neglected to mention that unimportant detail," said Shaw incredulously. "What did he want to talk about?"

"You wouldn't get anything out of it."

"Try me."

There was a knock at the door. Shaw raised the peak of his cap and glanced irritably at the wood panels.

"Go to hell, Renner," he called. "We're working in here. Find yourself another body."

He sat on the edge of the bed facing me.

"I'm listening," he said. "I'm listening to anything you've got to say. Now, maybe you know why you were set up, and maybe you don't; either way, we're going to sit here talking until I get me an idea."

I was growing tired of Shaw's folksy self-righteousness. I didn't trust him. Eyes like a judge; fists like gavels. But when he washed his hands at night, I was willing to bet you could write letters with the water.

"Go to hell," I said, warming up.

"I could turn you back to Renner. Renner's always good for perspective."

"Go to hell," I repeated. "Let's get a couple of facts straight. I've got an angle on Mayor Warren's campaign chest that'll put you in shit up to your earlobes. Push me hard enough and you'll be walking a beat in Sheep Dip, Newfoundland. You want to see your name in forty-eight point? Just ask me again."

Shaw gazed out the window where the forensic crew had chewed up the snow. Dusk filtered through the willows at the bottom of the lawn. He lit a new cigarette, and the glow made a fire against his chin

"That's as it may be," he said finally, patiently, with only a trace of exasperation. "I could do with a vacation. This town would get the kind of police force it deserves. I wasn't cut out for keeping track of so-called solid citizens. That wasn't the job when I signed up, you know. It's got to be that way lately. Beats me how to deal with it. I have to tell you, bub, they blindsided me on that slush fund fiasco. Warren and Playfair juggled those figures. I was probably the last man in Ockenden to know what happened. Makes a soul humble."

"Just the sort of place for a couple of quiet killings," I said.

Shaw paused to butt his cigarette before going on. His eyes looked out at me from under the cap.

"I've known Damon here since I was a kid. He taught me to shoot, tie flies, port a canoe, set traps for mink in the creek beds. He taught me everything I know about the woods. I've got every damn column he wrote. You could make a book out of them, and it'd be a good one."

"All right. All right," I said. "I was trying to get a line on a broad called Diana Barryhill. Yesterday, Damon found out and became highly agitated. I showed him a photo cut I copped at Rose Oxley's house after the murder. Today he called to say he wanted to tell me about Diana Barryhill. While I was unconscious, somebody frisked me and stole the cut. Now you know everything I know."

Shaw betrayed not a flicker of interest in my confessions. He went on regarding me with those shrewd, solemn eyes, taking in every word I said like a machine.

"Was it Barryhill's picture?"

"It looked like the head and shoulders of a man to me. The face was scorched in the Oxley fire. But Damon must have recognized it. That's the reason he was killed. Has to be."

"What's the connection with Rose Oxley?"

"She was killed to keep her mouth shut, too. You cops missed the point on that one. The fire was set to cover up her gossip files, not her murder."

I wrapped the last bit up in a rush and had the satisfaction of seeing Shaw a little rocked by it all. He gave a low whistle and removed his cap to wipe the sweatband with his index finger. He shook his head.

"Looks like we got a multi-murderer on our hands, doesn't it? Beats me to hell. You know who he is, by any chance?"

"Or she."

"What?"

"Diana Barryhill is the key."

"Shit, Elliot, Di wouldn't —" He stopped and a look of bewilderment settled over his face. "Barrett was her father, man. She was his little girl."

It was my turn to be shocked. I was the subject of assaults and menaces. I had been told the dead were alive. And now I was meeting myself coming round a corner.

"Barrett was his pen name. Not many remembered who he really was. And those who did never brought it up because he preferred it that way. But Damon was a Barryhill. I just can't figure why anyone would kill him for it. You got any leads on the woman?"

I told Shaw about the Jarvis Street rooming house, saying he might have more luck with the landlord than we did. For a while after that he gazed out the window without saying anything, working his jaw nervously. With the uniform on, he looked boyish and grave in the twilight. I was thinking about Barrett and the misery he had felt and how it was over.

"That all?" asked Shaw finally. He didn't seem to care if I answered the question. "You might as well beat it, then. You aren't going to leave town, are you? No, I expect not. You hear anything more, you let me know. Damon spoke highly of you to me. Don't let him down, now that he can't complain."

"Renner!" he shouted. "Let Elliot go." The door began to slide open. "And don't come in here, shit-for-brains! I want to think for a minute."

He paid no more attention to me, so I left. As I slipped through the door, Shaw called out, "Be good, Precious! Say hello to Amy. I ain't hardly talked to her in years."

He wasn't smiling.

18

I dragged myself through the snow to a street with traffic and then couldn't flag down a cab. It took forty-five minutes to walk from Barrett's to the American. My head ached, I was beginning to cough again, and I had the dry heaves in a snowbank before I made sanctuary.

Taking refuge in the can, I had one of the waiters bring me a double Hennessy and a bag of ice and sat amid the damp and stink and oracular graffiti trying to pull myself together. The waiter didn't mind; he owed me a table of draft beer after an insane wager on some lumpen hockey team.

I scanned the written notices on the cubicle wall. My name appeared twice in compromising company. At least no one accused me of improper syntax. How would they know, anyway?

After a while I struggled into the hallway, where a new ice age was starting at the foot of the outer door. I tried to telephone Amy at the house, but there was no answer.

I ordered another brandy to my private office and then went out to find Ashcroft's car.

In an hour, as dusk blotted up the last of the daylight, I was threading Toronto-bound freeway traffic and risking death by exposure in the unheated VW, with a wood-panelled Ford station wagon trailing discreetly in the distance.

My senses agog with paranoia, I had noticed the Ford parked halfway down the block with its engine running as soon as I left the American. It just wasn't the time of year for two men to sit in a parked car drinking coffee from Styrofoam cups, masticating bags of Mrs. Miniver's takeout hamburgers. Not the time of year at all.

As the little VW engine sputtered into life, I had sat staring at the Ford's exhaust plume, doing a deep breathing routine to quell panic the way they had taught us in flight school. It made me dizzy. And then I had the happy thought that the Ford was really a good sign after all. Liggett and the syndicate behind Barryknoll were worried about Ashcroft's news story. The tail was a way of finding out what he was up to as well as a not-so-subtle threat. If the two men in the Ford had had anything to do with Barrett's murder, they wouldn't have waited around watching the kid's old car.

Chances were they didn't know anything about the killing. Liggett was a respectable front man, a "three-piece suit," as Jerry had said. He might not be averse to a little muscle play when it wouldn't get noticed by the cops, but he would never get mixed up in anything as messy as a double murder and arson. That meant the killer had been acting on his own account, moon-lighting. Maybe Liggett didn't even know about the Oxley murder; there had never been an obvious connection with Barryknoll. But there *was* a connection via Diana Barryhill.

As I headed out of town toward the freeway with the station wagon in tow, I almost felt a surge of affection for the hoods. A low-grade threat was no threat at all compared to Barrett getting croaked like that. I was being protected. The killer was probably scared as hell the syndicate would find out he was lumbering their profitable land swindle with dead bodies. For the first time since Rose Oxley had died, I felt as though I could see the board, even if I couldn't make out all the other players yet. At the very least I could drop Diana Barryhill's name in the right ears, duck, and see who was left standing when the shooting stopped. In my altered state of consciousness, that somehow looked like progress.

Arriving in Toronto, I took the parkway downtown and parked the VW on top of a snowbank beside a snow route sign in Cabbagetown, in front of a grave Victorian house with a double door and bay windows. The Ford stopped a block away under a broken streetlight. I trudged up the neatly shovelled walk into a carpeted vestibule and rang one of the row of buttons fixed above the wainscotting. A female voice crackled through the mesh speaker.

"Yes?"

"It's me," I shouted doubtfully.

"— sus! I knew it!"

The door clicked and buzzed, inviting me in.

The woman who opened the door of the second-floor apartment was in her late thirties but didn't look it. Her tawny hair, cut in a pageboy, fell like a portière, concealing her dark clever eyes. She had a ripe figure, packaged in tight black trousers and a white silk shirt open halfway down her torso. Her breasts swung free, pushing against the shimmering cloth.

In the subdued lighting of the apartment, she looked arch and exciting, and the furnishings complemented the effect. Deep velvet sofas in soft colours, thick pile carpeting and Turkish throw rugs, antique brass lamp stands, framed serigraphs on the walls, gilt mirrors, and a low glass coffee table with a chess pattern etched on the top and a set of ivory and ebony pieces squared off against each other.

As I stepped through the door, her sexy pout mellowed into a warm amused smile.

"Precious, it had to be you!"

"None other. Weren't you expecting me?"

"For the last seven years, or when was the last time?"

"Who's counting?"

"The years haven't been good to you, darling."

"Flattery will get you everywhere. I need a drink."

I dropped my coat on the end of a couch and threw myself backward into its mossy depths. The apartment was warm, the air humidified. I was so tired that I started to doze off.

"Don't make yourself at home!" She laughed, a pleasant husky laugh, full of erotic entendres. "And I won't get you a drink."

"Brandy. I'm not staying."

"Tsk, tsk. You always disappointed me. Why was it I could never get you to stay still?"

She laughed again and disappeared into the other end of the apartment.

Rini Carillo, that was her name, had the distinction of being the second Mrs. Elliot at a time when we were both struggling young things. I had been struggling to hold fast to some illusions; she had been struggling to get rich. I don't think she made it, but by the time I left she had ulcers, hypertension, no gallbladder, and a $22,000-a-year job with the provincial government. And no illusions whatever.

As I have said, she was one of those people with projects and contacts. When we were together, she worked sixteen hours a day and flew to Montreal or Ottawa every other weekend for conferences and study groups. In public she played the beautiful, cool, tough, intelligent, sophisticated woman about town. In private she was a mad diet freak, cat lover, exercise fanatic, and gobbler of chintzy romances. She was terrified of pregnancy, and the bathroom shelves were lined with douches, foams, pills, and ointments. She was a Grade-A spermicidal maniac.

Rini was now in intergovernmental affairs, an executive assistant. She was a wheel, as we used to say in Ameliasburg. She made sixty grand and had sat most decoratively and expensively on a royal commission on youth. Once she had been photographed sipping Black Russians with the prime minister's wife in an out-of-the-way eatery in New York. She had not married again.

She returned from the kitchen with a large tortoiseshell cat, a bottle of wine, two tulip glasses, and a compressed-air bottle opener balanced precariously in her arms.

"This is Link," she said. "He's a notorious womanizer. Aren't you, love?"

The cat appeared to have fallen asleep hanging head down from Rini's elbow. Like all of her cats, this one seemed to treat her in the most offhand way. It was something she liked in cats and men. The more she was taken for granted, the more baby-voiced and obsequious she became. Of course, this was only in private.

She plopped the cat on the couch.

"Link wants to sit on Precious," she prattled.

I gave Link the back of my hand. I wanted to make a bad impression on him early.

"Oh, Precious, you're so cruel to animals! Open the bottle like a good man. There! Don't get annoyed. You know I never serve brandy. My, you have grown haggard. Tsk, tsk. What's this? Fighting in bars again?"

I brushed her hand away as it started to dab at the lick of hair hanging over my latest contusion.

"Oh, but that's all right. You never were the distinguished type. You were vulgar. No! Rough-hewn. Manly. So manly. And you still are, aren't you?" She looked into the middle distance wistfully. "You're the only man I've ever known who could come home in rags, babbling drunk, covered with blood and dirt, and still exude that certain something that made me drip like a leaky tap."

"Jesus, Rini!"

She laughed, a throaty lilt. She started to touch me hungrily, straightening a shirt sleeve, picking off a thread, pushing a stray strand of hair into place. I opened the bottle and poured the wine. Then I took a cigarette from my deck and lit it. I thought how Rini had always come on too strong, how she was crude because she wanted to look tough, and how she threw herself at men because she didn't know any other way of showing affection.

She pouted momentarily.

"Well, what did you come here for?"

After all was said and done, she really thought men were only good for bedding.

"I'm in a jam, Rini."

"Oh, Precious. I have no influence with the police. Or has hims got a nasty bar tab?"

"Cut it out. I need some information. I'm betting a Queen's Park angle."

"Oh, Lord! It's not a story, is it? That's low even for you, darling. I was thinking about the papers the other day. Not hearing from you for so long. And then I saw that odious little Billfold man eyeing the secretaries on their lunch break. I thought to myself how it must be an omen."

"It's Bellfield."

"Well, whatever."

"It's not a story. A man was murdered today. A harmless, foolish old man who was trying to find his daughter. I know it sounds silly, but people get killed for that nowadays. The murderer tried to pin it on me. The cops let me go on the grounds that anybody found lying beside a corpse with a gun in his hand is too stupid to have committed a crime. This assessment of the situation could alter at any moment. Right now there are two heavies outside watching this house because I'm in it. But that's not really important. Someday I'll tell you the whole story."

Rini, who hadn't believed a word I said, smiled unpleasantly and said, "In another seven years?"

"Don't hold your breath."

The cat attempted to have an intimate relationship with my left calf. I punted it over the glass table, knocking some of the chessmen over with it. The cat whined faintly and staggered out of the room, looking disgruntled. When I looked up, my ex-wife had tiny angry tears caught in the corners of her eyes.

"Why are you always so cruel to me?"

"You ask for it." I remembered those tears. She could turn them on and off like a movie star — but never in public.

"You're such a fool, Precious. I could give you so much."

"Cut the crap, Rini. You think you give so much, but all I remember getting was an occasional roll in the hay and a quick kiss over burnt toast."

"That's not true."

"Listen, I need to know what's going on in a place called Ockenden. Your plane would fly over it on the way east."

She straightened her shoulders and turned away from me, suddenly developing an interest in split ends. Underneath the pantomime she was transforming herself into the tough female executive, one of the ones who had to be ten times as tough as the men to get ahead. In the old days Rini could draw blood with a quip at twenty paces. I had seen bureaucrats lose everything but their shirt collars in conference with her and not realize it until they were blocks away recovering in a bar.

"There's nothing going on, Precious," she said icily. "It's just like you to take advantage of an old relationship to get something out of me. I should throw you out."

I stubbed out my cigarette and walked over to a window, beckoning Rini to follow.

"They're in that station wagon. You can see the exhaust," I said. Rini looked worried.

"Christ, Moss, you don't expect me to hide you? You can't come here when you're in trouble like that. I'm not involved. You should leave."

She stood against my arm. The skin around her neck looked cool and white. The expanse of her chest was marbled with veins, her breasts still large and firm. She turned her face to gaze up at me with her bedroom eyes.

I knew I had to make an exchange. For the information I wanted, I would have to go through the motions with Rini, show her I still loved her after the long separation. Years before, as the marriage faltered, it had been the same. She needed reassurance, and she got it in bed. Then she would be smug and self-satisfied until I couldn't stand it anymore and left.

Now she was excited by the strangeness of the situation, my being there and needing her, the men outside waiting for me. I took her in my arms and kissed her hard. It wasn't so difficult after I had made up my mind. But there was a price to pay.

"Oh, stop, Precious. You're revolting."

"Come on, love. We used to be good together."

"Too good. I knew it wouldn't last."

"Where's the bedroom?"

"You bastard. You goddamn arrogant bastard."

She was crying now, really warming herself up. Love for Rini was measured on some scale of emotional ferocity. There had to be effects, possession, rejection, intoxication before she was fulfilled. Inevitably, she doomed herself to disappointment. I pitied her. She had never learned simply to enjoy the closeness of another human being.

After a few minutes of cajoling and mawkish seduction, she dragged me into the bedroom. She was so anxious. And I remember her gasping, "Say things to me, Precious. Tell me how good it is. But, oh God! don't say anything you say to other women." It made me think of Amy.

For a while we lay in bed, smoking and talking. Rini ran her hands over and over my body in some fervid rite of possession. I relaxed against the pillows and waited.

"Darling, honestly, it's not my field," she said.

She could lie better after sex.

"Don't protest to me, Rini," I said flatly. "I've got enough already to go to the newspapers. I'm very good at spectacular innuendo. I used to work for the tabs, remember? I've got two murders, arson, and a bent land-development company that holds options on hundreds of acres on the east side of town. These guys are bidding grand slam all the way and we both know there's nothing there except . . ."

"Except what?" she snapped.

"In that part of the country, government is the last virgin natural resource."

She was sitting on the edge of the bed, a sheet wrapped around her body from the breasts down, picking her manicure and calculating.

"Damn you, Precious! Are you sure about this?"

I nodded.

"There are people down there buying land?"

"Right."

"Eeeeeyuck!" The childish exclamation was part of Rini's cute repertoire.

"I'm guessing Barryknoll's ahead of you four or five months. The options are half-year renewable. All they have to do is wait for the province to announce the plans someone has already leaked. See, I know that much already. But the new game is called murder and I need verification. Get it?"

I could see she was coming around. She was ready to ask for her cut.

"Okay. You give me names. What's that?"

I reached into my jacket on the floor beside the bed and handed her a photocopy of Ashcroft's draft plan. She flipped through it greedily.

"You're not shitting me, are you. It really is blown! This is an outline for Omniplex."

"For who?" I asked stupidly.

"Precious, we've got twenty-three companies lined up to go in there. We were going to start banking land in the spring, break sod in the fall. It was going to be an instant Detroit, Canada's own Ruhr Valley."

"But there's nothing there."

"Precisely. Only a computer could have found it. Ockenden has available land on current transportation routes. It's got easy access to the U.S. and resources via the Great Lakes. But best of all, it's got deep water, which means inexpensive international trade ties. It's the only port on Lake Ontario that can take twenty-seven-foot ocean-going vessels without dredging. Even Toronto can't bring them in that big."

I gave a low whistle.

"You mean they're going to build something like Omniplex just because it's there!"

"Well, it's not just that. In the seventies the cabinet got worried about oil scarcity. We contracted ahead by fifteen years for Mexican oil at higher than world prices just in case. Now we've got to use the damn stuff or pay anyway. Atlantic Richfield has contracted to build a refinery; we're going to build an oil-fired generating station. We've even made a deal with Con Ed in New York to buy our surplus power, though we'll take a beating on the price differential. That's why we developed Omniplex. The province may still take a loss, but at least we'll have all these jobs and plants to show for it."

"Great politics," I said, "a factory in every backyard."

"You're so cynical, Precious. We marketed Omniplex by emphasizing a timetable, cheap land, and the concept of an interlocking manufacturing community. If what you say is true, we may not be able to deliver. And once one of these companies pulls out, the rest will stampede through the door."

"Too bad you people can't be honest or keep your mouths shut or both."

I was going to say more, but Rini was no longer paying attention. She was off in some other jungle, calculating how best to handle the revelation she was about to drop on her boss's desk Monday morning. She lit a cigarette from her bedside table, then turned on me.

"Damn it, Precious. How do you know this? How did they find out? I need to know."

"A bad business," I said, shaking my head with mock severity. "A rogue newsman."

Before learning about Omniplex, I had been feeling my way on hunches and assumptions. According to Bellfield, Spandrell, the muckraking journalist, had had a reputation for using blackmail to extort the juicy details of his investigative bomb-shells. After the scandal that forced him to leave the *Daily News*, he'd gone straight to Ockenden with enough cash to buy the *Star-Leader*, giving him a handle on local public opinion. At the same time, mysterious development companies with links to Spandrell and the *Star-Leader* began cornering hundreds of acres of nearby farmland. Omniplex was the key, the motive I'd been hunting for. I gave Rini the gist of what I suspected.

"He's Burton Spandrell, publisher of the Ockenden *Star-Leader*, my boss. A year or two ago, he was running a string of investigative reporters for the *Daily News* in Toronto. My guess is that one of his sleuths struck a politician with a lurid love life or a bureaucrat with his fingers in the till, and this politician or bureaucrat leaked Omniplex to Spandrell in return for keeping his name out of the papers."

Rini's face had turned to stone. Her eyes were luminous with contempt. I knew what she was thinking: she hated the messy side of public life, the unfettered press, the elected representatives, the people. Rini was a born autocrat — democracy was the bane of efficient government.

"It's a safe bet," I continued, "that Spandrell sold the whole scheme to a syndicate in return for cash and equity in a company that is in the process of beating Queen's Park to the real estate. Of course Spandrell got caught but not before the damage was done. As far as I can tell, the provincial government and Spandrell's former employers colluded on a cover-up. The whole thing was swept under the carpet."

"Shit!" Rini's mouth dropped open. It was pleasing to see that her reserves of sang-froid were not infinite. "Somebody already knew it was blown, and they let us go ahead."

"Some people are just vile," I observed cheerfully.

"I can't just go in and shoot my mouth off. I'll have to find out who knows and let him know that I know. Then I can figure out what to do."

Rini's mind sprinted into the corridors of power again. I had another cigarette by myself with her statue sitting beside me. Later, she got up and in a trance put on a dressing gown. I heard a toilet flush after she left the bedroom, then came the telltale tapping of a typewriter in a far room.

I hauled myself into the bathroom to revive my spirit for the trip back to Ockenden. I had steamer trunks under my eyes, my cheeks were inflamed, and I needed a shave. I filled the sink, ducked, then stood gaping at the face in the mirror as the pearly water drained its geography, listening to the typing down the hall and wondering if I had been right not to fear those two men in the station wagon. As if you could trust anybody these days.

19

It was three a.m. when I finally guided the VW into the space beside Amy's Datsun, switched off the ignition, and sat while the engine subsided. A balmy southwest wind had blown up suddenly, squeezing the mercury above freezing. I could hear water trickling in the gutters, the siren sound of a false Canadian spring. My unofficial escort drove by and nosed up against a lawn a few doors down the street. Did those guys ever sleep?

The mist haloed Amy's porch light. At the top step I paused for a deep breath that triggered a coughing jag. I lit a cigarette to soothe my lungs. The ache from the bump behind my ear where the sap had struck was like the chiming of church bells inside my head. My forebrain felt like Cream of Wheat. My body was shivering, though I didn't feel cold.

Inside, I threw my hand up to cut the porch light, plunging myself into a darkness the texture of India ink. For an instant I lost orientation like a pilot without a horizon. I stretched instinctively for the wall, missed, and found the night spinning round me like a wagon wheel.

I seemed to fall and fall, and then I was hitting the sling couch, which held for a split second before capsizing me onto the coffee table. Magazines, plants, and fishbowl exploded in the gloom. I groaned and collapsed in the bog of a wet rag rug and rested there, feeling immensely sorry for myself.

A dagger of light stabbed beneath the bedroom door, then ballooned to fill the room. I blinked. Amy was standing, poised in her nightgown in the doorway, ghostly with the light at her back, her face pale and taut. Was I projecting my own guilt and fear? Or did she really look on the verge of hysteria?

"Sorry, darling . . . tried to call you," I mumbled graciously.

She was beside me. I felt warm hands lifting me gently by the armpits. My fingers brushed her face and came away scalded

with tears. She lowered me into a chair, peeled off my coat, and
dashed to the kitchen.

"I've got coffee on. It won't take a minute."

Her voice was breaking.

"I'm sorry," I repeated. "Tried to call."

"No, no, Moss. I'm sorry. I don't care what you were doing. I
guess I would drive anybody crazy the way I acted yesterday. And
then I heard about that Barrett murder on the news, and I was so
worried for you."

What could you do with a woman like that? I was guilty and
she was apologizing.

"Are you all right?"

She was beside me again.

"Just tired."

"It was that talk about Diana Barryhill, Moss. I couldn't
stand it. You were making me remember, it wasn't your fault.
You forgive me?"

I hated her self-chastisement. I pulled her head to my chest
and cradled her for a moment so she couldn't speak.

"My God! The fish!"

He was flopping forlornly at the edge of the rug near the front
door, his scales sparkling dully. As we watched, his struggles grew
weaker. For a moment he stopped altogether and lay there, his gills
heaving. I pushed myself out of the chair to kneel over him. He
tried to swim again as I lifted him on my palm.

"Oh, Pogo!" cried Amy. "I'll get some water."

"His bowl is broken. Get a jar or something."

I heard water rushing in the kitchen, the rising note of a jug
filling quickly under the tap. The tiny fish seemed to burn me.
It was like a holy relic, something wildly prosaic but full of
significance. Watching it struggle, I felt sad and weighed down.

"Moss, you're crying!"

There was awe in Amy's voice.

"Moss, love, the fish will be all right. Don't worry, please.

Give him to me. There you go, fish. Lots of water. A little adventure is good for the soul. Are you all right, Moss? I've got your coffee."

Her tone was efficient and matter of fact. She was at her best when someone needed her. She placed the mug of coffee in my hand and waited until I took it. While I sat, dazed, in the chair she quietly cleaned up the mess I had made, discreetly allowing me the privacy of my feelings. And I knew, as I watched her intent comings and goings, that I needed Amy Ranger, at that moment, more than anything in the world.

It was half an hour or more before I could summon the strength to break her spell.

Finally, I said, "I have to know about Diana Barryhill, Amy. I have to know. You're the only one who can tell me."

I couldn't even look at her as I spoke.

"Why?" she asked wearily.

"For a lot of reasons, darling. But mostly because of Barrett, who was killed today after promising to tell me about her. I think Rose was killed on the same account. If I find the missing broad, I'll find a murderer."

"But why? Why can't you just let it go? You didn't care about Rose before."

Amy's voice had grown cold and hoarse.

"I know too much now. Knowing somehow makes you responsible. I didn't know Rose, but I knew Barrett, and I think I know who killed him. If I had a motive, I could nail him. I can't walk away anymore. Besides, this killer already suspects Ashcroft, and he probably knows I put Damon onto his trail. When he finds out the cops aren't holding me for manslaughter, he'll . . ."

Amy clapped her hands over her ears to shut out the sound of my voice.

"I was a little girl then," she wailed. "How could I know anything? Couldn't we go away?"

I shook my head.

"There's a car outside. They're watching this house right now," I said, only half-truthfully. I was getting a lot of mileage out of Ashcroft's playmates. Taking Amy's hand, I led her to the window and pointed to where the station wagon's exhaust clung to the damp street.

"They all hated me," she said weakly. "They didn't want me around. I was locked in a room. I wanted to forget it all."

Amy's face seemed to crumple in an onslaught of tears.

I took her to the bedroom and drew her down upon the counterpane beside me. I thought it might be easier for her to talk if she felt protected. Her head nestled like a small animal against my shoulder. After a while, when her sobbing had subsided, I went to the kitchen to heat milk and mix it with brandy.

Suddenly Amy appeared in the doorway, her eyes puffy and grief-stricken. From bedroom to kitchen, her personality had altered completely. Her hair stuck out at odd angles; her jaw was slack. She was wearing a tatty housecoat I had never seen before. She demanded a cigarette in a voice I scarcely recognized; I handed her the pack. With trembling fingers she struck a match and lit up, then placed the package on the table between us like a wall.

"Brian Oxley was a pretty boy!" she began. "So they told me, though I don't remember myself." She stopped, seemed puzzled, brushed non-existent ashes from the collar of her housecoat.

The words had come in a strident singsong, a kind of childish prattle, but in the voice of a woman you might meet in a bar with her vocal chords pickled in alcohol and nicotine. It scared me to hear it, but I told myself it wasn't Amy, just a voice from the past, an unpleasant stranger I had summoned from the seedy rooming house at the back of her mind.

"Mummy and Daddy met on a dock in England, you know," she said finally, picking up a new narrative thread, taunting me by evasion. "A romantic beginning! She was a Nova Scotia librarian, a spinster named Grace Ludlow. When the war came, she went for overseas duty in hospitals, for the excitement and the men. Loads of men!

"Daddy came off a ship in a stretcher, all smashed and mangled, oh, ghastly. Through the bloody haze of his poor burned eyelids, he thought he saw an angel — it was Grace. He wanted to marry her there with a bollard for an altar, but she wouldn't have it. She waited a week, to be sure. And when Daddy was able, they got me."

Amy stopped to take a pull on the drink I had set before her. She wiped her mouth with the back of the hand that clutched her cigarette. Her lips twisted in an ironic smile at my solicitude.

"That was the best part, before I was born. Mummy was lewd. Daddy was a venomous little man, a printer with ink for blood, a union steward, a drinker of long pints with his mates. The year we came to Ockenden, one of his army pals, Uncle Albert I called him, arrived on a visit, and stayed and stayed. Daddy got him a job at the paper, and I remember the endless kitchen evenings with the two of them drunk and arguing and passing humorous remarks about Grace.

"Until one day when Daddy caught Grace and Albert on the parlour sofa together. Albert got a nasty case of lead poisoning after that — though I'm not sure what Daddy meant by it — and Daddy went to jail for three years. When he got out, Grace and Albert had run away, leaving him the daughter he didn't want."

She paused again and blinked innocently. Her face wore an expression of pop-eyed surprise. Then she looked away from me and began afresh.

"Brian Oxley was a pretty boy, don't you know? He could skate like Rocket Richard and played dirtier than Gordie Howe — but he never got blamed because his face was so sweet. Though it wasn't so sweet after the fire, I suppose.

"Trash to ash," she chanted bitterly. "Trash to ash. They said he threw me out a window, wrapped in a blanket, and perished.

Poor boy! Though I don't remember. I hit my head! Amy hurt . . . Amy hurt.

"The floor collapsed beneath him. Diana told me. He ran into the fire to save me and burned. He wrapped me in a blanket from head to foot. A hero he was. Don't you know?"

"Was it Diana Barryhill?" I asked. "Was she there?"

"She's the one you wanted to know about, isn't she? Everyone wanted to know Diana." Suddenly, there was a new subtone of anger in Amy's shrill monologue. "Why did all the boys chase Diana and leave Amy out of the fun?"

Her eyes sparkled coyly.

"Stop that!" I interrupted. "Answer me straight. Was it Diana Barryhill?"

"Yes, she was there."

"What happened to her?"

"Gone away."

"Where?"

"Rose knew! Rose knew!"

"Rose Oxley knew where Diana went? Is that what you're telling me, Amy?"

"I don't know, Moss. It was so long ago. Why are you asking all these questions?"

"Let's go back," I said. "There was a fire, your stepbrother got you out a window, the floor gave way, and he was killed. What was Diana Barryhill doing there? What's she got to do with it?"

Amy ignored me, fumbled for another cigarette, and took up her weird narrative where she had left off.

"Daddy and I came to stay at the Oxleys'. She was a widow, he a widower, or so he said after a while. He was not, of course, and she held that over him. Brian was the sunrise and sunset of her life, such an elegant imp, so charming to ladies. He shoved the door open when I went to the bathroom. I told Rose and she whipped me; she called me a slut. He cut off my fingers. You see? You think I'm a slut, Moss?"

Reaching across the kitchen table, I grasped her hand and held it, trying to send her a message. I didn't know what exactly.

She seemed so harsh and pathetic. She looked at our hands, seemed to make an effort to pull herself together, then went on.

"There was no one but me in the house that night. Rose and Daddy went out somewhere. I woke up and saw Diana with Brian. She didn't want to be there. She was crying and pleading with him to let her go home. He locked me in my room so I couldn't talk to her. At first I tried to call out to her through the door. She was sobbing, pleading with him. 'No, no, no, no, no.' But I went to sleep. Later the yelling woke me up. And Diana was screaming for somebody to help. It must have been Brian and Aaron fighting."

"Aaron?"

"Why, Aaron Raftis! They called them the Terrible Twins, though I couldn't see any resemblance. They played hockey together. They were both after Diana."

"And this was the night of the fire?"

"When Daddy and Rose were out, Brian would drink their liquor. He'd get Diana there, and that always made Aaron mad. There was a terrible crash. Something broke. I could hear them yelling when I woke up. I was scared. Then Diana screamed — I remember that, I'll never forget — before it all went quiet.

"Someone came into my room. It was dark, smoke was coming up under the door, and he wrapped me in a blanket. I hit my head on the window going through and fainted. Then I remember the house burning and Diana holding me out in the yard and the sirens and the crowds of people and Brian inside not making a sound, everyone asking where Aaron was.

"I remember the funeral and everyone saying how brave Rose acted. At the inquest, a man behind the big table asked me if I knew what happened to little girls who didn't tell the truth, and I told him they went to the other place, the opposite of heaven. The audience laughed. I wanted to tell the truth, Moss. But I was so young and I hit my head."

"How did the fire start?" I asked. "What happened to Aaron? Where was he when the house burned?"

"I don't know, Moss! You ask such hard questions. I was only little . . . little. Diana said Brian hit Aaron and ran him out of our place. The house caught fire while they were fighting, like in the movies. Diana told me out on the lawn. She made me remember. She made me repeat it. I'll never forget. I heard them whispering in the hallway."

"What were they saying?"

"I don't remember. I don't remember! I told them Brian was trying to put the fire out, and Diana was begging Aaron to help. She said he laughed and walked away. I didn't want to get him in trouble. I didn't mean to."

"You don't believe it, do you, Amy?"

"Don't know!"

Her voice mocked me; her face twisted like a mask.

"Tell me exactly how the fire started."

She looked bewildered, lost, and then she squinted across the table at me as if I were a stranger she was trying to place. Suddenly her hand went to her mouth and she gasped.

"I — I . . ."

She choked on the words.

"I wasn't there. Diana told me what to say. We — we were outside, watching the house burn, waiting for the fire trucks. I told the inquest. She said we should have the same story. I heard them whispering! She told me . . . I lied. Don't be angry, Moss. I was little."

"What happened afterward? What happened to Aaron?"

"I don't know!" Amy's voice became a wail. "They went away. I had to answer all those questions. I was all alone, and they kept asking me."

"Did Diana and Aaron run away together? You have to remember!"

"No. No, they didn't. Aaron went away the night of the fire. When he heard Brian had died, he ran away. No one ever saw him again. Diana stayed for a while."

"How long?"

"A month. Two months. They said she was bored; she went to the city to get a job. I didn't . . ."

Amy's mouth started to form words without sound. I touched her shoulder to reassure her.

She said, "I didn't want to lie, Moss. Aaron was always nice to me. But he wasn't there. He fled. He used to let me ride his shoulders. I didn't mean to hurt him, but they were all mad at him afterward. Amy didn't mean it."

She stopped speaking, and I decided not to ask her any more questions. Her secret was out. I could guess the rest. She had given the inquest the story Diana Barryhill had rehearsed with her. She had condemned Aaron Raftis with her testimony. She didn't know the truth, but she instinctively understood that Diana had prompted her with a lie. Worse than any of Rose Oxley's gossip and slander, her words had broken up families and ruined lives. Or so she believed.

She was staring at me, her eyes expressing a mixture of shame and revulsion, as though I had convinced her to perform some perverted act. I wanted to tell her she was a victim, not a criminal, that Diana had used her, that Aaron had run away, that her stepmother had refused to console her. But I couldn't find the words.

Instead, I helped her to the bedroom. I took off her slippers and tucked her in. By the time her head hit the pillow she was out. Just like that. Skin like vanilla ice cream, sweat dripping on her temples, soaking her hair. I shut the door, hoping that she would sleep for hours and that the sleep would heal her.

In the kitchen, I drank the last of the coffee, took some philosophy from a brandy bottle, and popped a handful of Wide-a-Wakes for the extra caffeine. The room smelled pleasantly of coffee grounds and bacon. Outside, false spring murmured up and down the streets; I could hear melting snow running in the gutters. Amy's goldfish paddled weakly just beneath the surface of its water jar.

At 6:05 the phone rang, nearly stopping my pulse; it was Chief Shaw

"Elliot," he said, in a voice that sounded a hundred miles away, "I want you to come to the station right away. I've found her. I've found Diana, and I wish to God I hadn't."

20

I hurried to the bedroom; Amy was curled against the wall, her back toward me. After what she had just gone through, it hardly seemed right to leave her alone. I had been trying to convince myself that talking about the past, Rose, the fire, Brian's death, and the inquest would do her good in the long run. But I couldn't shake the sick feeling that I had wanted to use her like all the rest of them.

"I heard voices," she mumbled, as though she were still remembering the whispers outside her door twenty-five years before.

"Shaw called," I said quickly.

She resembled a streetchild, a waif, with the bedclothes wrapped around her. She was like some female Lord Jim; she carried a private disaster in her heart, and the disaster was this: the little girl had become an accomplice, her innocence used to back a lie, without ever learning what she concealed or whom she betrayed.

"He's found Diana Barryhill," I said. I had made up my mind not to hide anything from her. Yet, almost immediately, I had to hedge.

"Who is it?" she asked coldly. "Who killed them?"

"He didn't say. He'll have suspects. The woman, or more likely someone trying to protect her. She must have caught up with Aaron somewhere. I think that was Barrett's theory."

"You *know*," she said, without turning her head.

I tried to ignore the contempt in her voice.

"Rose must have suspected all along that Brian's death was no accident."

"Bri —!"

The rest of the name was lost in a sob. It was the first time since the inquest she had talked about that night. It may have been the first time she had consciously faced the question of what really happened.

"I'll have to go," I said hurriedly. "Shaw is sending a car for me. Will you be all right?"

She didn't answer.

"I'm leaving the number. I think you should stay in. At least until I find out what's going to happen. Those bozos in the station wagon will probably abandon us when they see the police are involved. If they don't, if anybody comes to the door, don't even look, just telephone Shaw."

A car horn sounded in front of the house.

"I'll call," I said.

I wanted to say more, but there was no time. I needed to explain myself, as well as the murders, and I still didn't have the complete lowdown on either topic. Tomorrow we would talk it out. Someday we would have all the answers.

There was a knock at the door. It was a stocky, moon-faced constable, a kid; I had seen him once or twice as I walked to work, earnestly tugging at doorknobs and shining his flashlight on window displays. He was polite, a brand new experience for me. His car was parked on the street, its roof lights making elliptical patterns in the snow. The watchers had vanished; the constable had not even noticed them go.

Shaw was waiting like a Minotaur at the centre of a maze of temporary office dividers. Another non-sleeper. He motioned for me to sit down.

His office was furnished with the usual rows of legal files, steel cabinets, framed diplomas, a Woolworth desk triptych displaying a trio of smiling brats, and two tarnished hockey cups. On the wall behind Shaw hung a black-and-white photograph of a younger, crewcut version of himself, in pads and skates, shaking hands with Toronto Maple Leafs' trainer King Clancy.

Shaw's eyes followed mine.

"Training camp, 1960," he said. "The Leafs called me up from police academy in Aylmer for a tryout. Two weeks later I was back in Aylmer. Clancy said I'd enjoy walking a beat more than warming a bench."

I looked carefully at Shaw's face. He was played out, defeated. The caginess, the facade of worldly power were gone.

"At times like this," he went on, "you look back and you know, you *know* you've never done anything better in your life. You remember a couple of games, maybe just one shift, or a goal, when you were freewheeling across the blue line, lying yourself flat on the ice to turn, and every move felt like it was meant since creation and no one could touch you. Now everything falls apart."

Abruptly, he stopped talking and tried to straighten some papers on the desk. Shaw seemed naked without his peaked cap as a prop.

"Hell, you don't know what I'm talking about!" he said finally. "Anyway, we've got work to do. You were on the level about Barrett and Diana yesterday. At first I thought you were blabbing nonsense to save your skin, but I spent all night looking, and this morning I found her. Now we're going to catch Damon's killer if I have to tear this fucking town apart to do it!"

"Where did you find her?" I asked. "I did some legwork last night, too. I know she's the key. Show me Diana Barryhill and I'll tell you a story that'll make your toes curl. You must have been around when Brian died — that's part of it."

"I remember," said Shaw, looking satisfied. Anger acted on him like a tonic. Briefly, his eyes had sparkled with their old cunning. Then the veil fell once more.

"She might as well be dead."

His tone was distant and gruff.

"I went to Toronto myself last night and leaned on the little landlord fellow for a while."

I pitied the Portuguese, but not too much. I wondered why

Shaw wanted Diana Barryhill so badly, whether the Toronto police had helped or whether he had broken all the rules and gone freelance.

"She stayed there awhile two years ago," he said. "The rent was paid through a bank. Some social worker type brought her food. She still gets mail there — a cab driver picks it up at the end of each week.

"She was crazy, you understand. She'd been in and out of the Clarke Institute for booze and depression. The Jarvis Street room was part of a halfway-house program, which means she made it halfway back to the world before they had to put her away for good."

Shaw glared at me as though it were my fault.

"The landlord didn't know where. It took me half the night to find a Mountie friend with influence enough to get her file pulled at Queen Street. She's in a private home north of Thornhill. Somebody is taking damn good care of her, Elliot. Conscience money!"

"Maybe he just wants to keep her out of sight," I said. "Who pays?"

"Bastards wouldn't tell me. By the time I'd bluffed my way in to see her, some smart-ass doctor who'd seen too much American TV wised up enough to ask for my warrant. I nearly had the local cops on my tail.

"But I saw her. She's got what they call senile dementia. Can you beat that? She isn't old, not much older than me. It was the bottle and the life she led that got her. They had her doped to the gills with Thorazine. She don't talk. She don't look . . ."

"When do the hospitalization records start?" I put in.

"Just over three years ago. She'd been getting treatment already."

"Where?"

"No record."

"Was she married?"

"She's registered under her maiden name, damn it. What are you after, Elliot?"

"Just my hunch. I'll tell you when you finish."

Shaw's jaw worked furiously against itself. I had thrown him off track with my questions. He hesitated before speaking again.

"The boarding house was just temporary, like I said. The doctors at the Clarke Institute had let her out for a while, but she got booze, probably from the landlord, and grew worse. They had a community care worker, but they were still afraid she'd take sick from self-neglect or kill herself. You . . . she'd tried to kill herself once before. In front of a car. She'd lost a hand."

His head shook slowly from side to side. For a moment he reminded me of Amy, sunk deep in her past.

"Spandrell," I said quietly.

Shaw's eyes brushed over me impatiently. He waited for me to explain.

"That's who is paying the bills. I don't know exactly how he works it. Diana Barryhill is a company officer for Barryknoll, Bar-Tor, and the others. The insanity part fits — he must have power of attorney. Spandrell hides himself behind her name, then hides her in some loony bin. Technically she must own everything, but he reaps the benefits."

"What the hell are you talking about?" snarled Shaw. He was more surprised than angry. "Spandrell? The newspaper publisher?"

"That's right. Ever seen him?"

"No."

"I'll bet you haven't. He set up Bar-Tor, which controls the *Star-Leader* and Barryknoll. But aside from hiring on as publisher he has no apparent connection. The money for Bar-Tor must have come from Liggett and his syndicate in return for the Omniplex leak."

Shaw was at a loss. I backtracked and told him about the province's grandiose plans for an instant industrial enclave on the shores of Lake Ontario, how Spandrell had finessed the news story, his involvement in the subsequent cover-up, and his sudden emergence in the world of high finance and stock manipulation

"But what's that got to do with Diana?"

"She's his wife, or was his wife. It doesn't matter. He came to Toronto from England three years ago with an alcoholic wife who later disappeared, some said she had died. Now we know. Get a couple of warrants and we can prove all this. There's nothing illegal about it, though it'll be awfully embarrassing for Liggett and Queen's Park."

"I'll send Renner after the warrants this morning." said Shaw. "But I still don't get it. Who killed Barrett? If there's nothing illegal going on, why kill anybody?"

"The land swindle isn't the motive. I think I can tell you what it is, though. First fill me in on the night Brian Oxley died. Amy says she lied at the inquest. Diana Barryhill put her up to it. Does anybody know the real facts?"

"Not a soul. Those two kids disappeared. They were the only witnesses. Amy's story never counted for much."

"Tell her that," I said. "She's been living with the damn inquest like a hook in her jaw for twenty-five years. She came close to a nervous breakdown last night when she told me."

"Calm down, Elliot. What I mean to say is that Diana was the star witness. The coroner knew little Amy hadn't seen much. Everybody knew there was something funny going on because Raftis ran away, but there was no way to prove it. Practically speaking, there wasn't even a body. Oxley was just a pile of ash.

"Believe me, I reopened that file the minute I came back to work here. I made inquiries across the country and in the US through the FBI. I rechecked every lead from the original disappearance. Of course, the inquest had ruled that Brian died by misadventure. If there had been any hard evidence of manslaughter, the police would have searched more carefully in the first place. Besides, it was easier in those days to change your name, get papers, and whatnot. You could really lose yourself, if that's what you intended."

Shaw sighed wearily, rubbed his eyes, and leaned heavily against the articulated back of his desk chair.

"You have to see how it was," he said reflectively. "Diana was a princess, kind of fast, but cute. She wasn't mean; she was mischievous. I'm not denying she was a handful," he added with a dry chuckle. "Damon shot a load of rock salt over the head of more than one anxious kid. I guess every male in Ockenden fell for her at one time or another."

He stopped again, looking inward, tramping around the remains of a past that suddenly seemed sharp and full of possibility. I could understand the nostalgia. For Shaw the present was a patient in a psych ward and a middle-aged hockey player who never made the cut. But it also annoyed me because I couldn't shake the idea that Amy was back there, too, trapped in the same ambiguous past, waiting for someone to deliver her from its violent menace.

"After the fire," Shaw continued finally, "people said a lot of foolish things, worse when she skipped town. But whether she had always intended to meet Aaron, which was what folks believed, or whether the good citizens drove her out, we'll never know. Her dad always thought that if people like Rose Oxley had just let her alone, the girl might have stayed."

"What Amy said is true, then," I interrupted. I wanted facts, not might-have-beens. "Brian and Aaron were both after Diana. It sounds like things came to a head. Maybe Brian was trying to rape Diana. Aaron found them. It's possible they had a fight at the Oxley place that night."

"I'm not disputing that," Shaw said evenly. "They were tough lads, used to throwing elbows and punches on the ice. The official line — that's Diana's story — is that the fire started during a fight and Brian Oxley died rescuing Amy in an upstairs bedroom. Unofficially we think Aaron decked Brian. Maybe he hit him with a chair or something. Maybe he killed him; maybe he just knocked him out. Aaron stood over the body, shouting for the kid to get up and fight. Diana screamed when she saw how badly he was hurt. That's what Amy heard from the bedroom.

"So Aaron panicked — what would you have done? He got

Amy out in a blanket so she couldn't see anything, then torched the house and the body. He likely jumped a night freight to Toronto after working out the alibi with Diana, thinking things would cool off one day and he'd be able to sneak back. But he calculated wrong. Running was the biggest mistake of his life."

"And a couple of months later," I put in hurriedly, "Diana followed him. If they found each other — Barrett thought they did, though he wouldn't admit it — then Spandrell is Raftis. That's his motive. He *did* come back. He'd changed so much even Damon didn't recognize him until I shoved that cut under his nose. It was a kind of poetic justice; he was going to make a mint screwing the town that had exiled him and his girlfriend. He even flaunted her name to add spice to his triumph."

"Does that mean Rose Oxley was going to turn him in?" asked Shaw.

"Perhaps," I said. "She could have been blackmailing him. Or maybe he just got tired of her knowing."

Shaw peered at me thoughtfully, scratching his forehead where his policeman's cap had left a furrow.

"He must be nuts," he said doubtfully.

"Look what it did to Diana Barryhill. I'm no psychologist — maybe he went crazy, too, the way things worked out for them. Guilt — he lost everything, family, future. Grief twists you up." I thought of Amy huddled on her bed and my own improbable career. "It gets us all one way or another."

"By God, man, I don't kid myself that you haven't heard about my woman troubles," said Shaw, "but when I saw Diana last night, it all hit me. What she . . . what I could have been."

He subsided into his chair with a gesture of futility. And I let him sift among his memories without interruption, wondering all the while what kind of woman she must have been to snare so many fancies and wreak such havoc.

At last, he stirred. "Well, we'd better pick him up." He flicked the office intercom to ON and shouted, "Renner, get in here!"

Renner shambled through the door almost immediately, looking half-asleep, wearing a purple leisure suit and a string tie. Shaw issued commands in clipped no-nonsense tones.

"I'm sending Renner to Toronto to see about opening Liggett's offices and verifying that Spandrell's paying Diana's bills. You're probably right — we can't charge him over this land deal. We'll leak it to the papers in a day or two.

"We should get on to Spandrell's editors at the *Daily News*. Another good job for my assistant. They'll run around bleating freedom of the press and protection of sources crap, but it'll be worth it. Renner never leaves a dignity unwounded!

"Get a typewriter in the outer office, Elliot. Give me names, companies, those secretaries, editors, everything you've got."

After half an hour of scrambling Shaw had deployed his troops, Renner had left for the city, and there were two marked cars loaded with cops waiting for us in the fenced parking lot behind the station.

Shaw detailed one car to drive the coast road to Spandrell's house, the other followed his four-wheel-drive truck as we turned toward the *Star-Leader* building downtown. The back of the truck was full of ice-fishing gear, a portable duck blind, saws, and back issues of *Popular Mechanics*. On a rack behind our heads, there were two 12-gauge shotguns.

We parked in the breezeway where the circulation vans were loaded, and I followed Shaw up the grim stairs to the newsroom. Miss Lana, bright and birdlike in the face of all that male authority, was crestfallen to report that the publisher had left the office half an hour earlier, only minutes after arriving. Would we like an appointment?

"That won't be necessary, ma'am," enjoined Shaw, with backwoods courtliness. "We'll just help ourselves to some chairs and wait. Precious, where are those tapes?" I pointed to the morgue. "Dexter, stand by that door. No one in or out." The receptionist squawked a feeble protest as Shaw led his band of cops past her desk and into the stunned silence of the newsroom.

Ashcroft was sitting with his feet on his desk, telephone cradled against his ear, notepad on his stomach, pen in one hand, a doughnut dripping jelly onto his shirt from the other. His eyes grew wide at the sight of all the uniforms.

I motioned to him and he hung up the phone without a word.

"I was just taking a break," he said hesitantly. "Gratz is on the rampage about something. It's the only way I can get any peace."

"Never mind that. Where'd Spandrell go?"

"Dunno, Precious. Came in mad, wanting to know where you were, then steamed right out again with Amy. I didn't know they were friends."

"Amy!"

"She was waiting in his office when I got to work. I was just going to say hello when —"

"Jesus!" I shouted. I felt Shaw's hand on my shoulder. "Jesus!" I thought of the first time I'd met her, the hair hanging in her face, the picture on the wall. Then I thought of Barrett, dead in his bedroom, and Amy's goldfish gasping on the floor, and Rose Oxley's cold, sooty house.

"When was this?" Shaw asked. "Know where he went, kid?"

"Half hour ago. Just for a coffee, I suppose."

"Jesus!" We had missed her by thirty minutes. Talking hockey. I nearly exploded.

"What's going on?" asked Ashcroft. "You're Chief Shaw, aren't you?"

The eyes of the newsroom were trained on us. I made a dash for the door. Shaw nodded to one of his men, who put out an arm and stopped me.

"Call the house," he said.

"He's got her," I cried. "She must have known this morning. She guessed it from what I said about Spandrell and Raftis."

I tried to break away. I couldn't stand the chatter. I wanted to get her back without knowing how. All I could think of was Amy alone in the house, finally deciding to seek out and face the thing she feared most.

"What's up?" asked Ashcroft inconsequentially.

"Where are you going, anyway?" said Shaw. He scanned the room. "I want all you people to go about your business without leaving the building. My sergeant here will take a deposition from each of you. I want you to cooperate. Damon Barrett was murdered yesterday. We are here to investigate. Sergeant, I'll be back shortly."

He turned to me. "Come on. Let's get to a radio!"

21

In the kitchen I made whoopee with an Indian named Hennessy Five Star. He did wonders for my metabolism. That is my prescription for what ails you: Hennessy and a little Kundalini yoga. In a pinch you can forget the yoga. Since Shaw had dropped me at the house I had come to terms with Death and the Infinite. By noon I planned to be One with the Absolute.

Then I saw that the damn fish was dead, floating belly up in its jar like a kid's toy. It must have been the shock, I thought. Poor fish. Miserable wet death. I ransacked Amy's cupboards searching for a plastic sandwich wrapper to use as a body bag. Dead soldier fish. I was going to take him downtown and match him up with a live fish so that she wouldn't know the difference. I was amazed at my own intelligence.

"She beat us to it." Shaw had said that. Shaw was never a man for ignoring the obvious.

"She's not dead yet." This was meant to encourage the distraught lover. "Show me a damn body, Precious, and I'll say she's dead. He may try to bargain with her. If he's thinking of escape, he might take her along as insurance."

What else? An acute analysis of the criminal mind: "He could walk into that newsroom in the next ten minutes or he could be on his way out of the country — there are half a dozen airports within twenty miles. Depends on whether he knows we're after him or not."

What was I to do?

"Stay by the phone."

We had driven fast from the *Star-Leader* to Amy's house in the Rifle Range. Shaw wanted to see if she had left a note. She hadn't. Along the way he put in a call for every available off-duty cop to get back in uniform and report for assignment. He got patched through to the Ontario Provincial Police, letting them know he had a kidnap-murder suspect on the loose. By the time we reached the house, his radio was crackling continuously with flat metallic voices requesting information.

The patrol car reported in: Spandrell's house by the lake was deserted. A neighbour had spotted his wife leaving with her suitcases the previous evening. The police had found two small bags packed with a man's clothing inside the front door, ready for departure.

"That's good," said Shaw, "good for Amy, I mean. Spandrell's not completely crazy if he's got an escape plan. I reckon he sent the woman ahead, thinking he would try to ride out the storm. Pretty damn cool when you think of it."

"Look what he did to Rose Oxley," I said.

We had just finished searching the house. I hadn't noticed the dead fish yet. We were arguing tactics. I didn't know it then, but Shaw, too, had a scheme — and he wanted me to remain at the house, out of his way, on the off chance that Spandrell might try to get in touch. Never at my best under stress, I was coming to pieces. But I had made up my mind to play Shaw's shadow until the case broke. Shaw won.

"Stay put," he said, "or I'll get you a babysitter."

"Jesus!"

"Call if you hear anything." On the porch he paused, removing his cap and wiping the sweatband with his gloves. "Precious, there's something missing. Suppose Aaron did kill Brian in a fight. Suppose he did set the fire and run off with Diana. Even suppose he dreamed up this Omniplex scam, like you say. It still doesn't make sense to murder two people. It's out of proportion."

I glared at Shaw while he ran amok in the field of forensic psychology. He was a man of action. Now that he had an operation to command, he seemed tranquil, almost happy. He even had time for idle speculation on histories and motives.

"If you'd known Raftis, you'd understand. Off the ice he was just a good-natured lunk. Folks thought he was a bit slow." Shaw tapped the side of his head with a forefinger. "But I guess he was just thoughtful. At the time of the disappearance, he had quit school and was working as a house painter. I remember he had an old Hudson he'd restored, and it always seemed to me that Diana admired the car more than she did Aaron."

"Can we find Amy and talk about this later?" I asked impatiently. Shaw seemed to ignore me.

"What's it take to change a man like that? He should have made her a good husband. Instead, he drove her crazy."

"Why don't you ask him?" I said. "It's probably something simple. Jealousy? Suppose he murdered Brian Oxley. Forget the manslaughter angle. Suppose it wasn't an accident. Suppose Raftis discovered Oxley and the girl together, killed him, and then forced Diana to lie to the inquest."

Shaw was silent for a moment. I was a little stunned myself, for I could see that all at once I had put the puzzle together. Diana Barryhill's clumsy lie about the accidental fire and Brian dying after running back into the house to save Amy had never been meant as anything but a loss leader. What she intended, and what she succeeded in doing, was to use her aura of youth and innocence to convince everyone that her lie was just a panicky teenager's ill-advised attempt to stick up for her friend. Because the cops had already bought the panicky teenager act and discounted Diana's lie, they never doubted their own reconstruction, that Raftis had set the fire after accidentally killing Brian in a testosterone-driven brawl. In their minds, it was the story of a hockey fight gone wrong and a guilt-stricken boy making things worse by trying to hide what he had done. No doubt Diana Barryhill quickly figured out how to encourage this comforting fiction. No one suspected Aaron Raftis of cold-blooded murder.

At length Shaw shook his head and started for his truck. "Forget it," he said, his voice gruff, not as breezy or self-confident as before. "Spandrell's the man of the hour — whoever he is."

Since then I had been drinking and telephoning the police

every ten minutes. On the fourth or fifth try the switchboard operator got wise and asked me to think of Amy and not tie up the line. Guilt-stricken, I wandered from room to room, muttering and stumbling. All I could think about was Amy, but that wasn't getting me anywhere. For a while I sat in the kitchen trying to reassemble the tattered remnants of my philosophy.

Once it had seemed to me that the Creator had conceived the world for the sole purpose of man's enjoyment. He had generously filled the mortal abode with four great sources of gratification: food, booze, women, and sleep. But He had also planted weeds in this marvellous garden. He had made man with a soft brain that could easily be persuaded against the fourfold path, that abstractions such as money, power, fame, and glory were more attractive than the four great gratifications.

My war had never been with the Creator, whom I regarded as an eccentric philanthropist. My war was with the misled legions who had forsaken the sacred way. In this war I was a refugee. My foreign policy was live and let live. If the enemy grew insistent, I moved on. Once in a bar in Rome I had met a man who thought he was the pope. I told him my theory and he made me a saint of the church on the spot. Saint Precious of the Saloon of Lost Illusions. We were drunk together for six days, and on the seventh day he vanished.

At noon my hands stopped shaking. In truth I was in a state just shy of dematerialization, my hopes zero, my heart pumping Bloody Marys, my corpuscles reeling in my veins like gangs of sailors on a spree. I glanced out the window and was not surprised to see the now-familiar Ford station wagon bellying up to the curb. Like a mechanical figure on a church clock, it had rounded a distant corner in ominous silence to take the place of Shaw's truck. Who were these guys?

I reached for the telephone. What if they were in contact with Spandrell? Eschew the bureaucratic approach, I told myself. Personal attention demanded. After all, wasn't I a trained killer courtesy of the Royal Canadian Air Force? At twenty miles. With a six-million-dollar Starfighter strapped to my ass! Johnny Canuck Flyboy!

The phone rang in my hand. It was Spandrell.

"Jesus!" I said. Amy's life depended on my saying the right thing. But what do you say in a situation like that?

"What did you tell the cops?" he asked, a gruff interrogative that betrayed no anxiety. "Amy says they hauled you in this morning for a chat."

"Nothing. Nothing at all." There didn't seem to be any point in making him angry.

"Talk about Diana, did you? Billy Shaw must have enjoyed that. He was always sniffing after her when he was a kid. He tell you about it?"

"He wanted to know more about Barrett. You heard he was killed yesterday?"

"Cut the crap, Precious. Do they know about Omniplex yet? You tell them? Spill it. Amy's right here if you need motivation."

"Honest, Spandrell!"

"What are the cops doing at the paper, then?"

"Barrett. They're making inquiries —"

"I want *you*, Precious. Just to talk, mind! Call it an editorial conference. I'll let her go if you come alone. Is it a deal?"

"You can't get away," I muttered.

"The hell I can't. Meet me on the waterfront at eight tonight. Bay's frozen. Walk down from Boot Hill's through the vacant lot where I can see you, then onto the ice, straight out for a couple of hundred yards, clear of the breakwater. You'll see a light in the west — head for it. Half-moon tonight, Precious. No clouds. If you bring Shaw, I'll be able to see him. If you screw up, you'll hear Amy scream. Then you'll know you did wrong."

Spandrell hung up.

It was twelve-thirty. My hands were shaking again. I had a drink. I was ready to make the sacrifice, anything to get Amy away safe. Then I'd tear him apart. I could indistinctly recall hitting other men in the past, usually in bars. Twice I came to in hospitals. A buddy of mine once said I was a born brawler with a glass fist. Make a fist, Precious! Show the people. It was boney, white, and inoffensive. I needed help. I needed another drink.

My overcoat caught me in a half nelson as I tried to dress. Staggering through the front door, I executed an Olympic-class sit-spin on the porch ice. "Moss, run out and get some salt for the steps or we'll kill ourselves in the spring," she had said. It wasn't bad enough that strange men were threatening me, spying on me, and saying mean things about me — I had to make a fool of myself in front of them. Gathering up the shards of my dignity, I supported Amy's house to the driveway.

The station wagon surged out of its mooring and followed as I aimed Ashcroft's VW downtown, forming a cortege, somewhat funereal, in my wake. Unfortunately, I conceived the idea of outdriving it. Shoving the accelerator pad to the floor, I shot ahead. The old rustbucket burped up to forty-five miles an hour in second gear, its engine whining, tires skidding. In the distance an intersection hovered like a mirage. Suddenly I was braking, declutching, and frantically steering to no effect as the car floated majestically sideways into oncoming traffic. I stiffened to take the impact, but none came. A long-haired man in a black van with the words GET HIGH painted in Day-Glo orange on its panels sat on his horn and abused me verbally. The VW stalled.

Half an hour later, after driving aimlessly through the new subdivisions, scanning the ragbag of my memory for a ruse, I reined the white dwarf to a halt outside the American. Pausing to fumble at the parking meter, I made sure my tail was still with me, then marched bravely into the bar.

As usual, steam was rising in clouds from Mrs. Miniver's stainless-steel bins of roast beef, creamed corn, and instant potatoes. Steam also rose from the lunchtime crowds, sitting before their beaded beer glasses, looking as intimate as puppies in a box, happy about the warm weather.

I lurched toward the cigarette machine, an old enemy.

Although the Ontario government had outlawed slot machines, trying to buy tobacco at the American was not unlike playing the one-armed bandit. Sometimes I got a book of matches, sometimes I got another brand of cigarettes, and sometimes I got three lemons. Feeling in the mood for prophylactic violence, I kicked the vendor before inserting my change. It catapulted a pack of Lights into my hand.

"Your lucky day," said a voice behind me.

I glared balefully, an alcoholic basilisk stare guaranteed to petrify.

"Goodness, Precious, you look awful," said Bernie Tassio with genuine unconcern.

"Here!" I stuffed the cigarettes into his stubby hands. "Fuck 'em. If I can't smoke something fatal, I won't smoke."

"Touchy, aren't we? Let me buy you a drink."

Leering at Bernie's shiny rotund face, I ordered a triple Hennessy with a beer chaser. Without recalling how I had done it, I congratulated myself on manoeuvring him into the role of benefactor.

"I don't mind," he said, much too cheerily, his skin oozing sweat in the roast beef sauna atmosphere. "I owe you a lot. Two hundred and fifty thousand dollars. That's what they paid me for that old place, honey. A quarter of a million! I'm kissing Ockenden goodbye, going to San Francisco for a month, then Toronto. And I owe it all to you." He raised his glass in salute.

"Are you crazy, Tassio? What did I do? It's a mistake. A thing like that would never have happened while I was alive."

"The stable, Precious. The tip about Liggett. It panned out a thousand percent. I made a killing."

At first, thinking I had misheard Tassio, I nodded complacently in my chair, waiting for an explanation; then, as the import of his words began to traverse my synapses, I felt sick. The air around us was suddenly foul. He sipped his drink triumphantly, grinning at me with what looked like blood glistening on his lips. His out-thrust index finger stabbed the air to make a point. I knocked it roughly aside.

"Take it easy, Precious. What's the matter? Look out! Are you going to puke or something?"

Staggering to my feet, I picked up my drinks and stumped away from Tassio's table with the air of a man who has just shut the door on a very disgusting display. Almost immediately I lost my balance, dashing against a table crowded with lunching bank tellers dressed in boobs and rapier eyelashes.

My friend the waiter-punter, his face ascetic and wise, came up in the manner of a priest at High Mass and gently assisted me through the rear door to the can, muttering unintelligible *te deums* in his tavern vernacular. I commanded him to summon a taxi, then sat on the pot to wait, finishing my brandy in peace and privacy.

Five minutes later I dropped a butt into the toilet, where it hissed and sputtered like a mad ferret, then skipped out the back exit at the sound of the cab's horn to the rear parking lot, where the Ford station wagon was waiting for me.

"Just move. Around the block. Anywhere," I ordered the driver in a huff. Taxi drivers had had a hand in this, too. Wasn't it a taxi driver who had piqued Ashcroft's interest in the Oxley murder? Likely the kid would never have become involved if it hadn't been for the siren lure of the inside dope, the real story. Gossipmongers!

This one was going into a song and dance about the cold and his metal leg. He was slamming his leg with a tire iron he kept on the seat beside him. Didn't they have laws against cripples driving public conveyances?

"I would like to visit the liquor store and a sporting goods emporium," I sniffed airily, to demonstrate that I was not impressed by his crude exhibitionism.

He was squinting in the rear-view mirror.

"That car following you, mister?"

Mind your own business, I thought. Ignore him. I feigned boredom and poor hearing. He shrugged.

At the liquor store I spent the last of my cash on two bottles of brandy and proceeded to lug them to the taxi like a diver with a pair of air tanks clutched desperately to his chest.

"I would like to buy a gun," I told the smart young man behind the counter with the punk hairstyle and elevator shoes.

"What kind?"

"Something with treads would be nice."

"Perhaps you would prefer to come back some other day, sir."

"Perhaps I wouldn't, kid. Give me that one. Yeah, that one. It looks big enough."

"Skeet gun, sir."

"Skeet, eh? Get many of those around here, kid?"

"Perhaps —"

"And a box of bullets," I said quickly. "You take cheques?"

Reclining on Amy's sling couch, I sucked the urine-coloured booze and lovingly fingered my brand new Remington 12-gauge over-and-under skeet gun. This was a truly modern weapon, I enthused, as I broke the barrels and examined the ejection system. It was no Starfighter, but I could feel the power of its chambers. They seemed to vibrate in my hands. It scared me to peer down the glossy blue-metal tubes, even with the gun cracked, when all I could see were the tips of my shoes.

I could bend the wills of men with this gun. I could call my own shots with those bastards in the station wagon. What had they thought, watching me emerge from the store with that telltale parcel, grinning maniacally? I cracked the barrels once more, loaded and reloaded. I estimated how close I must be to injure a man with this gun. Morbid curiosity — God knows I didn't want to hurt anybody — but it made me happy.

Truth was, I had never fired either a rifle or a shotgun. We had been given small-arms training on the prairie. Big mother .45s. We were trained to stand off the whole Red Chinese army in case we were shot down in enemy territory. I titillated myself with daydreams based on the movie *Guadalcanal Diary*, mowing down the slants with my trusty Colt. But one day, on a bet, I shot a gopher and got sick at the result. Truth was, I was a city boy, though it was a damn small city. Pool was my dangerous game, small-time hustling. Later I graduated to drinking and left off sports altogether.

This gun, THIS GUN, I thought, made me a man of action!

I peeked out the window, my heart doing a Fred Astaire number against my rib cage. Still there. Two doors down in front of Missy Malchak's sty. She was probably running coffee to them in relays, she was that kind of spiteful woman. In the distance a white ghost hove into view, a washing machine on wheels, a drunken whore on crutches. Ashcroft's auto.

I fumbled with the chain lock and deadbolt to let him in. He was lovably familiar in his yeti-skin outfit, his nose running, his eyes pouchy and bloodshot.

"Ashers," I said. "What are you doing here?"

He eyed me gravely.

"The paper's been cancelled for the day. As soon as the police let us out, the whole staff went across the square to the American to talk about it. I found my car. You left the keys in it."

"I see."

"Are you sick, Precious? What's going on?"

"I think I've had too much to drink. Purely an error in judgement. I have been ill for some time."

"What the hell is that?"

"Artiller-iller-illery!"

Ashcroft gave me one of those superior withering looks, as only the Oakville Ashcrofts can give, due to their being less well off than the Rosedale Ashcrofts, hence closer to God the Teetotaller. Explaining how he had been detained by the police most of the day, though never questioned except concerning the location of the bathroom, he shed his coat and proceeded to the kitchen to make coffee. I followed and stood helplessly in the middle of the room while he fiddled efficiently with the grinder and watered the kettle. Then I went to the head for a leak.

"You're shaking, Precious," said Ashcroft when I returned. "Sweating, too. Drink this." He shoved a cup of something black that barely poured under my nose. I took stock; the kid was right.

"I'm under a lot of pressure," I said. He was beginning to give me the superior look again, eyes slitting, lining down his lacerated nose. "Spandrell's the killer, Ashers. You may not believe it but the guy is a wrongo. And what's more he's got Amy; he wants to meet me tonight. If I show up, he promises to let her go. Now you and I both know that old Precious was not, I repeat, was not, born yesterday. It smells like tuna to me. I can't get help from the cops; one glimpse and . . ." I groped for words; it was tough being tough. "To top it off, those guys in the station wagon have been hanging around like vultures waiting for me to croak since Barrett was killed. They started when I picked up your damn car and they're still out there!"

Ashcroft was superbly matter-of-fact. He moved like Jeeves, without apparent pedal activity, to the front window and returned, saying, "That's what I figured. I twigged as soon as I saw my car."

"I backdoored them," I said, swaying smugly until the kid put a chair against the back of my knees.

"You sure did, Precious."

22

Why, then, was I sitting in the bathroom? Was I asleep? Had I passed out? Was it day or night? Had I missed the appointment with Spandrell? In the nick of time I remembered my wrist-watch; it was six-thirty. From the living room came the snap and hiss of a match. It suddenly dawned on me that I had retreated to the bathroom for a shower — that explained why I was wearing only my trousers and a sock. I wondered whether I had fallen asleep before or after I took the shower. Must ask Ashcroft . . .

Struggling painfully to my feet, I took a quick inventory: my mouth tasted like the inside of a coke oven, I was getting hot flashes like some cinema Frankenstein with jolts of artificial lightning zapping his ears, a tiny man inside my head sang smutty songs and rattled a tin drinking cup, the floor trembled. I coughed for a while to get my circulation up, then oozed over to the door.

Smoke and flame billowed from the sling chair by the window, where Ashcroft meditated with his pipe, his legs stretched before him, his tweed vest unbuttoned and ajar. His face, pale above where the cream streetlight fought its way into the darkened house, was rubicund and devilish below from the glow of his match and tobacco.

"Still here," I said.

"Oh, yes. I was about to call you. Time we were on our way, I expect. Lucky you fell asleep in there. I had no idea what to do with you."

With a forefinger hooked over his pipestem, he arched and yawned, then, sitting forward, rubbed the bridge of his nose between his fingers. He was doing his Sydney Carton routine, complete with assumed mid-Atlantic drawl and feigned boredom. I half expected him to call me Old Top or break into "It is a far, far better thing . . ."

"Got a cigarette?" I asked.

"You can have these." He tossed me a fresh pack of Gitanes. "Keep them. I'll never know how you stand to smoke that terrible stuff."

Brushing aside the curtain, I checked the station wagon, watching the pinpoint glow of a lighter in the front seat give birth to two tinier sparks.

"There's coffee in the kitchen — still hot."

With my back to Ashcroft, I poured coffee and killed the last of the brandy. I couldn't tell whether I was shaking from fear, excitement, DTs, or nervous collapse. In a cupboard I discovered the rest of Amy's Wide-a-Wakes. By the time I returned to the living room, I was feeling fit enough to run a marathon.

Ashcroft was back in his chair, all suited up in his parka, pulling woollen glove liners on like a surgeon. He had blackened his face with shoe polish.

"What are you going to do, Ashers, sing 'Mammy'?"

"It's camouflage."

"I know that's what you think it is."

"How else are we going to sneak up on them?"

"Maybe they'll laugh so much they'll hurt themselves."

Nearly passing out in the struggle, I fought my way into a coat. I jerked a balaclava over my head and face, which Ashcroft approved as a camouflage measure, then retrieved the Remington from the bathroom towel rack.

"You'd better put these in," said the kid, handing me the shells. "I took them out — you were going to practise on Amy's spider plants. I've got more."

Though there was no immediate threat, we both flattened ourselves against the wall on either side of the front door in preparation for departure.

"You don't have to do this," I whispered. "I can manage on my own."

"Is that your only plan?"

"I'm a trained killer," I said. "Once Amy's safe I'll jump him."

"What about these guys in the station wagon?"

"That's your job, Ashers. We're going to outdrive them."

"I see," he said doubtfully. "Ready?"

"Watch out for the ice."

"Precious, what the hell are you doing with a dead fish in your shirt pocket?"

The question was rhetorical. Not waiting for an answer, Ashcroft swung the door open and shoved me through. I waved the gun wildly a moment to get my balance, then stood, legs apart, while he slipped behind me. Spandrell had been right — the sky was clear. A phosphorescent mist rose from a street drain. Tree branches cracked arthritically in the cold.

Ashcroft skated to the car, while I glared at the station wagon. The VW exploded into life. I edged back along the walk to where he was holding the passenger door open for me. The Ford glided forward slightly, then seemed to hover.

"Go! Go!" I shouted, bracing myself against the dashboard.

The car lurched backward down the driveway, then along the street toward the Ford, as Ashcroft shifted into neutral. We hung there a moment.

"Go!" I cried.

Ashcroft fiddled with the gear shift; the engine revved hysterically. There was a clang of angry metal, and the car wrenched back suddenly as the tires bit into a patch of bare pavement. The vehicles collided with a thump, a crunch of fenders, and glass tinkling forlornly in the aftermath.

"Sorry!" yelled the kid wildly.

The VW engine whined out of gear. He was waving the stick up and down like some insane opera conductor.

"Goddamn!"

I shot the safety catch on the Remington and hit the door with its polished stock. Momentum carried me out of the car onto a bank of dirty snow, where I lay for an instant clawing the air like an upturned beetle. Then I was on my feet, covering the Ford's windshield with the gun.

"Stay put," I shouted. "Don't move!" To Ashcroft, "Get it going! Get it going!"

With a profound shriek, the gears engaged. The VW jerked away from the other car, then halted a yard away, sputtering aimlessly.

"Okay!" yelled Ashcroft.

Lowering the Remington's sights, I blasted a load down the choke bore into the glistening radiator cage. The two heads vanished behind the dash. I stepped closer and shredded the near front tire with my second shell.

Momentarily, I hesitated, gazing with amazement at the mechanical carnage. The roar of the report seemed never-ending as it echoed through the icy streets and building blocks. Then I threw the shotgun into a snowbank and leaped for the open car door. Ashcroft's hands clenched the steering wheel like death, his eyes were frozen on the road ahead. I stared at him, and for a long time nothing happened.

"Did you kill them?" he asked shakily, without looking at me.

"Are you kidding? Get the hell out of here!"

As though released from a spell, he pumped the accelerator and jumped off the clutch, spinning the tires, and we inched slowly away from the station wagon where it lay like a beached whale at the edge of the silver lawn.

"Sorry, Precious," breathed Ashcroft. "I was nervous."

"Shit!"

A ghostly patrol car, its lights flashing, slid into the intersection ahead and skidded to a halt. Almost at once a second jammed the street closed. Ashcroft twirled the steering wheel, running the VW onto the sidewalk, then reversed and tried to turn. Two more cruisers had pulled up behind us.

Constables with pistols were dragging the two men from the Ford's front seat and splaying them over the hood for a search. In a side mirror I caught sight of Shaw striding toward us, shouting over his shoulder for someone to find the shotgun, a phalanx of uniforms at his back.

A half-dozen hands hooked the two of us out of the Volkswagen like grain sacks. I raised an arm to shield my eyes from the glare of police spotlights. Someone shouted, "Watch it!" A sap hurtled through the sky, black, then red like the blast of a shotgun. My knees buckled. Shaw had me by the coat front, hefting me with one fist, battering me against the car door. "What the hell are you doing? Trying to kill somebody?"

"Leave him alone!" — the kid, screaming.

Suddenly I was stretched out on the street watching my breath melt a tiny snow wall at the tip of my nose. I did not remember how I got there, but the descent had evidently been accomplished without hindrance and with a minimum of discomfort. A snooze would be wonderful. I could hear them arguing like Greeks and Trojans over my corpse, Shaw and Ashcroft, but they were far away and the topic not so very interesting. One thing had seemed utterly important only seconds before, but now, watching the ice crystals melt, I had forgotten what it was.

23

Peace didn't last. I came to consciousness almost immediately. Ice broke under me like cinders. Everywhere I looked there were boots, mostly in pairs, supporting uniforms. Ashcroft tried to hit a policeman. A very large albino gentleman wearing a trench coat screamed absurd accusations.

My brain cells took a strike vote. Many had been severely damaged in the past week. The aggression index hovered at the top of the scale. Someone slapped my face. His hands felt like frozen fish fillets. Someone rubbed the back of my neck with a mittful of snow. Pneumonia stamped on my chest like a quarter horse.

All the same, the situation had its comic side. There I was, a middle-aged newsman whose articles had appeared in at least ninety-eight journals worldwide, lying in a snow-choked gutter surrounded by what looked like a plenary session of a doormen's convention. Suddenly I was an underworld celebrity, guilty of every heinous crime from international jewel theft to attempted murder. For the first time since I had arrived in Ockenden, I had something akin to respect.

The two men in the Ford had been stunned by the gunshots. As soon as he realized I was helpless, Otto Kleppinger was after me like a hydrophobic white rabbit. It was all one policeman could do to keep him from stamping on the back of my head. It was Kleppinger who brought up the emerald pendant caper. He had had the American staked out all week, hoping I would panic and lead him to the jewel. Right away, Renner believed his story. Ashcroft's face brightened. All of a sudden my character sparkled with exciting new facets. Kleppinger's sidekick, his bald Korean houseboy named Lou, thin as a whippet, had fainted.

Almost as soon as I had subsided to the pavement, Shaw's men searching the station wagon had discovered a .22-calibre target pistol and a lead-pipe mace studded with spikes. Kleppinger had handed Shaw one of his cards; Shaw had ripped it in half and dropped the pieces in front of my nose. I wanted to make a statement but was encountering technical difficulties. My mind was skipping like a cracked LP. Shaw ordered a make on Kleppinger. Car radios sizzled like fried fat.

Kleppinger turned out to be the scion of a freeze-dry food fortune, a distant nephew who rated a couple of codicils in the family will and a five-bedroom condo on the lakeshore. He really was a painter; he had once designed a duck stamp for the post office. But strikes and rate hikes had nixed the issue, and Kleppinger had suffered a nervous breakdown. In its aftermath, the family had hired Lou as nurse, amanuensis, and watchdog.

Kleppinger was not licensed to do detective work; he couldn't even get a license to drive a car. Panadakis had hired him through a classified ad. He was thirty-two and already had a dozen convictions for auto theft, shoplifting, and assault on various members of his family and post-office personnel. He was currently awaiting sentence on a mail-fraud scheme involving a non-existent sex introduction service which had netted him ninety-seven dollars after expenses. He had once kidnapped himself.

Somehow he had enlisted Lou's aid in his plot to shake me down for Anne Delos's missing pendant. They had barely finished congratulating each other on the success of the venture and their arrival at the threshold of big-time crime when the shooting began. Neither had ever experienced gunfire before. Under questioning, Lou admitted that Kleppinger was a psychopath. Kleppinger said Lou had masterminded the whole project. The Ford station wagon belonged to Lou's sister-in-law, a Korean woman whose name also happened to be Lou.

While Shaw sorted out recrimination and confession, I huddled in the snow, Ashcroft tried to hit a second policeman, and the rescue operation hung in limbo. At length, Shaw squatted on his hams, scratched his forehead, and asked me if what Kleppinger said about the emerald pendant could be true.

I opened my mouth and passed out. It was only then that the kid managed to achieve a plausible explanation of events, shouting into the police chief's face at the top of his voice, and got the wheels of justice in motion again.

I was absolved of attempted murder but was not to be resupplied with a gun. The hot-jewel allegations would pend until Shaw checked with Interpol. Kleppinger and Lou were removed from circulation in a squad car. It was 7:35 before we were on the road, four of us, Ashcroft, Shaw, myself, and the moon-faced constable of the morning, all wedged together in the Volkswagen for camouflage. The remaining police cars streamed silently through back streets to take positions well clear of the waterfront rendezvous.

While Ashcroft drove, the constable methodically stripped and reassembled a long sniper's rifle with a telescopic sight. I was on automatic pilot, impervious to everything but certain low-level internal stimuli which governed breathing and heartbeat. I was not snoring, as the kid said afterward. And I have always denied that upon being led through the public room at Boot Hill's, I shouted, "Haven't we passed the drinks, boys?" and took a death grip on the bar moulding.

By seven-fifty we were in the back room at Boot Hill's overlooking the vacant lot where the burned out warehouses had once stood. Beyond, abandoned transhipment cranes rusted and the shadows of pier pilings marched into the lunar ice as it crept toward the open lake where gentle waves cupped the moonlight. At least that was the way Ashcroft, in a characteristically literary effusion, reported the scene later, much later, when I was conscious and near enough sober again to understand. Somehow, betwixt a sip of this and a shot of that, I had slipped right out of myself, proof positive of a self-preserving inability to pretend to be a hero in anything like a clear state of mind. I didn't love Amy Ranger. How many times had I said this to myself? I'd certainly never stick my neck out. No, never.

At 7:55 Shaw positioned his marksman in a darkened upper

storey of the tavern and returned to find Ashcroft trying to lift me from a recumbent position by my armpits. I had fallen, he explained, while endeavouring to read my wristwatch.

"Brandy may sometimes be given to the dying," I intoned, according to Ashcroft, who remembered it as a gem of boozy wit — not to be trusted.

"He can't do it," muttered the kid. "He can't even walk. Let me put on his coat. He won't have a chance if he goes out against Spandrell like this."

"Let him go," said Shaw. "I don't want that bastard getting wind of a set-up. If Precious can distract him, we may get a clear shot."

"Shoot him!" exclaimed Ashcroft, for whom events had taken on a sheen of brutal realism undreamed of in his romantic fancies. "But —"

Shaw quickly explained how a routine CPIC check that afternoon had turned up a Restricted Firearms Registration in the publisher's name for a U.S.-made M1 semiautomatic carbine and a Webley & Scott .38 revolver.

"Use this if you get a chance," said Shaw, slipping a Police Special into my coat pocket. "Don't shoot yourself."

I waved an index finger in his face. "Tell Daniel Boone upstairs not to shoot me either. I pay taxes."

At eight o'clock sharp Shaw shoved me unceremoniously into the street and repaired with Ashcroft to the sniper's aerie from which the lakefront spread like a fan beneath them (Ashcroft's simile).

Striking out with a fragile, boozy determination, I made straight for the shoreline, my image quickly resolving into a black silhouette against the reflected moonlight. (What I remember — not the details but the feeling of the moment: cold, wet feet, thirst, the beginnings of a sore throat, the urge to lie down in a drift and take a snooze, the pitch and yaw of the horizon which gradually I realized had nothing to do with the horizon, and terror — for myself but mainly for Amy, that I might fail her. A life made up mostly of evasive manoeuvres had not prepared me for action on the epic scale. Not to mention the alcohol I had recently consumed. It occurred to me that in the future, if there was a future, I might ease up, not teetotal, mind you, but something tentative in the nature of moderation. But I digress. Of the events which followed I have no recollection whatever.)

Then for several anxious minutes Ashcroft and Shaw watched as I stumbled zigzag patterns in a minefield of snow-covered debris. Once I tripped outright, leaped up with a cap of snow on my head, and jogged a few yards toward town before reorienting myself. Another time I stopped to inspect a boxcar coupling.

"He's taking a leak," said Shaw.

"Yes," said Ashcroft.

"What's he doing now?"

"It's the breakwater. He can't get down."

"He's so damn drunk he should have fallen over it."

As they looked on in disbelief, I wrapped my arms around a piling, gingerly lowered a foot over the low concrete parapet, then delicately raised it and tried the other without success. For a moment or two I stared down at the ice with my hands in my pockets, a figure of dejection. Then I jumped to the parapet top and began swinging my arms and flexing my knees as a prelude to descent.

"If he doesn't go, so help me, I'll shoot him myself," said Shaw.

But after a few seconds of arm swinging and knee-flexing I straightened up and replaced my hands in my pockets. It was only then that I lost my balance, pitching out of sight, headfirst, without any warning. For a long time I did not reappear, and when my head finally showed, bobbing above the horizon of the breakwater, I was already fifty yards from shore.

The constable now knelt, without hat or gloves, at the open window, his elbow braced against the sill, following me with the crosshairs of his telescopic sight.

When I was about two hundred yards out, he said, "Can't guarantee a shot if he walks any further."

"Turn now, Precious," muttered Shaw.

As if on command, I did stop, but I didn't veer to the right the way I was supposed to. Instead it looked like I was trying to count my footprints in the thin snow crust above the ice. Abruptly, a single headlight needled out of the darkness about a quarter of a mile to the west. All three of them saw it before I did. A small motor coughed and revved. That finally caught my attention and I set off toward it.

"Snowmobile," said the constable.

"Spar Cove out there," said Shaw. "He was lying low in a fishing hut. Damn if I shouldn't have thought of that."

The headlight began tracking in my direction, slow at first, as though Spandrell smelled a trap, then faster, jouncing as it came over the drifts and ruts, that engine sound humming wide open, coming closer and closer. Soon they could see him, crouching low over the cowling, Amy bundled on the pillion seat, holding on for dear life.

"Woman's in the way," said the constable, as he swept the waterfront with his sight. "I'm as likely to hit her as him."

A thin spurt of flame snaked ahead of the snowmobile. The sound of the shot seemed to take minutes before echoing off the harbour buildings.

"He's using the Webley, Chief," said the constable. "The M1's on a shoulder strap. Banana clip. Our guy's out of range for the Webley, but the snowmobile is closing."

"Shit! Is he hit?"

Spandrell had fired again. The shot sent me sprawling facedown. The snowmobile was twenty yards away, then ten, its skids vibrating on the hard-pack. At the last instant Spandrell swerved aside, spattering me with snow.

"I think he just fell down," said the constable.

"Where are you going?" demanded Shaw, as Ashcroft headed for the door. "You can't help. We got a chance if he keeps assing around like that."

The snowmobile made a wide easy arc between the break-water and my body, then straightened out and flew toward me, leaping tiny drifts as it came. Then I was on my feet and running, first to his right, then left as Spandrell turned the machine to cut me off. He fired the pistol twice and I dropped, rolling to avoid the runners as they knifed by my shoulder.

"He's got the woman's arms tied around his waist," said the constable. "She keeps knocking his gun hand. I can see her through the scope."

Almost as he spoke, Spandrell throttled back and dragged to a stop a stone's throw from where I lay. For a second or two he fumbled with the rope that tied Amy's hands, then, swinging round, he jerked her out of the saddle one-handed and shoved her onto the ice.

"That's it!" cried Shaw. "Can you get him now?"

"Too close," said the constable. "She's too damn close for a long shot."

They saw Spandrell's face flash white as he shouted at me; they couldn't hear the words. Then he gunned the engine and catapulted into a tight fast turn, his torso hanging over the ice like a racer's as he fought to hold it.

I was on my knees, then sprinting, struggling with the Police Special in my pocket, as he straightened up. He fired twice; I was ten yards from Amy. The snowmobile sliced toward us like a chain saw, its engine whine pitching higher and higher as he wound the throttle open. I tumbled, trying to aim and shoot, but I was too late.

The cowling caught my right side and arm as I sprawled, spinning me down like a rag doll, sending the revolver flying. The snowmobile leaped away toward the breakwater again, Spandrell yanking the M1 from his shoulder as the lone headlight swept the harbour front. The constable's first shot pinged off a runner strut.

For an instant Spandrell gaped at the shoreline in surprise. The constable's second shot popped a tiny geyser of snow by his foot. Jamming the snowmobile to a halt, he rolled sideways for cover, squeezing off two quick bursts on automatic over the seat.

Shaw and Ashcroft, emerging from the tavern exit, dove for the gutter as bullets smacked the brickwork behind them.

Oblivious of the chattering M1, the constable aimed and fired twice more. The first round seemed to startle Spandrell, snapping his head to attention. The second punched him backward to the ice, his awkward hands flailing the air. He died where he fell, blood pooling under the snow crust beside him.

When the kid reached us, Amy was bawling hysterically. We were both standing, swaying together, and she had me by the collar, tugging to get my attention, showering my face with kisses, like breathless pecks between sobs, and whispering urgently.

"It was Brian," she said. "It was Brian come back!" Her voice was husky and strained with horror. "Rose knew all along it was Aaron's body in that rubble. She drove them crazy, Brian and Diana, with her knowing. It was Brian, Moss. It was Brian come back to kill . . ."

I wasn't listening. Later everything she said would make sense, but for the time being I could only stare, as if hypnotized, at Spandrell's body and Shaw seated on the snowmobile, equally absorbed. The harbour was suddenly alive with lights and sirens. Crowds of superfluous policemen came tumbling over the breakwater.

"Geez, Precious, you're shot!" said Ashcroft in awe.

My right arm hung limp and useless, oozing a dark fluid that spattered the snow.

"Just don't light a match, kid," I said, "or we'll be in deep trouble."